Was AJ about to kiss her?

Mary Hannah stared into his intense blue eyes, wondering if the heated intent was real or an illusion from the dash lights. She should just open the door, get the hell out of his messy all-terrain vehicle where these even messier emotions were jumbling up inside her. She would hop the gate to the Second Chance Ranch and run all the way to her studio apartment.

But she couldn't seem to make her hands let go of the edge of the seat.

PRAISE FOR
THE SECOND CHANCE RANCH NOVELS

SHELTER ME

"There is indeed plenty of love to go around, and animal fans in particular will be swept away by it."
—*Publishers Weekly* (starred review)

"A story about the redemptive power of love told with heart. With *Shelter Me*, Catherine Mann delivers another unforgettable romance."
—Cindy Gerard, *New York Times* bestselling author

"*Shelter Me* is contemporary romance done right! Brimming with wonderfully *real* characters, hard-hitting emotions and enough sexual tension to light my e-reader on fire, I couldn't put it down!"
—Julie Ann Walker, *New York Times* bestselling author

continued . . .

Berkley Sensation titles by Catherine Mann

Second Chance Ranch Novels

SHELTER ME
RESCUE ME

Dark Ops Novels

DEFENDER
HOTSHOT
RENEGADE
PROTECTOR
GUARDIAN

RESCUE ME

CATHERINE MANN

BERKLEY SENSATION, NEW YORK

THE BERKLEY PUBLISHING GROUP
Published by the Penguin Group
Penguin Group (USA) LLC
375 Hudson Street, New York, New York 10014

USA • Canada • UK • Ireland • Australia • New Zealand • India • South Africa • China

penguin.com

A Penguin Random House Company

RESCUE ME

A Berkley Sensation Book / published by arrangement with the author

Berkley Sensation Books are published by The Berkley Publishing Group.
BERKLEY SENSATION® is a registered trademark of Penguin Group (USA) LLC.
The "B" design is a trademark of Penguin Group (USA) LLC.

For information, address: The Berkley Publishing Group,
a division of Penguin Group (USA) LLC,
375 Hudson Street, New York, New York 10014.

ISBN: 978-0-425-26989-3

PUBLISHING HISTORY
Berkley Sensation mass-market edition / February 2015

PRINTED IN THE UNITED STATES OF AMERICA

10 9 8 7 6 5 4 3 2 1

Cover illustration by Anna Kmet.
Cover design by Diana Kolsky.
Interior text design by Kelly Lipovich.

To my husband, Rob—thank you for always supporting me in my animal rescue efforts, for listening when I ramble endlessly about the latest cool thing I learned about animal care and for holding me when I cry for the ones I couldn't save.

Acknowledgments

As always, I am deeply grateful to my editor, Wendy McCurdy, and the entire Berkley team for the opportunity to tell these animal rescue stories that are so near and dear to my heart. Endless thanks also goes out to my longtime agent, Barbara Collins Rosenberg, for always being in my corner. My critique partner and very best friend, Joanne Rock, is truly one in a million—I appreciate you, my friend, more than I could ever say. Many thanks as well to my super beta readers—Haley Frank and Jeanette Vigliotti—I adore you both and appreciate your always being there for me at the drop of a hat.

I'm also lucky to have the most amazing street team, led by Ann, Vickie and Stephanie. Wow, y'all are the best! I'm so grateful for each and every one of you—for your cheers, your support and, most of all, your friendship.

Daily, I'm blessed to work side by side with my friends in the animal rescue community, in particular the staff and volunteers at the Panhandle Animal Welfare Society. I want to send a shout-out to a few of my shelter volunteer friends who so deeply embody the heart of rescue—Susie, Zo, Virginia, Debbie and Dixie. I want to be just like you when I grow up.

Lastly, all my love to my two-legged family and my four-legged pack. Thank you for loving me back!

Prologue

FOR TWENTY-EIGHT YEARS I had three names—Bitch, Fat Mama and Dumbass.

I didn't dare ignore the voice that growled more fiercely than any animal. I didn't question if I deserved to have a single name of my own. My existence followed a pattern. Hungry, not hungry. Hurt, healed. Pregnant, nursing. And above all, obey or pay.

Looking back, the contrast from then to my life now is staggering. Some people have said they wonder how I survived so long in that cabin with limited human contact, only the drone of game shows on television and the bubbling mix in the kitchen to break the tedium. How I kept my spirit intact. How I didn't turn into a mirror image of the voice that both fed me and hurt me. I have to confess I came close to becoming like the soulless monsters that drifted in and out during those early years.

Until I was saved from crawling into the dark hole of hurt and misery forever. I was given a hint of hope beyond the rank four walls of my home.

I smelled honeysuckle.

Just a whiff of the perfume drifted through an open window one summer Tennessee day. At first, I thought I'd imagined it. I tipped my nose into that gentle breeze curling through the half-cracked pane, each puff parting the despair one ripple at a time. Overriding even the constant hum of quiz shows.

Then there it was again. Honeysuckle. Sweet. Soft. Light. Everything opposite of what I'd known from birth.

Desperate for more, I crawled to the window, slowly, praying no one would see me. Life was easier if I stayed hidden, because otherwise I feared I would one day have to fight back. Still I was willing to risk detection to breathe more of that flowery perfume.

I have a particularly keen sense of smell, so living in a filthy meth house for twenty-eight years took a toll on me. And just to clarify, twenty-eight human years equates to four dog years for me. As a dog, that explains why the stench hit me hard.

Did you know that canines can identify smells up to ten thousand times better than a human? Well, we can. I learned that about sniffers on *Jeopardy!* My brain has forty percent more capacity devoted to smell than yours. Not that I mean to sound condescending or call you inferior. Facts are facts. I have more than two million olfactory sensors in my nose. You have opposable thumbs. Truly, aromatherapy is wasted on you people.

I like facts. The endless television programs offered that much at least, game show after game show. Back then, I embraced those quizzes, soaking up data, anything to prove I wasn't a dumbass at all. If I'd been a human and hadn't started having babies so early, I've often thought I would have become a professor with thick black glasses. I would have sequestered myself in an office lined with books, solitude. Peace.

But back to my sniffer.

Back to the honeysuckle.

And how all that relates to the day I found freedom in a splintered door.

To be clear, I spent my life watching methamphetamine being cooked, smoked, shot, sold. The rancid odor of the drug left me groggy. Sometimes even made me snarl, when that's not my nature. The smell of it saturated the walls, peeling the paper down in strips I chewed in moments of frenzied boredom. It permeated the saggy sofa I never sat on. Even clung to the mattresses on the floor in both bedrooms where junkies had sex. Worst of all, the toxic clouds hung in the kitchen, counters packed with everything from drain cleaner to funnels to my bowl full of scraps.

But that afternoon during my fourth summer, when I discovered honeysuckle, I considered that maybe, just maybe, there was something better for me, if only I could wait long enough to escape farther than the chain in the yard allowed.

Easier said than done, because I was a moneymaker, just like that steaming meth cooker. My litters of boxer pups were worth a lot, so I ate well, periodically. No one kicked me for a while. Until my babies were taken away so I could breed again. They always took them too early, and then I was alone.

You may already be thinking *puppy mill*, but that's not one hundred percent accurate. The woman who owned me—I won't bother to distinguish her with a name—would be more appropriately labeled a backyard breeder who used me and other dogs to supplement her meth income. Up until that honeysuckle moment in my fourth summer, I thought my mission in life was to have babies for people to love even if I never got to experience that feeling myself, other than for the few brief weeks I was allowed to keep each litter, their warm, tiny bodies snuggled up against me.

By the fourth winter, I wondered if I'd imagined a honeysuckle world just to survive. I began to lose hope, drawing in nothing but the fumes that made me mean.

Then, on the bitterest, coldest morning, my world changed on a larger scale with another beautiful scent. Peppermint.

It's still my favorite perfume, even above honeysuckle. Those two beautiful smells outnumbered the one evil stench of that cabin. There was more out there past my chain. So much more.

And I thank the Big Master who made us that the peppermint-scented lady understood I was not at my best the day she and the sad-eyed policeman broke down the meth-house door to rescue me.

One

DETECTIVE AJ PARKER started kicking down doors at five years old in hopes of becoming like his idol, Chuck Norris. The first attempt had landed AJ in the emergency room with a broken leg.

Thirty years later, though, he'd perfected the skill. By then he'd gotten a lot of practice as an Atlanta detective. Too much practice. The very reason he'd relocated to the sleepy town of Cooksburg, Tennessee, for a more low-key life. Still, a sixth sense honed from too many years undercover in narcotics told him he would have to channel his inner Chuck before high noon this Christmas Eve.

Raiding a home on a holiday wasn't particularly holly jolly, but there had been a report of neglected animals inside, and dogs left outdoors without shelter, in imminent danger of dying due to the frigid weather. His boots crunched along the caked snow as AJ approached the isolated cabin with caution. Footsteps crackled behind him—his police-department partner, Wyatt, his cousin who'd gotten him this job.

Oaks and pines circled the clearing, creating a wall of

privacy with only one icy path to the cabin. Which also meant there was one lone escape route, and so far no signs of animals or people coming in or out.

A brisk wind cut through his thick coat and bulletproof vest, chilling him all the way to his Southern roots. He and Wyatt accompanied an animal rescue team that had been instructed to stay safe and warm in their van for now, the engine purring softly.

Sunshine glimmered off the icicles spiking from the railing as if nature had decorated for the holidays even if the occupants of this ramshackle place ignored the season. Not so much as a wreath or tinsel in sight. Even the windows were blacked out with thick curtains, making the porch less than inviting.

Not to mention dangerous, depending on who lurked behind those darkened windows.

AJ breathed steady white bursts of air into the December afternoon. But inside AJ's gut, his instincts were on fire.

Adrenaline burned his veins as he scanned the front yard, deserted except for an old gray truck with a camper top. There wasn't snow on the hood, so the vehicle had been driven recently. The place was silent other than the grunt of a distant deer and a crisp wind whistling through the trees, boughs burdened with snow.

His cop senses burned hotter with each step closer to the cabin. Complicating matters, he had that contingent of animal rescuers behind him in the van. He held up a hand reminding them to stay back.

Then he saw it.

A thick chain, almost covered with snow, glinted through the powdery white like twisted garland spilling out of an overturned trash can. A brown mass of fur was curled up in the back. A large dog that didn't growl, bark—or even move.

Shit. They might already be too late.

He heard a car door open and caught the movement out

of the corner of his eyes a second before one of the rescuers shot past. He didn't have to guess who it had been.

Mary Hannah Gallo.

A fearless dynamo in a paisley parka.

And a giant pain in his butt.

His first night in Cooksburg, they'd had an impulsive one-night stand of crazy-good sex—his first since his life had gone to hell in a handbasket. The connection had sizzled so damn hot he'd been stunned stupid when he woke up the next morning and found she'd left the motel room already.

Worse yet, she'd given him a fake name. Francesca Vale. Not even a good made-up name. And he fell for that shit in spite of more than a decade collaring criminals.

He hadn't discovered her real name until his cousin tried to set him up on a blind date. AJ's only consolation? Miss Fakey-Pants Francesca Vale had been every bit as shocked to see him as he was to meet her for real as Mary Hannah Gallo. A buttoned-up mental-health counselor who had a wild-child hidden side. Very hidden. Apparently she'd assumed he was just traveling through town on his way to Nashville like most people at that truck-stop bar.

That bar.

That motel.

That night.

He willed away the steam-charged memories. He couldn't afford to think about anything except getting the job done and keeping those with him safe. Especially the Queen of Mistruths making her way to the dog in the trash can.

He understood her urge to charge ahead for the animal's sake, but damn it, caution saved more lives in the long run. He'd learned that the hard way. And wasn't that a memory-lane trip that could walk him straight to hell like in some bad teenage horror film?

"Gallo," he hissed between his teeth. "Get back to the van."

Without even turning, she waved away his concern and crouched near the toppled trash can, a blanket tucked under her arm. The winter gear hid how freaking petite she was as she crawled closer. And that petite frame hid a will of steel. She hadn't wanted anyone to know about that night at the bar, and she didn't want to have anything more to do with him. Fine by him. Except they'd been made the target of matchmakers determined to pair them up, in spite of how many times he and Mary Hannah told them no. No. And hell no.

It wasn't surprising she'd been sent with him today.

Now she was a great big stubborn distraction a few feet away. She wasn't budging unless he threw her over his shoulder and forcibly moved her. Which she would know full well he didn't have time to do.

Or even think about.

At least she would be on the side of the house when he pressed ahead. All the action would be focused at the front door. Left with no choice, he hauled his attention off Mary Hannah's fine ass in blue jeans and back to assessing the cabin.

Mewling and muffled woofs swelled from inside the cabin. The animals had picked up on his arrival, which meant any people behind those blacked-out windows would know soon as well. If they didn't already. He climbed the slick steps with sure feet, no hesitation.

He thumped the door with his gloved fist, launching a fresh blast of barks. "This is the police. We have a warrant to search the premises."

He pounded again. Only more woofs responded. "Police," he said. "Open up now, or we'll be forced to enter."

Still, no one answered.

He glanced at the rusted pickup with no snow on the hood. Screw waiting. "This is your last warning to comply. We have a warrant."

Notice given. He kicked the door. It held. Shit.

Snow showered down from the frame. The hefty bolts sent his instincts on a higher alert. This crappy cabin had a stronger door than he would have expected, a lot sturdier than even those at his rental cabin with top-notch security.

Bracing his feet on the icy porch was an iffy thing, but the element of surprise was gone now. He had to act fast. He booted the door again. The force jarred his teeth. But the door gave a little. He felt it.

He slammed his shoulder against the panel to finish the job. Wood cracked and splintered. A plank fell inward.

Yes.

His relief was short-lived.

The smell hit him hard. One whiff was all it took for total recognition after all the drug cases he'd worked in Atlanta. Snaking free, the unmistakable stench of meth stung his lungs. Not just a single pipe burning, but the thick stink of a full cooking operation.

This was supposed to be a sleepy little town. Most often cops dealt with the standard teenage vandalism and an occasional bar fight. That's why he'd chosen to move here. He'd intended to leave this kind of high-level crime nightmare behind.

He shouted over his shoulder to warn his partner, "Smells like a meth house. Call for backup, then secure the rear." He thought of Mary Hannah on the side of the cabin with the trash-can dog. "Civilians, return to your vehicle. Gallo, do you hear me? That means you. Clear out. Now."

His fingers closed around the grip of his 9mm Glock. With his other hand, he tugged his shirt collar up over his nose as a makeshift filter. He kicked the door the rest of the way open. It slammed against the inside wall. He prepared himself for whatever animals he might meet. At least his winter clothing added some padding.

Except nothing charged at him—human or canine. He was greeted with woofs from inside kennels. Four large and filthy

crates lined the living room. Two were full of poodle and
schnauzer puppies and two held nursing mama schnauzers.
There wasn't a person in sight.

Had someone already escaped out another door? Did
Wyatt have that entrance covered? God, he hoped Mary Hannah had taken her paisley, perky self back to the van.

AJ edged past the saggy sofa. An old-school console
television was turned on, the volume lowly chiming game-
show reruns. Not even a Christmas parade.

His heart slugged in his ears as he swept the two-bedroom
cabin, sparsely furnished. Definitely not enough here to call
the place a home. A framed yarn-art owl was faded with age.
A wagon-wheel lamp cast a yellow glow through a dingy
shade. He'd seen plenty of places just like this, even lived in
them during undercover assignments.

Wood floors squeaked beneath his feet, his steps muffled
by a rag rug. The one bathroom was empty other than a
nasty toothbrush caked with spit. A poodle slept in the tub,
curled up and snoring. The black ball of fur peeked through
half-open eyes then drifted off again, uninterested in the
stranger in her home.

Very un-doglike. Probably groggy from the fumes. Poor
little gal. The rescuers outside would have their hands full.

Soft footsteps from the kitchen had AJ spinning back to
the main area. Someone escaping? His eyes narrowed, and
he closed the bathroom door to make sure the poodle didn't
suddenly sprint out to trip him up.

Whoever was leaving, Wyatt would be ready for them. AJ
stepped deeper into the toxic haze toward the kitchen, ready
to have his partner's back. AJ reached the linoleum floor in
a 1970s-era orange kitchen just as the rear door creaked.

A shriek split the air. A female scream.

AJ's muscles bunched.

"Ma'am," his cousin Wyatt's voice rumbled through, cutting the shout short. "Put down the baseball bat and place
your hands on top of your head. Now!"

"Okay, okay, okay," the woman's voice answered, raspy like a chain smoker's. "I surrender. I was just here to pick up some puppies. I wasn't doing nothing wrong."

The click of handcuffs snapped. One problem down, and so far no one else in sight. Still, his muscles stayed tensed, ready.

AJ scanned the dirty kitchen full of a grocery list he knew by heart—everything needed to cook crystal meth. Ephedrine, butane, brake fluid, drain cleaner and more lined the counters along with other ingredients. Dishes were stacked in the sink with food caked on them from meals eaten here in spite of the dangerous fumes.

His mind churned with memories of another bust, another time, of finding a child hiding beneath a bed with a sippy cup full of drain cleaner.

Bile roiled in his gut.

He stuffed down the image before the past sucked him under. He needed to focus on the present. To give one hundred percent to a job that should have been nothing more complicated than doling out speeding tickets and catching underage drinkers.

"Wyatt," he called, "appears all clear inside. Dogs are contained in crates." His nose twitched under the shield of his collar. "Since it's a meth house, we'll need masks and latex gloves."

"Shiiiiit." His cousin whistled, then let out an "ooof."

"You okay?" AJ started toward the back door.

"Just securing the lady in the cruiser. You deal with the inside. I've got this." Wyatt's voice grew fainter as he walked farther away. "Don't even try it again with the knee, ma'am."

AJ forced his hand to relax on the grip of his weapon and turned back toward the living room. Now they just had to deal with the animals. Tragic, yes, but not as dangerous as a bunch of meth dealers. Mary Hannah and her friends at the local Second Chance Ranch Rescue could step in now and do their thing.

A mewling drifted from the far bedroom—half human–, half animal–sounding, stopping him in his tracks. His grip tightened on his weapon again. His thoughts firmly planted on that other bust, the child under the bed in agony from a sip of drain cleaner.

AJ followed the noise into the smaller of the two bedrooms. One step at a time, he inched closer to a rocking chair with a ratty afghan draped over the seat, preventing him from getting a clear view. Crouching, he lifted the trailing corner, slowly. A low growl gave him only an instant's warning that the mewling cry hadn't been human.

And that his first search hadn't uncovered all the animals.

A big brown dog shot out, toppling the rocker onto AJ. The beast darted past until the tether bolted to the floor went taut quivering with tension. The dog—a boxer—cowered only inches from the door.

Blocking the exit.

Crap. There was no way out except past the growling canine. His winter police-issue jacket wouldn't last long if that animal decided to take a serious bite out of him. The dog snarled louder, teeth bared as it flattened to the floor, pulling at the restraint that wouldn't survive another serious lunge.

Even a regular Joe with no animal rescue experience could tell the boxer was clearly freaked out and terrified, ears back, eyes wide, drool dripping from its mouth. He'd learned on past assignments that a scared dog could be every bit as dangerous as an aggressive one.

Much like people.

He wasn't the type to cry uncle, but animal rescue folks used tools for this job for a good reason.

"Um, hello," he called lowly. "Can someone bring a catchpole before Cujo in here turns me into a Milk-Bone?"

Hopefully someone outside heard him. The team of four

consisted of two employees from county Animal Control and two from the Second Chance Ranch Rescue.

"Shhh, shhh, shhh." He made what he hoped were soothing noises. "I'm not here to hurt you, puppy. Be good and there are people here who will get you a bed and food. I'll personally make sure you get a grade-A hamburger if you keep your teeth to yourself."

A one in four chance Mary Hannah would show up. She was thin, short and not particularly intimidating. He envisioned her comforting the little poodles, not wrestling with this muscular creature.

Except the odds were not in his favor today.

Mary Hannah appeared in the open doorframe, a catchpole held in a fierce grip. Her sleek dark hair slipped free from a low ponytail to brush the shoulders of her parka. Her wide brown eyes saw everything.

But through pretty rose-colored glasses with heavy black frames.

The woman was a whirlwind of naive perfection who seemed to think the world could be changed with sweet words and a soft touch. She might take a brief walk on the wild side now and again, but she hadn't come close to seeing what he had. He'd witnessed firsthand that some evil just went to the core. There was no talking it down with a warm, fuzzy hug.

He wasn't judging. She just hadn't seen what he had. She would get there someday if she kept assisting in these kinds of "rescues."

Someday.

But right now she was all that stood between him and a wild-eyed animal high on meth fumes.

SMELLING THE METH made Mary Hannah's mouth water, made her nose burn.

And made her senses sing like sirens luring her back into the bottomless pit of addiction.

Mary Hannah Gallo had made a lifetime's worth of mistakes by twenty-four. She'd spent the next four years making sure she never screwed up again. Too bad Detective AJ Parker was a sexy, hot temptation begging her to break every one of her rules for a calm, structured future.

One night. Just one weak night of mourning in a bar, thinking she could have a no-strings fling to ease some of the pain, grief, hunger, and now she was stuck bumping into temptation every time she turned around in this closet-sized town.

Not that she had time to check out Detective No-Strings with a full-sized, growling boxer straining on a tether. The bolt in the floor inched upward.

"Parker . . ." She kept her voice soft and low-pitched. She peeled off her gloves so her grip would be more secure on the pole. "Keep your eyes averted from the dog until I loop the catchpole over its head."

She monitored the fawn-colored boxer out of the corners of her eyes, cataloging details about the animal. Her OCD came in handy sometimes. The dog was female, trembling, jittery, likely from living in this disgusting place. Mary Hannah took another step, assessing, inching warily until she was finally close enough. Slipping the loop at the end of the pole over the dog's head would require finesse.

The boxer lurched toward the door, away from the cop. The bolt in the floor wriggled at the strain. AJ's hand twitched just over his gun. Mary Hannah winced. Shooting the animal would be a last resort, and one she prayed wouldn't happen here. She couldn't stomach the thought that this was the only life that poor dog would know. She had to give this animal a chance. Mary Hannah took another, final, step, extending her arm. The loop at the end was . . . almost . . .

There.

She tightened the loop until it was secure. The pole gave her distance from the dog for now.

A sigh of relief shuddered through her, and she allowed herself an instant to breathe, just breathe a thankful prayer that AJ was okay. Her eyes skated to him as he stood slowly, taller, taller, taller still and filling out that cop uniform oh so very well.

God, he was too sensually appealing for his own good. And for her sanity. It wasn't about the handsome features, either, or the way his coal-black hair curled at the ends, just a little too long in a rebel kind of way. He epitomized tall, dark and studly in the manner that made teenage girls flock to vampire movies.

It was his crystal-blue eyes that drew her in, those haunted windows to his soul that made her consider he and she might not be complete opposites after all.

This wasn't anywhere near an appropriate time to be thinking about how sexy he looked. Maybe the fumes were affecting her judgment.

"Hey, Mary Hannah?" he said without moving, the tension in the room so thick she could swear his Southern drawl vibrated across in waves. "How about getting some more help before the beast knocks you over? I'll hold the dog, with my eyes down checking out the peeling wallpaper."

Sure enough, wallpaper pieces curled and spiraled like macabre ribbons on a package. Except why was she checking out the decor of this filthy place, for God's sake? She needed to get her head in the game and shake off whatever had hold of her, whether it was the fumes or the holiday doldrums.

Mary Hannah tightened her grip on the cool metal pole, bracing her feet. "Everyone else is outside working to medically stabilize the male boxer found in the trash can. So I'm all the help you have."

"He's actually still alive?" he asked, glancing her way.

"Barely. He may not make it. Damn it, avert your eyes," she reminded him sharply. Herself, too. Except she needed to look away from the man. "Dogs perceive direct eye contact as a sign of aggression. Now keep yours focused on the floor while you slip out and find another catchpole. Then we'll have more control to walk the boxer to the vehicle and into a crate. Or you could also ask someone to sedate the animal, but we'll still need her safely restrained until the drugs take effect."

AJ snorted. "Or like I said before, *you* could pass over control to *me* before that dog runs you over."

"Quit going all macho man on me." She kept her voice low and even, doing her best not to rile the dog. "Do your job. I'll do mine."

The wild-eyed animal strained against the loop, making Mary Hannah's arms burn from the force. She'd already noticed the dog was female, and given her saggy underbelly, she must have puppies around here somewhere or had recently.

"Parker, stay loose as you inch past. She's clearly had a recent litter. Mother dogs can be protective, which makes them more aggressive. Maternal instincts kick the aggression into possessive overdrive."

Understandable, really. Mothers should do anything to protect their babies. Anything. Her eyes stung. Her heart, too. But there could be no more attempts to indulge in just one night to forget.

AJ walked in a slow half circle past the mama boxer. "I haven't seen puppies that look like hers around here. Only small-breed pups."

"Good to know." Mary Hannah's arms ached, but she had to hold on only a little longer. AJ was at the door now, just behind her. "Shhh, shhh, Mama, it'll be all right. We want to help you."

Mama lifted her head, a low growl rumbling in the back of her throat.

AJ locked his arms around Mary Hannah in a flash, his hands eclipsing hers. "Careful now. Mama here's high—"

"—on meth." She swallowed hard and held herself very still in his arms again for the first time since that impulsive, stupid—mind-blowing—night five months ago. "Mama's high on meth," she repeated. "Right."

That made her want to help save this dog all the more, to give the girl a chance to show who she really was underneath the drugs. This horrible existence couldn't be the end for the dog, especially not because Mary Hannah was distracted by the feel of AJ's arms around her again.

His chest was a solid wall of muscle behind her, the scent of his aftershave a tempting relief from the sting of drugs in the air. She swallowed hard, her body tingling to life— and at such an awful time it was surreal.

His breath was warm against her neck. "Mary Hannah? You can let go now."

"I understand the need to be careful." In more ways than one. She was always careful and tried to do the right thing, except on those rare occasions when she messed up, she went all out. Big-time. "I'm not in danger . . . from the dog."

"For some crazy reason I'm not reassured by your pink snow boots."

She ground her teeth together before blurting out, "That's sexist."

But sexist or not, the heat of his breath on her neck was too much. She needed to get out of this room, away from this man.

Mary Hannah passed AJ the catchpole. "Fine then. Since you insist. You can hold her, and I'll get more help—"

Before she could finish the sentence, Animal Control Officer Martel—a big burly guy who could have passed for a lumberjack—ducked inside the room and added a second catchpole over the dog's neck. "Nice job, you two. Take this and I'll give her a quick injection."

A shudder of relief went through AJ that shimmered right into Mary Hannah, warming her freezing-cold toes before he stepped away and took the other restraint pole. Martel pulled a capped syringe from his pocket, tugged off the cover and tucked the needle in the boxer's left haunch before she could blink.

The Animal Control officer stepped back fast. "That

should kick in soon and make her easier to handle." He took the catchpole from Mary Hannah. "I've got her now."

"Thanks. I'll see if they need help outside." She couldn't run from AJ fast enough.

She stumbled away in the living room, through the front door, gasping in the crisp afternoon air to clear away the jumble of too many emotions and sensations intensified so much during the holidays. Everything tangled up inside until even the good was overshadowed by the bad.

And oh God, there were so many sad memories of another man's touch. Her husband's. Her *ex*-husband's—Ted's.

She couldn't even blame him for walking out on her. She'd gotten hooked on prescription drugs, of all things. So damn cliché and too easy to access when she was a college student afraid of disappointing her parents, then terrified of not being accepted into grad school.

There was a seductive allure in those pills that seemed socially acceptable. They'd been prescribed by a doctor, after all. Then two, then three different doctors.

Then through other avenues.

After that, she'd deluded herself into believing that she used to make sure her studies didn't inconvenience her husband, only to lose him and so much more.

She blinked back tears. She didn't have the luxury of time to indulge in a pity party right now. The yard was filling fast with more cops, another team from Animal Control and the head of the rescue she volunteered with—Second Chance Ranch.

Her friends. Her new family of sorts, especially since she'd so royally messed up her chance at a real family.

She and Ted hadn't planned on having children until she finished college. She'd thought she had plenty of time to get over her "little problem" with drugs. Except she'd accidentally gotten pregnant and couldn't avoid her demons any longer. Her addiction threatened the well-being of the life growing inside her. She'd thought confessing to her doctor, then to her husband, had been the toughest days of her life.

Not even close. The worst day had come later. When she'd miscarried her baby while in rehab. There was a grief in that she would never get over.

Never.

Ted hadn't been able to get over it, either. He blamed her for the death of their baby, and she couldn't disagree with him. It was her fault, and she had to live with that. The only way she could stay sane—stay alive—was to spend the rest of her days trying to make amends. She didn't expect forgiveness. She just wanted peace.

Mary Hannah sagged back against the icy slick wall of the cabin. The cold against her was nowhere near as intense as the chill inside her.

Not all junkies looked like the skeletal woman sitting in the police cruiser.

Some of them wore pretty paisley to cover ugly secrets.

Two

That injection made my head spin like a
Wheel of Fortune.

—FEMALE BOXER, FOUR YEARS OLD,
BROWN/BLACK CONFISCATE #8

A J CAME FROM a family of cops. It was in his blood.
He tore off his surgical mask and tossed it in a hazardous-
waste bag set up outside the cabin, the routine familiar, similar
to countless other days on the job in Atlanta. His dad had risen
to the rank of police commissioner and had been proud of AJ's
speedy promotion to detective.

Papa Parker hadn't been too thrilled over AJ pulling himself off the fast track to move. Not that there'd been any choice.
After his last undercover sting, he'd been on a crash-and-burn
path of reckless behavior, shit for brains. His cousin Wyatt
had somehow seen it in his eyes at a family reunion and mentioned the opening in his small-town force along with a great
rental cabin next door to the Second Chance Ranch Rescue.
The offer had come a day after AJ had almost gotten his partner killed. He wasn't cut out for the big-city crime scene anymore, and his old man would just have to live with that.

AJ reached for his surgical mask only to remember he'd
already tossed it. He may have made it through this bust

with everybody in one piece, but he was rattled. He never should have let Mary Hannah get away with running around outside, much less entering the house to save his ass.

He eyed the Animal Control van loaded with crates. Mama lay inside with her head on her paws, ears plastered back against her head in fear. She'd been given a tranquilizer, but her eyes were still so wide with terror the white showed in a whale-ish look that made him want to crouch down in front and talk softly to her.

Promise her . . . what? That everything would be okay? Because that was a lie. He didn't know what would happen to her.

The thought twisted his gut so hard he didn't notice his cousin approaching until Wyatt clapped him on the back.

"Poor Boxer Mama," Wyatt drawled, the laid-back soul of the family. "Mary Hannah said the dog looks newly weaned. Puppies have probably already been sold."

"The truck looks like it was driven today, no snow on the hood. Maybe they were dropped off earlier and we still have a chance of tracking them down."

Wyatt pulled his keys from his coat pocket. "Maybe the news coverage will help."

AJ glanced at the woman under arrest in the back of the cop car. She wore a gray wool coat over a sweat suit. Her lank blond hair hung down her shoulders. Years of drug use showed in the dark circles under her eyes and her pocked, acned skin. She could have been twenty-five or fifty. Meth gave a person a timeless look—and not in a good way.

With luck, the meth woman would cut a deal.

AJ looked back at his cousin. "Has she confessed to anything yet?"

"She says it's her boyfriend's cabin, and she was just here to pick up the poodle and schnauzer puppies to take to their new homes. The male poodle and schnauzer were found in the back of the covered pickup, huddled together to stay warm.

According to our suspect"—Wyatt flipped open his notepad—
"Evelyn Lucas, the litters on the property are all Christmas
presents due to be dropped off today."

"Then there are going to be a lot of disappointed families,
because those pups can't go anywhere." He knew the drill by
heart after past busts, a couple of them four times the size of
this one. "The dogs are contaminated with the fumes from the
meth cooker. They need a good wash-down straightaway. And
of course there are Boxer Mama's missing puppies. God, I
hope each family bathed them before letting their kids cuddle
up to sleep with the new pup."

Wyatt shuddered. "Once we get back to the station, I'll
make it a number one priority to get Ms. Lucas to give up the
names of the buyers." He tugged his stocking cap over his
red-tipped ears. "The place will be searched more thoroughly
once we get a team with suits in. If they find contact names,
I'll pass them along to Animal Control."

Doubtful that there were any records. And likely cash-
only transactions. He braced his hands on his thighs and
hung his head. "Some way to spend the holidays."

Wyatt swept off his stocking hat and finger-combed a
hand through his graying hair. "Hey, once we finish our
report at the station, you should come with me to Lacey's
for Christmas Eve dinner. I know she invited you for the big
Christmas Day meal, too. But you're welcome at both. Mary
Hannah will be there."

Of course she would.

AJ cricked his neck from side to side, searching for the
best way to duck out. Wyatt dated the quirky owner of the
Second Chance Ranch Rescue—Lacey McDaniel. The two
of them led the effort to set him up with Mary Hannah like
they were all in high school, for crying out loud, trying to
match up their friends for double dates to the movies. He
wouldn't have expected Wyatt to become such a romantic
sap, but he didn't intend to exchange locker-room stories with

Wyatt about the one-nighter with Mary Hannah and how she'd bolted before sunrise.

"I appreciate the offer," he said again, "but I'll be beat by the time I get home tonight. And I have holiday plans of my own for tomorrow."

"What plans?" Wyatt raised an eyebrow. "A microwaved dinner and a beer in front of the television?"

"My Christmas holiday. My traditions. My business. But thanks all the same." He glanced over at the van with Mama in her crate, her eyelids starting to slide down as the drugs kicked into high gear. "I'm going fishing."

"Seriously?" Wyatt snorted. "You're the worst fisherman I've ever met."

"Thanks." AJ winced but couldn't deny it. Not that it mattered. He didn't fish for food or sport. He hung out there with the line in the water, no bait on the hook, just searching for peace.

"Promise you'll think about the offer, okay? Lacey put a ham in the oven before she headed over here for tonight. And she's got a turkey in the smoker for tomorrow. Friends and volunteers from the rescue are bringing side dishes. She needs our support over the holidays. Even though it's been two years since her husband died in Iraq . . ."

"I'll try," AJ offered, guilt already stinging because he wanted to help his cousin, but he also knew he would be a big wet blanket. Better to stay away.

"Good. And hey, with her daughter and son-in-law coming to town, plus all those volunteers, the crowd will be large enough for you to stay quietly grouchy if you want."

Wyatt was ten years older and always had been in charge of looking after his younger cousin AJ. Apparently some things hadn't changed, and as much as AJ wanted to haul his own ass out of this dark pit he'd fallen into, it wasn't happening.

His cousin clapped him on the shoulder again. "I'll see you at the station later?"

"Yeah, as soon as I finish up here. I need to double-check all the Animal Control documentation."

So he could stay and watch over Mary Hannah even if he didn't plan to push for a second one-night stand.

Idiot.

"Later, cousin." Waving, Wyatt slid into the front seat of the cruiser and flipped on the lights, sending flashes streaking across the pine trees in the late afternoon as he took Ms. Lucas away.

It had been a long day of grueling work. He was sweating under his winter gear.

He'd accompanied other Animal Control contingents back in Georgia since dogfighting and drug trafficking often went hand in hand, but he'd never been on an operation that included a volunteer animal rescue, too, like Second Chance Ranch.

Mary Hannah had certainly pulled her weight today, loading filthy dogs and puppies into crates. That surprised him. Up to now he'd been so focused on reconciling that wild night with "Francesca Vale" with the image of prim Mary Hannah Gallo, who shut him down cold. Granted, he hadn't been himself that night, either, morose as hell after too long spent undercover and all too willing to indulge in a distraction.

But the woman he'd come to know over the past five months had her life in alphabetical order. So he'd been surprised today to see her be so hands-on in the rescue operation. She'd just yanked on two pairs of latex gloves and a surgical mask before wading right in, cuddling the terrified creatures matted with their own feces. She'd even already agreed to go with Animal Control to the county shelter to help intake the animals.

AJ peeled off his own gloves and tossed them into the industrial-sized waste bag on his way to one of the vans, which happened to be where Mary Hannah was working.

He stopped just behind her, catching a hint of peppermint

that stayed on her. Breath mints? Or shampoo? The question tugged at him like some great puzzle he had to solve.

"Hey," he called out softly, his hands twitching with the urge to rest on her shoulders. "I didn't get to thank you in there for saving my ass."

She jolted, just a slight twitch of her head, then her shoulders braced as she went back to the task at hand. Her eyes were so damn sad as she labeled the crate with the groggy boxer.

"No thanks needed." She knuckle-nudged her glasses up the bridge of her nose. "We were both doing our part to handle the situation."

Suddenly he didn't want to pile into the van yet with everyone else around them. He wanted more time to figure out this third dimension of a woman he hadn't come close to understanding in the five months since they'd crossed paths. Then maybe she would stop haunting his dreams. Naked. "How do you know so much about animal rescue as a volunteer?"

"I may be a volunteer, but I've gone through additional training." She tucked the paperwork into a waterproof sleeve.

He wasn't letting her brush him off so easily. Not this time. "But it's not like you're on the payroll with this group. You're under no obligation to work holidays."

She glanced over her shoulder, her brown eyes still shimmering with that sadness, her hand falling to rest on the crate protectively. "Most of the other volunteers have families. I don't have anywhere else to be, so I offered to assist."

Just like him. Other than a cousin. "So you don't have plans for Christmas—"

Her eyes went wide with panic. "Speaking of Christmas, I need to finish up. Have a great one."

What the hell? Had she feared he would ask her over for a microwavable turkey dinner and a visit with Francesca?

Her snow boots punched through the icy layer on her way to the van where Second Chance Ranch Rescue director

Lacey McDaniel jotted notes on a clipboard while an angry schnauzer charged the crate door. The reality of how badly things could have gone today hit him hard for the first time. An image of Mary Hannah wrangling that freaked-out boxer chilled the sweat on his skin.

He couldn't just walk away, not until he knew she was tucked in back home with visions of sugarplums dancing in her head. The sooner he wrapped this case up at the shelter and the station, the better. It would take a full afternoon of Christmas fishing to erase the memory of this day—and dreams of that one night five months ago.

THANK GOD THE shelter had a private shower, because Mary Hannah's nerves were shot.

She held the sprayer over her head. Exhausted. But relieved.

The male boxer was in the clinic in critical condition. All the other dogs had been cleaned, processed and settled in kennel runs faster than she would have predicted, thanks to the unexpected help from AJ. She'd done her best to keep him at arm's length since she'd realized her stupidly impulsive one-night stand lived next door to the Second Chance Ranch—next door to her since she rented the loft apartment over the barn. Sometimes she wondered if they should talk about that night, blame it on the two drinks, except they hadn't been drunk.

And she couldn't bear to think about what drove her to seek comfort. Or how much he enticed her to go back for more.

She cranked the water hotter, hoping to chase away the chill in her heart that seemed to go deeper today because of that mama boxer and her missing babies. Showering in the shelter's dog washroom wasn't optimum. But it was private with a locked door that would give her a few minutes to collect herself.

The patter of the shower water hitting tile muffled the

distant barking mixed with the low melody of Christmas tunes—ironically "Silent Night." This place was anything but quiet.

She'd bagged her clothes to be tossed—including her favorite parka and boots. Maybe they could have been cleaned, but there was no way she could wear them again. Each piece would serve as a reminder of the meth smell. She'd even eaten a whole tin of breath mints—homeopathic, all-natural for stress—trying to get the scent and taste out of her system.

Water streamed off her. Suds swirled down the drain. She'd scrubbed and scrubbed until her skin was almost raw. Still the smell lingered, reminding her of how easily she could be tempted to numb herself with drugs again.

Or sex.

Except her one attempt at that hadn't gone as planned. God, what were the odds she would have her one epic fling with a narcotics detective? The last kind of man who could forgive or understand her past. She needed to remember that and chalk up today's weakness to holiday sentimentality.

She shut off the water and squeezed the excess moisture from her hair. Her life consisted of one day at a time, staying clean, keeping her world in order and making atonement through her volunteer work at the Second Chance Ranch.

That place had a peace about it that had saved her, a peace she knew these poor animals needed. Once legalities were cleared up, these animals could be transferred to there—if they passed their temperament tests. She just prayed they would stay healthy here in the meantime with all the airborne viruses of so many animals in close quarters.

One day at a time, she reminded herself.

Get through the holidays, then she could focus on these animals and the upcoming My Furry Valentine Mutt Makeover competition. A group of animal-lover bigwigs from Nashville were sponsoring the shelter challenge, led by country-music legend Billy Brock. Trainers and foster families from across Tennessee and Kentucky would pair up with rescue dogs for six weeks to train, culminating in a Valentine's festival with music and a parade of the canine contestants. Then a big debut on Valentine's Day for love-match adoptions and a hundred-thousand-dollar grand prize to go to the winning shelter.

The perfect opportunity for Second Chance as well as the animals.

Some had called her a workaholic for volunteering all her free time, but she preferred to stay busy. She wasn't interested in partying. Her rescue friends kept her social calendar packed with plenty of events and camaraderie.

She had a full life, damn it.

So why was she so nervous about leaving this shower room and running into AJ again? She'd managed to keep her distance for five months. She could manage today.

Mary Hannah grabbed a couple of towels to dry off, the terry cloth bristly from so many washings with bleach. She tugged on the sweat suit with the shelter logo, and her gym shoes. She'd washed her glasses—five times. She finger-combed her hair. With no more reason to delay, she stepped out of the small washroom and into the corridor.

Where AJ waited. For her.

There was no mistaking the intensity of his piercing blue eyes. He leaned back against a wall beside shelves full of towels and blankets, garland strung along the edge. A big inflatable dog filled a corner of the lobby, the glowing decoration donated by a local ad agency, complete with a contribution box wrapped like a package.

AJ, all intense and brooding, looked so innocuous up next to that goofy blow-up dog with a wagging tail. And his sweat suit sure fit his leanly muscled body. The shelter logo stretched across his broad shoulders, his black hair wet and spiking. The fresh-washed scent of him was as enticing as any cologne.

"You're still here." She picked the hem of her sweatshirt

self-consciously, her hair hanging in a thick, wet clump over one shoulder. "Is something wrong?"

He waited until a male kennel tech walked past pushing a bucket and mop, then met her eyes again. "I wanted to make sure you're okay. And? Are you?"

She might as well be honest on that point at least. "I'm still a little shaken by what we saw at the cabin. The drugs as well as the horrible condition of the animals. I've never participated in a seizure with these sorts of legal ramifications."

"Hopefully they'll plead out and things will move faster to release the animals from here."

She simply nodded, her gaze darting up and down the hall, where a half-dozen kennel techs went about their daily routine of cleaning and feeding the hundreds of animals in their care, dodging around that inflatable dog. The Cooksburg Animal Control facility was a standard county shelter, with concrete floors and the thick scent of bleach, a clean, well-run operation. But it was still a shelter and a traumatic place for any animal to land. Much less ones that were already stressed to the limit.

AJ lifted a lock of her damp hair, rubbing it between two fingers. "I hope you'll have time to decompress over the Christmas break."

Her scalp tingled at his touch, her raw nerves soaking up the sensation, craving the distraction he could bring. Her mind flooded with memories of his hands along her bare skin in a motel room, the lights low and their inhibitions even lower as they'd both looked to forget about the world for that one night.

Except that one night had made her feel too much. Want too much. Even now.

She opened her mouth to tell him to stop. "Don't worry about me. I'm fine. In fact, I, uh, you should—"

He let go. "Your hair is going to freeze when you step outside."

She exhaled with relief that he'd changed the subject.

"All of me will freeze even though I feel like a snowman— or snowwoman—in this sweat suit."

"Christmas theme?" He tugged a flannel blanket off a shelf and wrapped a paw-print blanket around her shoulders.

"Um, thanks."

How surreal it was talking to him without discussing what had happened between them. But she'd made her position clear to him five months ago when he'd shown up at Lacey's with his cousin. There would be no repeat of that night, and the subject was off-limits.

His hands brushed her neck briefly, but the heat of his touch lingered. "Sorry the purple blanket doesn't match the red sweat suit."

She frowned, nudging her glasses. "That's an odd thing to say. Almost sounds like you're making fun of me."

"I apologize for being a rude bastard." He grimaced. "It's been one helluva rough day."

"Amen to that. I'm not sure there's enough aromatherapy in my arsenal to wipe away what we saw." What did he do to decompress? Images filled her mind, like the thought of showering with him five months ago. What it would have been like to shower with him today and massage the tension from his shoulders. "We sure didn't expect a meth house. There was such pain in those animals' eyes."

AJ leaned against the wall beside her, his shoulder touching hers. "Drugs have a way of casting a wide net of destruction."

She forced herself not to flinch as that comment hit way too close to home. "I'm just glad we could intervene." She needed to put distance between them. Now. She needed to find Lacey since they'd ridden together. "I'm sure you have work to do. Please don't let me stop you. Good night, Parker."

AJ stopped her with a hand to her arm. "Do you believe that Mama can be saved?"

She looked down at his fingers wrapped around her arm,

the feeling warm through the fabric. The world went silent for a second other than the *swish, swish, swish* of the inflatable dog's tail.

Mary Hannah stepped back until AJ's arm fell away. "It's too early to tell."

"But what does your gut tell you? How will she react once the drugs wear off?"

"That depends on how her temperament test goes."

"And if she passes, you'll work with her?"

"Me, or another foster home, but it's tough to say how much we can do for her even if she passes her evaluation. I do believe she has been . . . damaged. She appears to be undersocialized, possibly abused. We'll know more in a couple of days." Why was he asking so many questions? Did he want to keep her here? But to what end? "Although maybe we'll get lucky. Sometimes the animal needs a while to chill and rehab before being made adoption available."

"Even the boxer?" He still insisted on focusing on that one particular animal.

Ah, realization sunk in. He might try to appear all broody and badass, but he'd been touched by the grief in that dog's eyes just as she had.

She patted his shoulder, resisting the urge to curl her fingers around and hold on. "Even her. Lacey and I will do everything in our power for her. It's . . . unpalatable . . . to think that's all she will ever experience in life."

"I know that there are animals everywhere in need of homes that *don't* require the extra effort rehabbing. So why invest your time in this one?"

Had she misunderstood his feelings about the boxer after all? "Because of those drugs, we didn't see the real her today. Even so, Mama didn't bite in spite of being terrified and high. That's promising."

Or maybe Mary Hannah just desperately needed to believe the dog could detox and overcome all the odds to be redeemable. That *she* could be redeemable.

"You're an idealist." He tapped the rim of her glasses. "Seeing the world through rose-colored lenses."

"I assume that means you consider yourself a realist."

"Yes, although I would appreciate it if you didn't use the counselor skills on me."

The last thing she wanted or needed was him as a client. Right now she just wanted to leave. To shower again. To figure out how she could be attracted to someone she wasn't even sure she liked.

She searched his eyes as deeply as she searched herself and found . . . he was in as much pain as she was.

Mary Hannah touched his shoulder again lightly, tentatively. "Are *you* okay?"

"I'm fine, Dr. Freud." He winked, his smile almost managing to chase the shadows from his eyes.

Her hand fell away. "I'm not a doctor or a psychiatrist. I'm a mental-health counselor who specializes in patients with PTSD."

"Okay, mental-health counselor. Lucky for us, I'm fine. I'm the seasoned professional."

She should just leave, but the shadows in his eyes urged her to press on. "I'm not asking in that capacity. I'm worried, you know, one person concerned about another. I may not be in the line of fire, but I deal with fallout of days like this. I have some understanding that we're both going to have trouble sleeping tonight."

His eyes narrowed, and the air between them suddenly crackled to life. "Are you suggesting we distract each other?" He paused, taking a lazy step closer. "Again."

And just that fast, all the walls she'd built between them these past five months crumbled. That one reckless night was right there as vividly as if someone had turned their memories into a movie, replaying in explicit, body-melting detail.

Her skin went tight, her body aching. She swallowed hard, not having a clue how to make this stop but knowing she had to try to regain level ground between them. "AJ—"

He held up his hands. "Forget I said that. This isn't the time or place. We both do need to call this day over. I need to get things moving all the faster at the department in hopes of clearing away the legal paperwork keeping these animals here. The sooner I drop you off, the sooner I can go to the station."

The roots of her hair tingled. "Drop *me* off?"

"Didn't I tell you? Wyatt called right after Lacey left here to go home and check on dinner. He asked me to make sure you get home safe and sound. He even had my car sent over from the station."

AJ hadn't been waiting around to talk to her after all. He'd been here because he was asked to escort her home. That shouldn't sting, damn it.

But it did. "Don't you have to leave for the station right away?"

"Wyatt's handling our report until I get there." He spread his arms wide, inflatable dog glowing behind him. "So for now, I'm all yours."

Three

I'd always dreamed my first car ride would be like *Cash Cab* and I'd make it to my home, rolling in dough. But my ride got cut short . . .

—FEMALE BOXER, FOUR YEARS OLD, SHELTER #S75230

ALL MY LIFE I'd wondered what the world looked like beyond my chain. I'd fantasized that the places on television were real and I might get to experience running through a forest or sleeping in a clean home.

Never in my wildest fantasies did I imagine I would get stuck in a Sarah McLachlan commercial of save the shelter animals—for real. Yes, I was now officially the cowering animal inside a kennel run.

Roll the cameras.

I'd let my guard down with the peppermint lady that the policeman called Mary Hannah. She did something worse than loop a chain around my neck. I was stuck with a needle. Then they dragged me outside and stuffed me inside a crate. I felt betrayed.

Terrified.

Even with the knockout drugs they pumped in my system, I couldn't stop trembling because I'd never left the cabin or yard before. The shelter was technically better—cleaner—

than my old home and no one yelled at me. But it was so foreign. I didn't understand the rules.

How strange that there had been a comfort in the monotonous routine of my awful past life. A talk-show psychiatrist would have said I was suffering from battered-woman syndrome.

I just knew I was scared shitless. Literally. I pooped in fear when one of the workers put a bowl of kibble in my kennel.

Even with the Christmas music playing, I could hear the dogs from the cabin in the other kennel runs. But they kept us separated—something about detoxing and temperament tests. I knew from my TV watching that answering quiz-show questions incorrectly meant failure. Booted off the show. No prize. Huge disappointment.

What would that mean for me? I knew it couldn't be good. Except there wasn't anything for me to study, even if I could have stopped shaking long enough to ask. My heart pounded so hard it made me too ill to eat. Not that I could crawl out of my corner.

My eyes were closed, but I stayed awake long after the lights went out and the workers left. Breathing in the scent of bleach. Listening to the soft holiday music.

Until I surrendered to the groggy pull of those knockout injections.

AJ STEERED HIS restored Harvester Scout through the dark snowy streets. The road was mostly deserted other than a snowplow, a couple of trucks and a car abandoned in a ditch. Lampposts with wreaths lined the sidewalks, white lights twinkling in trees and store windows. Tools rattled in the back along with fishing poles and a jack. Standard mess.

With the not-standard addition of Mary Hannah Gallo sitting beside him, rocking the hell out of sweats and a blanket patterned with dog paws draped over her legs. She stared out the window, tracing one finger along the condensation. Her sleek brown hair was almost dry. He'd cranked the heater on high, the vents lifting stray hairs around her face like some kind of mystical aura.

He still wasn't sure why he'd agreed to drive her home. He could have paid for her cab, driven to the station to file his report—then gone straight to bed. But somehow, when Wyatt had made the latest transparent effort to pair them up, AJ had gone along. It had been almost comical. Except he wasn't in a laughing mood today.

The whole meth-house raid had him off-kilter. This day needed to be over, and yet he found himself extending the time he spent with the one woman who managed to get under his skin. When it looked like Mary Hannah would turn down his offer, he'd been too damn disappointed. He couldn't deny that he wanted to see her *messy* again.

Mary Hannah turned from the window and held her hands in front of the heater vents. "Thanks for the ride."

"You're welcome. I'm surprised you didn't put up more of a fight." He downshifted to gain traction along the ice as he turned a corner, the scenery shifting from shops to housing.

The holiday decor grew less coordinated; colored lights lined one roof. A big plastic Santa glowed beside the chimney of another. A crèche was lit by a spotlight in front of brick home with a driveway full of cars. Next door, a bundled-up man shoveled the walkway. Outside, the world was . . . normal. Cheerful.

"Everyone else has families and out-of-town guests. Parties to attend." She pointed to all the cars parked in front of houses. "It seemed wrong to ask them to wait around longer because I would have preferred to call a taxi."

"That's logical," he answered offhandedly.

"Is that a dig? Like with the blanket?"

He glanced at her in surprise. He hadn't expected a stray comment from him would affect her.

"Just an observation." He tapped his temple and added a smile for good measure. "Purely from a detective's objective perspective."

"Right, sorry for being defensive." She relaxed back into her seat, looking at ease for the first time since she'd stepped into his vehicle. "What else does your detective's intuition tell you about me?"

He thought for a moment, envisioning her life, her apartment. Thinking about Mary Hannah and "Francesca." Better to stick with the Mary Hannah side for now. "That your cabinets are alphabetized. You're stylish but thrifty, which cycles back around to that organization. You don't let things go to waste."

"I like myself the more and more you say."

He laughed, glancing at her and taking in the way her eyes lit up the night. "Now, I wouldn't have guessed you have a sense of humor."

Her smile went tight. "We all have our secrets."

"That we do, Francesca."

Her breath hitched, then she cleared her throat. "My career gives me insights into people, too."

Okay, mentions of Francesca were still off-limits. "Bet that takes all the fun out of dating."

"Or it saves me from more messy breakups."

"More?"

"I'm divorced," she said. "I thought you knew."

"I'm sorry. I didn't know. Wyatt and Lacey never mentioned it." And he genuinely was sorry. He'd experienced firsthand how much broken relationships hurt like hell even when the end was inevitable and completely right. "Does he live around here?"

"No, he moved away with his new wife." She picked at the edge of the blanket. "They live in Ohio and have a baby on the way."

"Are you okay about that?"

"Of course," she answered too quickly.

This conversation was getting heavy, fast. He needed to lighten the mood again. "So, Dr. Freud, what has your psychiatric intuition discerned about me?"

"That you're moody," she said without hesitation.

"A doorknob could figure that out." He tugged a lock of her hair again. "Come on. Play along."

The strands were even silkier dry, like whispery threads against his skin. He let go and put his attention back on the road, headlights pointed toward the tire-worn ruts in the ice.

"Fine, AJ. You want more?" She counted off on her fingers. "You're a loner, but I would guess you haven't always been. Something happened to send you running here," she continued with unerring accuracy. "Your family is large and tight-knit. That's why, even in your need for space, you still gravitated toward your cousin. Am I right?"

Too right. So much so he would almost think his cousin had been talking too much, except he trusted Wyatt. And Mary Hannah had such a wholesome honesty to her that he knew she wouldn't cheat, even at a simple guessing game.

His grip tightened on the steering wheel. "I was expecting more answers like you noticed I'm messy and eat a lot of carry-out food."

"Rookie info I could find from a simple search." She tucked her hand into the cup holder and pulled out an empty fast-food wrapper. "I bet I would find more like this under the seat. Or some empty soda cans rattling around with those tools in the back."

"If we're doing background searches, I would bet money you belonged to a sorority. Alpha Mega Hot."

She burst out laughing. "Has that line ever worked on a woman before?"

"It's an original, just for you." He winked, stunned she hadn't gotten mad, that she had an ability to take a joke about herself. That made her even hotter. He scrubbed a hand along his stubbly jaw. "You're just so . . . perfect. I can almost see you wearing pearls with that sweatshirt."

"Why is that a bad thing? Pearls are the universal accessory."

"I'm right?" He glanced at her and saw . . . he was right. "You wear pearls with sweatshirts?"

"A T-shirt, actually. Once. It was pink. It called for pearls. And they were fakes—good quality, though." Her lips went prissy tight again in a way that had him thinking of ways to ease them, part them open.

His body went hard at the thought, and he shifted in his seat. "Of course. The very best quality."

"Do you always deflect stress with smart-ass comments?"

Good question. And he wasn't anywhere near giving her the full answer about why his brain was as tangled as last year's Christmas lights.

Still, he owed her some kind of explanation. "What went down today—it was a crappy way to spend any day, much less Christmas Eve. I'm sorry if that's made me irritable."

"Apology accepted. I'm sorry you got roped into taxiing me around."

"No worries." He glanced at her. "And to be honest, it's probably time we declare a truce. Let the past be the past."

Her eyes went wide. "As in forgotten? No more veiled references and 'accidental' touches to make me uncomfortable?"

Was that what he'd been doing? Probably. "Yes, a legit cease-fire. We join forces to shut down the matchmakers."

He steered the off-road vehicle onto the two-lane county road that led to the Second Chance Ranch, located just outside of town. Lights grew dimmer, traffic sparser. The Christmas decorations were farther from the street and farther apart.

She half turned in her seat, hints of peppermint drifting from her, overriding the lemon scent of his air freshener dangling from the rearview mirror. "That would be incredible if we could pull it off."

"If anyone can pull off the impossible, you can."

She angled back. "Is that another dig or a compliment?"

"Hey, I just mean you're *extremely* competent."

She laughed softly. "Bite me."

The last two words hung there in the air. Sexy. Edgy.

And leaving him seconds away from breaking the truce before it started.

He turned from the county road into the driveway leading to the Second Chance Ranch. A security gate stopped them from traveling up the long dirt path leading to the white farmhouse. The Scout's engine rumbled in the night, the lights trained on the gate with a wreath in the middle. He jammed the Scout into park. He just needed to roll down the window and press the speaker call button.

But he didn't.

He turned in his seat to face her, the leather squeaking. His body ached from the attraction that had damn near knocked him on his ass earlier today. He saw the answering flicker in her brown eyes and wondered what she would do if he pulled those glasses from her face—to hell with the truce—and kissed her.

Four

I loved romance shows like *The Bachelor* and *The Newlywed Game*, but my favorite was reruns of the old-fashioned *Dating Game*. Such anticipation waiting for the verdict: "I pick bachelor number . . ."

—FEMALE BOXER, FOUR YEARS OLD, SHELTER #S75230

OH. GOD.

Was AJ about to kiss her?

Mary Hannah stared into his intense blue eyes, wondering if the heated intent was real or an illusion from the dash lights. She should just open the door, get the hell out of his messy all-terrain vehicle where these even messier emotions were jumbling up inside her. She would hop the gate to the Second Chance Ranch and run all the way to her studio apartment.

But she couldn't seem to make her hands let go of the edge of the seat.

Her senses had gone on overload, from the feel of the rough upholstery against her palms to breathing in the lemony scent of the air freshener with every gasping breath.

This whole Christmas Eve had been so upside down. She clenched the seat harder to resist the impulse to pull his beard-stubbled face toward her and make that kiss happen all the sooner.

"AJ, the security code is five-seven-three-two." She angled away to lean against the door. "We should hurry. Lacey will need my help getting ready for Sierra and Mike's visit. They're due in anytime now, if they aren't here already."

God, she was babbling like an idiot. Of course AJ would know that Lacey's daughter and son-in-law were due in tonight. And he likely knew why she was babbling.

He stared back at her silently for so long she thought he might ignore her words and kiss her anyway. She didn't even question for a second that the kiss would be explosive, powerful. Satisfying. She knew from experience.

She also knew she wouldn't be able to resist, and if she crossed that line with him as Mary Hannah—rather than Francesca—everything would get so damn complicated. She needed simple. Her sanity depended on it. Order helped her conquer the daily battle against addiction.

She couldn't afford even a kiss from this man.

Before she could have second thoughts, she leaned across him and lowered the window. The heat of his whipcord strength against her was tempting, melting through her like cotton candy on the tongue. She punched the security code in with extra force and sank back into her seat.

God, her heart was drumming in her ears.

She ground her teeth and willed the gate to open faster so she could . . . what? Hurry to her lonely studio apartment with her sad little tabletop tree and perfectly lined up nativity figures? A minute ago the place sounded like a haven. Now, not so much. How strange to suddenly feel so alone when she lived in a place full of people and animals.

The old Harvester Scout jostled along the dirt road leading to the white farmhouse where Lacey lived. A spotlight shone on a sign that read *Second Chance Ranch Rescue*. Garlands were draped along the top of that new sign, a part of the rescue's expansion over the past year and a half. Lacey had bought an extra acre when some cranky neighbors moved. She'd expanded fences to take in horses as well but rented out that cabin next door to AJ for extra cash to fund her rescue.

How different her life would be right now if she'd realized the guy she picked up at a truck-stop bar was the new tenant Lacey had been talking about.

Last summer when he'd moved in, the leaves on the trees had blocked her view of his home an acre away. But recently, through the icy skeletal branches, sometimes late at night she could see the lights glowing in his place, reminding her she wasn't the only one who had trouble sleeping. Avoiding each other was tough enough in a small town. Damn near impossible when they lived next door and shared a landlord.

Silently, AJ drove past Lacey's house to the red barn that housed many of the rescue's animals. Lights lined the edges of the roof thanks to Lacey's teenage son. Earlier this week a preschool class had come by and built snow cats and snow pups around the fenced play yard before feeding the animals treats.

Mary Hannah grabbed the door handle as the vehicle stopped near the outdoor stairway leading to her apartment. Best to pretend the almost kiss hadn't happened. "Thank you again for the ride."

Her feet hit the hard-packed ice, and she held on to the open door for balance. She refused to be disappointed AJ didn't say a word to stop her.

Then he was there in front of her, having moved from his side of the vehicle in a smooth flash. He held the puppy-paw blanket rolled up in his fist. "You'll probably go by the shelter before I will and can return this."

She took the cotton throw, the warmth of his hand clinging to the fabric.

"Thanks." She wrapped the blanket around her shoulders again. "And, uh, Merry Christmas."

"It's been a memorable one for sure." He took her elbow without asking and steadied her past those lopsided snow kitties and snow pups, toward the steps leading to her place.

A sled was propped up against a post at the base, caked in ice as if encouraging her to relax, to play.

His boots crunched with evenly paced strides. "Now that we've declared this truce, how do we get Lacey and Wyatt to back off with the matchmaking?"

"I wish I knew the answer to that. Lacey has done so much to help me, I'm not really sure how to make her understand without telling her everything and I just can't." She shook her head.

"Wyatt and Lacey seem to think everyone should be as giddy as they are—"

"Giddy? That's just not a word I would expect you to use." Her nervousness over that almost kiss made her latch on to the small thought. There was so much about him that confused her.

"When have we talked enough for you to form an opinion of my word choices?"

"That's my point. You haven't struck me as the chatty sort." Yet he'd spoken to her quite a lot today, mixing up that irritability with surprising concern and humor. "You seem like more of the grunt-and-point kind of guy."

"I thought counselors were supposed to be nonjudgmental." He stopped at the foot of the outdoor staircase, blocking the path upward.

"I thought cops were supposed to . . ."

"What?"

The one word puffed into the cold air between them, launching goose bumps along her flesh that had nothing to do with the freezing temperatures.

She sagged back against the barn wall. "Hell, I don't have a witty comeback."

"Seriously." A smile tucked one dimple into his cheek. "That's it?"

She nodded, hugging the blanket closer, her hair turning chilly from the last bits of dampness. "Blame it on the aftereffects of meth fumes and the adrenaline surge from the danger."

"Thank you again for coming to my rescue earlier. The way you handled that dog and the whole operation was impressive. I imagine that will be all the talk around the station, how you saved my bacon," he said without the least hint of concern or ego she would have expected from her ex-husband.

That quick the thought of Ted blindsided her too close to that almost kiss with AJ earlier by the gate. She needed to retreat upstairs, into her home. Alone. Because right now being by herself didn't sound sad and scary anymore. It sounded like a sanctuary from the mixed feelings that being with AJ inspired.

"Thank *you* for the ride home. We can call it even." She thrust out her hand to shake his. "Merry Christmas, AJ."

He clasped her fingers and tugged ever so slightly. "Merry Christmas, Mary Hannah."

He leaned in and for a heart-stopping instant she thought he was going to kiss her after all. At the last second, he veered up and pressed his mouth to her forehead. Such a simple kiss, but the warm press of his lips on her skin felt damn good. Her eyes slid closed and she swayed, willing him to put his arms around her so she wouldn't have to ask.

Except he didn't. He angled back and the cold night air swept over her. She scrambled for something—anything—to say to fill that awkward space between them.

"Did I miss out spotting the mistletoe?" she asked breathlessly.

"That had nothing to do with the holiday." His hands fell to rest on her shoulders.

His behavior was giving her whiplash. Frustrated desire made her edgy—hell, downright cranky. "I thought we agreed to ignore the matchmakers."

"Believe me, I'm not thinking about Wyatt or Lacey right now."

Then what was he doing? What kind of game was he playing?

She rested her hands on his chest, needing distance between them. "You're seeing me as Francesca, and I'm not. This is me, paisley and buttoned-up, an OCD girl. Let it go, AJ. I'm not interested."

He backed away from her, his eyes staying locked on her the whole time with that dark intensity as he whispered, "One of the benefits of being a cop for so long? I can tell when people are lying."

His wink sent a shiver up her spine. Then he walked back to his car, tucked behind the wheel and drove back up the long driveway, red taillights glowing. She blinked and the lights were gone.

Grabbing the stair railing, she hauled herself up the steps faster than was wise. She would be keeping her eyes off that window tonight.

AJ GUNNED THE engine, his Scout threatening to spin out on the ice as he left those lumpy snow kitties and snow pups behind.

He'd meant that forehead kiss to set a new tone of friendship. A symbol of their truce. Instead, what should have been a platonic peck had knocked him on his ass. He could still smell the hint of peppermint that would always remind him of her.

Damn. Just damn it. He accelerated away from the barn and sprawling fat oak trees, naked branches glinting with ice. He sped back up the drive until the lights along the front porch dimmed with distance.

With each mile away, he knew the distance and time wouldn't help. He still wanted her. Didn't have a clue how to stop. He just needed to figure out what the hell he intended to do about it. Preferably before he saw her again.

Which, given the fact that they were neighbors, would undoubtedly be soon.

The town lights grew brighter and closer. His day was far from done. He still needed to check in at the station. Theirs was a small police department. As much as he wanted to leave the memories of his undercover work behind, he couldn't avoid responsibilities. His experience in the world of illegal narcotics trafficking would be valuable.

He owed it to that little kid under the bed in Atlanta holding a pink sippy cup full of drain cleaner from a meth lab. The child he'd thought might one day be his daughter—Aubrey. He'd foolishly believed Sheila meant it when she'd said she wanted out of the gang and that she wanted to build a better life for her daughter. With him.

Like a total sap, he'd been so certain she was legit since Sheila hadn't known she was speaking to a cop. He'd been undercover, and while he'd hated lying to her, he'd known maintaining his cover was the best way to keep her safe. He'd fallen for her, never once suspecting that she was telling the worst lie of all.

The lie of an addict. Lying to herself.

Sheila had gone to jail for possession and child endangerment. Aubrey had gone into foster care. He'd used every contact he had to keep track of the toddler until a distant relative petitioned to adopt her. That should have eased the roaring in his head.

No such luck. Until one night he'd almost gotten his partner shot by hesitating because a woman with a gun looked like Sheila.

That made the decision to accept Wyatt's offer a no-brainer.

It wasn't like Mary Hannah reminded him of Sheila. They couldn't be any more different. Other than the fact they both interfered with his ability to think straight.

He needed to wrap up this case, lock away those responsible for the meth lab and send the animals on their way to homes. No more wounded eyes haunting him.

And after that?

It was time to accept he wanted to sleep with Mary Hannah even more than he wanted Francesca.

MARY HANNAH KNELT beside the Santa statue by her door and scooped up her house key. Her hand still trembled, goose bumps as real as the memory of a simple sorta kiss. Her very fertile imagination filled with images of them tangled up in stark white motel sheets and a polyester spread, of him sinking inside her. Of *her* sinking her teeth into his shoulder.

She rested her forehead against the slick door.

"Mary Hannah?"

She turned so quickly she almost slipped on the ice before she grabbed the handrail. Holding tight, she looked down at Lacey McDaniel stepping out of the mudroom door of the main house.

"Lacey? You startled me."

"Sorry about that." Lacey stepped the rest of the way outside, crystal wineglass in hand and a three-legged Lab loping after her. "I just wanted to see how everything went finishing up at the shelter."

"They're all settled." She started down the stairs. "All we can do is wait on the temperament tests and the police legalese."

Lacey picked her way through the snow wearing fuzzy bedroom slippers and a cardigan that kept slipping off her shoulder. Her caramel curls were gathered up in a loose bundle that always looked ready to explode but somehow never slipped free. She was quirky, no question, but she was a strong woman. She'd not only survived the loss of her husband, but she took care of her aging father-in-law and a teenage son and oversaw this operation that saved so many lives.

Mary Hannah admired her on more levels than she could count.

Lacey hugged her cardigan tighter and met Mary Hannah at the foot of the steps. "Sorry I wasn't of more help today."

"You have family responsibilities. Everyone understands." She rubbed the corner of the blanket between two fingers and thought of AJ draping it around her shoulders. "It's a lot to take on with the Valentine competition coming up. I'm here to help. So no more apologies."

"Fair enough." Lacey lifted her crystal glass in toast.

If they could pull off a coup at the My Furry Valentine Mutt Makeover, they stood a real chance at putting the Second Chance Ranch on the map. "You should go back inside and get warm. I'm going to change into real clothes."

"Actually, I've been watching the front gate. Sierra and Mike are due any minute now. The roads from North Carolina haven't been hit too hard by the storm." She leaned against the play-yard fence, her face tipped into the night breeze. "I imagine you'll want some best-friend catch-up time."

"We have the whole Christmas vacation." Mary Hannah had been introduced to the rescue by fellow graduate school student Sierra, Lacey's daughter. Now Sierra had moved to North Carolina with her army husband. This was definitely a night for girl talk over big bowls of ice cream.

A tone chimed from the security alarm, along with a squeak as the security gate opened. Only someone with the code could get through.

Lacey downed the rest of her drink before tucking the crystal into a fat wool pocket. "I sent Joshua and Nathan for dinner rolls . . ." Her father-in-law and son. "But Sierra and Mike are due, too."

A familiar truck drove down the dirt drive, exhaust puffing into the cold night.

Sierra.

Excitement sprinkled joy over the gloomy residue of the day, like snowflakes covering the wintery earth.

Dogs barked inside the barn, but thanks to volunteers,

they'd all gotten to tear around in the snow today before being given fresh bedding and food for the night.

The truck stopped alongside the barn; driver's-side Mike leaped out waving. "Hey, ladies. Merry Christmas."

"So happy you're here." Lacey hooked arms with Mary Hannah, approaching the truck.

Mike slid like an ice-skater toward the passenger side to open the door for his very pregnant wife. He held out a hand to Sierra as she stepped out of the truck. Her almost-seven-months-pregnant belly filled the brown wool coat—clearly one of Mike's—but Sierra had always had a natural beauty who didn't need glitz. Plus she now had that inner sparkle, magnified by the glow of pregnancy. "Careful, Sierra, hon. I've got ya."

Smile frozen on her face, Mary Hannah stifled a wince. As she looked at her friend's pregnant stomach, her husband's tender care, a wound reopened in her heart, a wound that had never quite healed. For so long after her miscarriage she couldn't even look at a pregnant woman because the ache of losing her child stabbed so deep. She'd only just started to feel the flutters of life inside her as she'd entered her fourth month of pregnancy.

Mary Hannah forced herself to say cheerfully, "Can I help?"

"I may look like a whale, but I can still walk." Sierra braced herself, holding his arm and the doorframe. She kissed her husband's cheek before stepping off the running board. "This will be my last trip before the baby's born, and I intend to enjoy it. Thanks, Mike."

"Sure thing," he said. "I'll be right in. I need to take Trooper for a quick run first."

A tan shepherd mix, Trooper leaped out of the cab of the truck in a blur of fur and energy. The midsized mutt had been Lacey's husband's companion in Iraq, and when he'd died, Mike had brought Trooper home to the McDaniel family. Now Mike was a part of their family, too. Trooper had bonded so tightly to Sierra and Mike that, when they'd moved, Trooper had gone with them.

If they hadn't taken him, without question, the smart pup would have escaped every fence on the property and tracked them all the way to North Carolina.

Lacey gave Mike a quick hug before she slid a balancing arm around her daughter's thickened waist. Mike waved again as he jogged to catch up with Trooper. The crazy mutt was already bounding through the snow, Clementine the three-legged Labrador close on his heels to catch her buddy, the two of them leaving crop circles of paw prints.

The wind cut through Mary Hannah's sweat suit and the blanket. She backed away, feeling guilty for trying to escape until she could get used to seeing Sierra's pregnant stomach. "Sierra, we'll catch up later. I should let you all have your family time."

Extending her arm, Sierra waggled her fingers for Mary Hannah, clearly not taking no for an answer. "You are family. Join us."

Mary Hannah surrendered to the inevitable and followed. "For a few minutes. I really do need to change soon."

Lacey tugged open the back door for Sierra, her daughter's ponytail swishing along her back as she waddled ahead up the steps. "I'm so glad you and Mike made it in tonight. Was the drive too awful?"

"Snowy, slow going. God, Mom, I never knew being pregnant meant peeing all the freaking time." Sierra shuffled toward the half bath tucked under the stairs. "And food, Mom, please," she called through the closed door. "I'm starving."

Lacey opened the refrigerator and pulled out a bag of salad. "Your brother and grandfather aren't back with the rolls yet, but I can make you a ham sandwich. Mary Hannah? Would you like one, too?"

"No thank you." She wanted to leave, but she was a people pleaser. She always did what she was supposed to—and if she didn't the world went to hell. She dragged in a ragged breath.

Sierra came back out of the bathroom with a huge sigh of relief and slumped in a chair at the scarred table. "Yes, a sandwich, please." She trailed her fingers along the cat circling her chair. "With cheese, too. And if there are cookies in that old Santa jar, I'll do the dishes for all eternity."

"Mary Hannah's bringing the cookies tomorrow. We're all running a little behind schedule." Lacey pulled bread from the bread box—an old-fashioned necessity that kept dogs from counter-surfing to steal a bag. "Today's hoarding situation turned out to be a lot more involved than we expected. They were running a meth-lab operation out of a home, plus a backyard breeding business."

"How awful. Are you two okay?"

Mary Hannah hugged herself. "It was sad. Beyond sad, really. I'm not sure I'll ever forget the look in that mother boxer's eyes . . ." She hesitated, the meow from under the table and the cuckoo clock in the hall filling the void, announcing seven fifteen. "Hopefully we'll have her here soon. Lacey? And you? Are you all right?"

"I'm fine. I didn't see the worst of it since I was outside the whole time." She sliced off a piece of ham and added it to the bread with cheese and mustard. "Then I left early to get back here. I owe Mary Hannah. She carried the brunt of the work helping out Animal Control and the police."

She set the plate with a sandwich in front of Sierra along with a glass of milk and a cloth reindeer napkin.

"Just doing what I can and hoping once they clear their systems of the meth, they'll get the green light to come here."

Sierra took a bite out of her sandwich and sighed blissfully as she chewed. "Remember Lucky, the one that ate a teenager's stash of weed? Once he detoxed from the pot, he was a great, adoptable dog."

Lacey tucked away the bread. "A dog that lived with a family. Sure, the teen had a drug problem, but everything else in that house was relatively normal. That sure wasn't the case today."

Sierra set aside her glass of milk. "When does Wyatt get here? I assume he's coming over."

"He's still filing a report on today's incident. He'll be here after he finishes up at the station and changes, probably later this evening." She checked inside the Crock-Pot. "You'll get to meet his cousin, too."

"Lacey," Mary Hannah warned softly.

"The new cop? The one you keep telling me is perfect for Mary Hannah. Who'd have thought you would play Cupid?"

"It was Wyatt's idea."

Sierra nodded, polishing off the last of her sandwich. "He probably liked the notion that you would have Mary Hannah to distract you so he can talk about a ball game or fishing with his cousin."

Lacey closed the Crock-Pot with a clatter. "That's a little cynical. He's a nice guy."

"I know. It was a poor attempt at a joke. I'm happy for you, Mom." She traced a scar in the well-worn family table. "The holidays just have me missing Dad. You deserve to be happy, and if Wyatt makes you happy, I'm all in."

"He does. But I miss your dad, too."

Sierra leaned to hug her mom tight, blond ponytail swinging around.

Mary Hannah felt like a fifth wheel, not to mention a self-pity wimp. This family had every reason to feel loss over the holidays, and unlike her, they'd done nothing wrong. Nothing to deserve this pain.

She eased back quietly to slip out the door.

Sierra pulled away from her mom and tossed the napkin on the table. "Wait, Mary Hannah. I really want to catch up with you before supper starts." She glanced at her mother. "Is that okay with you, Mom?"

"Absolutely. We have weeks to visit, and I need to tie up some loose ends now."

So much for making a clean escape. But she couldn't deny the relief of getting that girl time and ice cream after all.

Five

Who is *The Weakest Link*? I always thought it was me . . . until I learned strength comes in many forms.

—FEMALE BOXER, FOUR YEARS OLD, SHELTER #S75230

L ACEY McDANIEL WAS dog tired, in more ways than one. She hefted the ham out of the oven, grateful her crowd was happy with Crock-Pot mac and cheese, bagged salad and rolls for sides. Well, she would have rolls once her teenage son and her father-in-law got back from the store. Damn, she was scatterbrained these days.

The animal seizure at the cabin had taken a serious chunk out of her Christmas Eve. But when Animal Control had asked if she could step in to help on a hoarder seizure, she hadn't hesitated. In reality, this was the calm before the storm since she would take in the ones that passed their temperament tests.

She'd noticed how attached Mary Hannah had already gotten to the female boxer and hoped like hell she wouldn't get her heart broken if the dog couldn't be rehabilitated.

Moments like that, though, drove her to keep pushing through the exhaustion for the good of the animals. As director, she'd turned a home-based rescue group into a full-fledged operation. Soon, she might even be able to make that a salaried position, which would give her more time for the rescue if she didn't have to teach online classes to pay bills.

Though, in times like this, she questioned if she could handle the weight of running a full-on shelter in addition to juggling the needs of her family. Like today, knowing she should do more than stand outside and log in animals. Then she'd left before they were finished at the shelter. More guilt piled on top of frustration.

But she just couldn't step inside the meth house.

Lacey tore open the bagged salad with her teeth and dumped half of it into the colander in the sink before turning to tuck the rest back in the fridge. She automatically reached for a bottle of wine, only to stop short. The last thing she needed was a fuzzy head and a weepy, tipsy ramble.

Still, her Waterford wineglass brought her comfort, so she filled it with water and tossed in a lemon slice. The fine-cut crystal piece was the last one left from her wedding set. A military move had broken the rest, along with too many dreams to count.

The will to cook Christmas Eve dinner just drained right out of her.

Sidestepping two beagle puppies curled together by the table, Lacey slid into a chair, took a long sip and tried not to be bitter over the fact she should be celebrating the imminent arrival of her first grandchild with her husband. Her dead husband. Blown up by a roadside bomb in Iraq on what should have been his last deployment before he retired. His blond, lumbering presence had been the center of her world since high school.

Allen had told her once she would be the hottest grandma on earth. They'd been standing in this kitchen, talking about their children growing up. Dreaming of spending their golden years together. Instead, her husband had died two years ago, leaving her a forty-two-year-old widow. She was forty-four now. Sometimes those two years felt like an eternity.

She'd fought hard to pull herself through those stages of

grief into acceptance, and she was happy now. Truly. She had a grandchild on the way. She even had a boyfriend. Still, she couldn't deny landmark moments like this reopened the wound.

Bottom line, she needed to get herself together before Wyatt showed up for supper. He was a good man, and he didn't flinch when she mentioned Allen's name, even though she could see it bothered him.

Stroking her thumb up and down the beaded notches on the stem of the wineglass, she sipped her lemon water again while she stared at the spiral-cut ham that needed shifting to a serving platter. She took another sip, wishing she could just let alcohol dull this day into a warm haze. A dangerous thought. Only since she'd stopped drinking had she realized how close she'd come to being dependent on those bottles of wine.

She had too many reasons not to drink, too many responsibilities. Starting with her teenage son and father-in-law currently buying those dinner rolls. She glanced at her watch, worry niggling. The Alzheimer's had gotten worse for her father-in-law, Joshua, once a general in the army. Now he could barely talk, much less remember his family's names. He'd moved to an assisted living facility three months ago and they visited him every other day, but they brought him home for holidays. Her son, Nathan, offered to help. But was she asking too much of her son when Nathan was just finding his own footing after losing his dad?

Her phone rang with a country tune Wyatt had programmed into her cell as his ringtone. She pulled back with a watery smile.

Lacey scooped her cell phone out of her purse and stepped into the mudroom, the tabby cat following, circling around her ankles. "Hello, there, everything going okay?"

"Hey, babe." The rumbly drawl of his voice flowed over the phone lines.

"Hey, you." She tucked the phone closer to her ear and

leaned back against a wall full of dangling leashes. "Where are you? Supper's almost ready to go on the table."

"I'm running behind at the station, but AJ's going to have to come back here to finish paperwork." The familiar sounds of the station whispered faintly in the background, with other phone lines ringing along with a shout for him to hurry up. "Go ahead and eat without me. I know that puts a crimp in your plan for us all to be together tonight. Sorry about that."

Was it wrong that she was actually relieved not to have him here this evening? To have longer to level out? "No one could have foreseen what happened this afternoon."

He stayed silent for so long she almost thought he'd hung up, then he said hesitantly, "Are you hanging in there all right?"

"Just tired." And emotional. "Once I eat, I'll catch my second wind. You just focus on work."

"Actually, there's a reason for my call besides canceling. I wanted to give you an early Christmas present." He pulled away from the phone for a second and shouted, "Hang on, guys. I'll be there in a minute. Okay, Lacey, I'm back."

"A surprise? Sounds intriguing." Guilt pinched over her relief that he wouldn't be here for supper. He was clearly excited about something.

"Meant to tell you earlier, but got distracted this afternoon. I was talking to my captain yesterday about the station sponsoring a shelter dog for the February competition. The captain really went with the idea and came up with the perfect candidate to be the dog's handler."

"Tell me more."

"You may have noticed my cousin's wired pretty tight. We want him to have one of the shelter dogs and work with Mary Hannah if you can convince her. I know there isn't time to do a full-out service-dog training, or even complete the therapy-dog training. But isn't there another level?"

"Emotional-support animal."

"Right, sorry for spacing on the terminology."

"You've been amazing in how you've learned about my world. I appreciate it." And she did. She just wished she gave as much back to him.

"This is who you are. I accept you as you are."

She knew that, and appreciated what a rare gift that was, but she just wished things weren't moving so quickly and that she knew how to slow them down. "Um, Sierra and Mike are here, so I need to get dinner on the table. Thanks again for everything."

"No problem, babe. I'll see you in the morning. Love ya."

Normally, she said it back. But tonight her throat closed up like she'd taken too big a bite of food.

Of life.

She opened her mouth but could only push out, "See you in the morning."

Walking into the kitchen, she hung up and tossed the cell phone into her purse. She reached for her Waterford crystal glass beside the Crock-Pot full of macaroni and cheese. If ever she'd needed a drink, tonight was the night for it.

But Sierra wasn't the only one who had to watch what she ate and drank for a baby on the way.

WITH SIERRA CLOSE on her heels, Mary Hannah unlocked her front door and pushed inside her studio apartment. Pristine, neat as a pin, and she couldn't help but think how AJ would tease her for that obsessive organization all the way to her alphabetized spice rack and labeled recycling bins. She craved order more than ever these days.

Even if she could only make that happen inside this space of her own.

With pale green walls and refinished hardwood floors, the loft had a large television area and a raised platform for a bed under a skylight to watch the moon and stars at night. She wondered sometimes in the wee hours what it would be like to invite AJ into her bed and look up at the stars with him. To have a man in her life again. To figure out how to help that man trust her once he knew about her past. Hell, how to trust herself.

The risk was just too much. She drew in a deep, calming breath of the lavender and peppermint scents from her plug-in infusers.

So that left her with this celibate limbo life, treading water, and she wasn't sure how to move forward. Maybe she wasn't supposed to. Not yet. There was a lot to be said for simply not sinking.

She flicked on the living-area lights. Her cat, Siggy—short for Sigmund Freud—jumped off the back of the slipcovered sofa. She'd walked out of her marriage taking nothing except her furry Persian kitty. She'd rebuilt from the ground up with a shabby-chic-meets-flea-market restoration style.

She trained dogs, but didn't have one of her own. Not yet. Someday. For now, she got her dog fix through the rescue. She was lucky to have this place, her job and close friends. Like Sierra.

Mary Hannah kept her eyes off her friend's swollen stomach. "Come inside. Sit. Let's talk. I'm so happy you're finally here."

Sierra took off her boots and left them by the door. "It's been too long, and phone conversations just aren't the same."

Mary Hannah tossed the blanket on her butcher-block table with the mini Christmas tree. "I've missed you."

"Me, too, so much." Sierra hugged Mary Hannah as close as her pregnant stomach would allow.

The baby kicked between them. Mary Hannah felt that kick all the way to her bruised heart.

Pasting a smile on her face for her friend, she stepped back. "Just look at you, all glowing and pregnant. Not much longer, right?"

"Big as a house, I know, and I still have two months to go." She smoothed her hands over her stomach, glowing with happiness. "It's a boy. We didn't want to know, but during the ultrasound he just rolled right over and flashed his boy parts."

"Congratulations. I'm happy for you and Mike, truly."

And she was. Sierra was the best friend she'd ever had, and yet she'd never told her about the baby she'd lost. Or the addiction problem. Just that she'd gone to grad school after a painful divorce.

It hurt even thinking about that time in her life. She didn't know how to push the words free. But she wouldn't let her own ghosts rob her friend of the joy of celebrating. "Tell me everything about North Carolina and your work with the magazine. I want to hear it all. You talk, I'll bake. I promised your mom I would bring cookies for Christmas dinner tomorrow."

"I'll be your taste tester." Sierra grinned, sitting on one of the white ladder-back chairs around the table. "I can't eat the batter raw because of the eggs, so I guess I'll just have to wait until you bring them over tomorrow."

Eyes stinging, Mary Hannah turned away under the pretense of setting the oven on to preheat. "I've got a recipe for cookie dough that uses almond butter, flaxseeds and carob. I'll make some for you before you leave."

"Maybe you could just bring the dough to Mom's now since the ham is ready. The cookies can bake while we eat supper."

Mary Hannah glanced over her shoulder. "Thanks. But I'm kinda queasy from the rescue operation today. I'm going to need to shower at least two more times. Please, you all eat without me and enjoy your family time."

"You're family, too." Sierra reached to squeeze her hand.

"Thanks." But they weren't. Not really. Just best friends who'd met in graduate school. Mary Hannah pulled her container of dough from the refrigerator; all the cookies had already been rolled and cut. She only needed to bake and ice them. "I've got plenty to keep me busy, then I'm going to turn in early."

"Okay, okay. If you're not joining us for supper, I'll have to come right out and ask." Sierra leaned forward on her elbows, tapping the salt and pepper shakers out of line with each other. "I want to hear all the details on your hot cop friend Mom told me about. Don't bother denying he's sexy. She showed me a picture of him on Facebook."

Mary Hannah weighed her words as she placed sugar cookies shaped like trees, candy canes and reindeer on a baking pan. What was she supposed to say? That his coal-black hair curled at the ends when wet? Like when he began to perspire during sex? That he was great in the sack, like best-sex-of-her-life great?

She'd worked too hard for her peace to risk it. "My 'friend' had to go back to the station."

"And? Details, please. Tell me more about the Greek-god cop," she said with a wicked but determined twinkle in her blue eyes. Sierra wasn't going to give up.

"He's a police officer. Wyatt's cousin, which you probably already know." She pulled out another baking pan to ready more cookies for the oven. "AJ brought me home tonight to help Lacey and save me cab fare."

Sierra frowned. "You're really going to keep insisting you're not interested in him?"

She shrugged, unable to push the lie out in words.

"Well, I see you don't want to talk about him, which says all I need to know. So I'll just leave you with your hot thoughts and hot oven." Sierra pushed away from the table. "I should help Mom anyway. She's acting kind of strange. She didn't breathe any of those meth fumes today, did she?"

"Actually, no. She stayed outside the whole time logging in the animals, and left straightaway after delivering the crates the shelter." Which wasn't like Lacey at all. She was usually the last to leave. But then even the most seasoned rescuers could be shaken.

"Sounds as if she really does need my support tonight. You and I can talk more tomorrow." Sierra hugged her hard again. "I really have missed you, Mary Hannah."

"I really have missed you, too." And she meant it. She just wished she was able to talk as easily as she could listen. "Be careful on your way back to the house."

"I look more awkward than I actually feel." She paused at the door, tucking her feet back in her boots. "Merry Christmas."

"You, too, my friend."

The door closed behind Sierra, leaving Mary Hannah alone for the first time since she'd headed out this morning expecting to liberate hoarded animals. Her own pain was never far from the surface, but today had torn away all her defenses on so many levels.

Her work with the rescue usually brought her comfort, knowing she'd helped the animals and the people whose lives they would touch. Today, though, it was tougher to imagine how things would end happily for all the dogs they'd seized.

She'd seen such hopelessness in Mama's expression as she thrashed against the restraints. And if she was beyond rehabilitation?

Squeezing her eyes shut, Mary Hannah sagged onto the fat sofa, exhausted. Heart tired. One day at a time, she reminded herself. Get through the moment and control what she could. And above all, no self-pity.

Her head lolled back, and exhaustion tugged at her until she slumped to the side, a throw pillow under her neck. She swung her legs up on the sofa. Just a quick catnap and she would get back to the cookies.

In the late-night quiet her thoughts grew louder, memories swelling to fill the corners of her brain. Five months ago she'd been driving home after meeting with a new client, a soldier who'd lost an arm and leg overseas. He'd been out of it, but his wife and son had been with him, supporting. That frail family unit had tugged at her heart, shredding her professional objectivity all the more given it was her anniversary. Or rather it would have been except she was divorced.

Recognizing she was in no shape to drive, she'd pulled into a truck-stop bar/restaurant for food and time to recover her composure. Only to have that composure shattered all over again by a lean, sexy man with compelling blue eyes sitting at the bar with chili cheese fries and a beer.

She'd been drenched from a summer storm and ditched the professional suit jacket she'd worn over her silky sundress. The heat of his gaze had almost steamed the clinging fabric dry. His jet-black hair, a little long in a bad-boy way, had curled at the ends, damp from the rain. Without thinking, she walked past the private corner booth and parked herself on a barstool, leaving only one empty space between them.

Even now, her skin tingled and heat gathered between her legs. So much. Making her want to relive every second of that night until she found an echo of release.

Her fists clenched, and she sat up sharply.

No. She was done living in the past. She didn't know what the future held for any of them, but at least she had an idea how to make tomorrow a little more bearable for the animals at the shelter. She got off the sofa and arranged the salt and pepper shakers so they lined up again, then grabbed her iPad off the counter where it had been recharging. She tapped the app for dog-treat recipes. She wouldn't be sleeping in tomorrow after all.

Her Christmas morning would be spent at the shelter.

Six

Who would have thought *Top Chef* would
send their winner to visit me at the shelter?

—FEMALE BOXER, FOUR YEARS OLD, SHELTER #S75230

AFTER THE PEPPERMINT lady left, I didn't think I would
ever see her again.

When I felt that van lurch while I was in the cage, I forgot
all about peppermint smells. Sure, the crate was cleaner, but
the stink of fear fills up the smell sensors fast, taking over
everything else. I was scared of so much in those days. Even
the bath they gave me, not that I remember much of it since
once I started thrashing around under the water, they jabbed
me with another needle and then I got loopy. I woke up later
in a long concrete tunnel—a kennel run. There was an inside
and outside with a swinging door. I got to choose when I
went inside or outside.

Strange how even the thought of having choices terrified
me in those days. I held myself in tight, curled in a corner,
only relieving myself when the pain of holding it in was too
much to bear. I could see dogs in another kennel across from
me, a couple of chows that had gotten out when their family
was having a cocktail party. They were scared, too, but not
like me. Plus they had each other. They also had hope their

people would come looking for them. That didn't scare them the way the thought of my owner coming to take me back to the cabin still frightened me. She had friends and customers, too, and in my fear, there were moments I thought I saw a couple of those people.

But then I wondered if the drugs were making me hallucinate.

I listened to the other dogs around me howl and bark out their fears and stories. So much information piled on top of me, it was too much to process.

Then morning came. And with it, peppermint.

She came back.

The lady who'd smelled so sweet showed up at the shelter with food for me. Not scraps, either. But things I'd only ever seen on television. Treats.

Better yet, homemade dog treats.

The peppermint lady—Mary Hannah—sat on the concrete floor by my kennel, talking softly. The injections from the day before had worn off, so I was clearheaded, more than I could ever remember feeling, in fact. Every breath of that bleachy clean air swept out the residue of the meth fumes.

But without all those meds, my true feelings—and fears—filled every corner of me. I was too scared to crawl up to the gate, but I liked the sound of her talking. I stayed in my corner and listened. Her voice was every bit as sweet as the scent of her.

"Merry Christmas," she said, pushing a cookie through until it fell onto my kennel-run floor.

She pulled her hand away. Good thing, because I really wanted that cookie, but I wouldn't be so quick to trust her again. Not after the way she'd looped that choker around my neck and helped drag me outside with a pole. I didn't dare move. I wasn't sure if it was a trick. The woman who'd kept me all my life would do that. Lure me in, then kick me for doing what she'd asked.

Mary Hannah looked off in the distance now, rather than

at me, so I inched forward warily, picked up the cookie and scampered back to my corner to eat that treat.

Peanut butter and pumpkin flavored.

Might as well have been pure ambrosia.

Christmas had finally happened for me.

Up until that day, my only understanding of Christmas came from the television. I liked all the music that played behind shows during the holiday season. But quite frankly, *It's a Wonderful Life* seemed like fantasy fiction.

Little did I know that in the years to come I would discover all the smells that went with holidays.

Now the bleachy air in my kennel run held a hint of peppermint. I still didn't trust her, even with the cookies, but I liked the way she smelled as much as I enjoyed her voice. So if she maintained her distance and kept pushing cookies into my kennel, I wouldn't bolt through the dog door to hide in the outside portion of my kennel run.

Footsteps approached, and fear kicked into high gear. I trembled so hard the last bite of cookie fell out of my mouth.

"Shhh . . . Shhh . . . Shhh . . ." Mary Hannah chanted softly. "It's okay, Mama. It's going to be okay."

A shelter worker knelt beside her, a big strong guy, the one who'd put the second loop around my neck to haul me out of the cabin. "What are you doing here, Ms. Gallo? It's Christmas. No pulling animals for the rescue today."

"I brought you all cookies—and some for the animals, too. The director okayed it. I have her text." She glanced up. "What are you doing working today? You're not on cleaning or feeding patrol."

"Got a call to pick up a stray hound dog wandering in the cold. No microchip or collar. So he's spending Christmas with us."

"I'm sorry to hear that." The sadness in her voice made me want to inch out of my corner. "I promise to finish up here soon so the staff can leave to have lunch with their families."

"Take your time. Second Chance is welcome here any day. But the director's going to be pissed she missed your cookies. Which cookies are the human kind?"

"The ones in the break room." She pulled out another peanut butter pumpkin treat. "I also wanted to check on the dogs from yesterday.

"Last update, the male boxer was still hanging on. The puppies are all warm and snug, healthy so far. The mamas are a little freaked out over being shaved." He backed away. "Just don't open any kennels."

"I promise to stick to the rules. Girl Scout's honor." Smiling, she pulled out another cookie. "Here, Mama. I thought pumpkin would be fun, plus pumpkin settles your tummy, and I thought you might be stressed."

I inched one paw forward, slow like. Maybe I could just nudge the cookie over to me since she was on the other side of a fence. Maybe. I stretched my leg farther, farther still—

Ding.

The sound jarred me, and I snapped my leg back. Fast. Pushing my body flatter against the wall, praying I could just disappear.

"Damn it," Mary Hannah said softly, pulling out her cell phone. She thumbed along the screen, her eyes tracking as she read whatever had popped up on the screen.

I knew how cell phones worked thanks to commercials. The few people who came to the cabin also had them. Apparently all humans came equipped with one from birth.

Knowing the phone was a normal item, though, didn't help unlock the fear again. Not even when a huge smile spread over her face.

"Mama, good news. That was my friend Lacey. She heard from the police department that you and your animal friends have been released to go to a rescue if you pass your temperament test. You can't be adopted just yet, but we can get you out of the kennel run. If you come to the ranch, you'll get time in the play yard and lots of walks since there aren't as many animals there. If you get a foster home, you'll be living in a house all the time."

She rambled on in that soothing voice, and something inside me said *trust her*, but I couldn't make myself move out of the far corner of the run to take the treat out of her hand even though the smell had me salivating.

Or maybe I was drooling out of abject terror. It was tough to tell.

"It's okay, Mama. You don't have to trust me if you don't want to. You can still have another cookie. Eat up so your tummy will be full and happy for your temperament test tomorrow." She pushed the treat through the gate. Then pushed three more after it. They fell onto the concrete floor. "You can enjoy those after I go."

She still didn't leave then. Not right away. She sat on the cement outside my kennel run, humming along with the Christmas music on the sound system. It was almost like she didn't have anywhere to be on Christmas Day, which didn't make sense. Everyone on those TV shows had somewhere to go with tables full of enough food that I would never go hungry again.

The burly guy came back again and knelt beside her. "We've finished the morning shift. We're headed home for turkey time. You can come back when we do our evening cleanup and feeding if you want."

"I won't disrupt your schedule anymore. Thank you." She pushed another treat through my gate. "Be a *good* girl for your test, Mama. Please."

Something about the way she said that last word made me look at her just for a second. An instant was all I dared, but it was enough to see. She was every bit as scared as I was.

And in that moment I knew. I would do anything to make her happy again.

* * *

A BLINDING LIGHT sliced through AJ's dream. A damn good dream of peeling a wet silky dress off Mary Hannah's body . . . except she'd been Francesca and he'd been an even bigger mess that night than he was now. He'd still been reeling from too much time undercover, from Sheila's betrayal. And wondering if moving to this place would make a difference or just sink him right back into hell.

So that night he hadn't questioned the instant attraction. He'd taken the moment. Taken her.

And God, she'd taken him right back. The feel of her against his skin was so warm and soft that he didn't want to wake up to a morning where that night didn't exist anymore.

He hauled his pillow over his head to block the morning sun streaking through his window, except he could swear he'd pulled the curtains shut before bed. He'd gotten home late from the station last night, staying as long as he reasonably could so he would fall straight into an exhausted sleep. And those curtains, he was damn sure he'd closed them so he wouldn't have to see Mary Hannah's loft apartment through the forest branches.

His plan hadn't taken into account the fact that Mary Hannah would haunt his dreams.

He peeked from under his pillow and found his cousin standing by the window, heavy drapes pulled wide and blinds opened. Groaning, AJ buried his head again.

"Cousin? AJ?" Wyatt called, his voice unmistakable even through the pillow. "Ho, ho, ho, wake up for Santa Claus."

"Seriously?" AJ tossed the pillow at his cousin and sat up, covers pooling around his waist. "How the hell did you get in here?"

"How did you not hear me breaking in?"

A disconcerting question, for sure. "Fair enough. You've made your point. Close the blinds when you leave."

"It's almost noon." Wyatt pulled a pair of jeans off the back of a rocking chair and tossed them at AJ as he got out of bed. "We're going to be late for Christmas lunch at Lacey's."

He caught the jeans against his chest and stepped over a pile of laundry on the floor. "I told you already. I'm going fishing."

"For an undercover cop, you're a crappy liar. Now hurry up." Wyatt backed out of the bedroom into the hall. "I'll make coffee while you get dressed—*to go to Lacey's*, not fishing."

AJ tugged on the jeans and padded barefoot out of his bedroom into the great room. The place had come furnished. Simple. Functional. Rustic. A little messy. It worked for him. "You're not going to let up, are you?"

Wyatt pulled ground coffee out of the cabinet. "I'm worried about you."

"Domestic life is making you soft." He joined his cousin at the stone counter and opened a box of Pop-Tarts, taking one and tossing the rest back on the counter beside a pile of mail. "Pass me the peanut butter there beside you."

Wyatt handed it over with an ill-disguised grimace. "That's not much of a Christmas breakfast. Lacey's son-in-law made the most freaking awesome sticky buns from scratch. The food over there is crazy good."

"I remember a time not too long ago when you considered blueberry Pop-Tarts with peanut butter to be a delicacy." He bit off a corner while Wyatt finished prepping the coffeemaker.

Once the pot started gurgling java, Wyatt turned to lean against the counter. "Higher-ups at the station are concerned about you—hell, I'm concerned about you. The captain wants you to talk to the in-house doc."

"The shrink?" He bit off another quarter of the Pop-Tart and chewed while choosing his words carefully. He thought he'd left behind this crap in Atlanta and salvaged a life here for himself. At least he'd thought that until yesterday. "I'm doing the work. No slacking. Am I being sent to ride desk duty?"

"No, not at all. We need you. You're a damn good cop. Everyone here knows that."

"Then why are you all busting my chops? And why the hell was our boss discussing it with you?"

"We know the signs of burnout." Concern creased Wyatt's forehead. "He asked for my opinion as your partner and your relative."

The last thing AJ wanted was a pity party behind his back. "Hey, if I'm causing you trouble, I'll quit. You called in favors to line up the job interview here. I owe you."

"You don't owe me jack shit." Wyatt pulled two mismatched mugs out of the cabinet. "We're family. That's why I want to give you the heads-up."

"Heads-up about what?" He pushed the pause button on the coffeemaker and filled both mugs.

"The captain has a plan to reassure himself your head's on straight. And when the doc or the captain mentions it, you are going to say yes." Wyatt lifted an eyebrow and his mug in a toast.

AJ blew into his mug of steaming java. He wasn't going to win this argument with his cousin or the department, and it hadn't escaped his notice that Wyatt didn't answer his question. Bottom line, he didn't want to put anyone at risk if he was screwed up. So whatever it was that Wyatt thought would make him run from this plan, he would just get over it.

Drinking his coffee, AJ eyed his cousin over the mug. "Sure, fine, of course I'll go see the shrink. You got me the job and I don't want to cause friction for you at work."

"Don't do this for me. Do it for yourself. And to be clear, you got the job based on your merits. We don't have a force big enough to give away positions."

His merits had only bought him burnout. He was weary with the job, the devastation, the sense that no matter how many criminals he brought down, he'd scraped only the first layer of scum off a bottomless pit. And apparently Cooksburg wasn't much different from Atlanta when it came to the meth business.

Undercover work almost nonstop for seven years had raked him raw inside. He'd experienced a weak moment yesterday, which also explained his lack of control around Mary Hannah. He just wanted to hole up with his television today and recharge. Yes, he would go along with the shrink's plan, but that didn't mean he had to give up control.

"Dude, I appreciate the concern and you coming by to wish me Merry Christmas." He set aside his mug, using a magazine as a coaster. "Now you can leave. This is how I want to spend my day off. I told you that yesterday. Don't you have somewhere to be for lunch?"

"As a matter of fact, I do." Wyatt smiled in a way he hadn't for a long time. Not since his divorce. "I told Lacey I wouldn't come back without you."

"Your promise is not my problem. I'm not up for eggnog and 'Deck the Halls.'"

"Then I guess I'm not going to Lacey's because I can't leave you alone on Christmas." He extended a hand. "Pass me a Pop-Tart. I'm starving."

"That's emotional blackmail, cousin." And it was pinching at his conscience. "I'll toss you out, if I have to. Trust me, I can."

"I believe you. I learned that one the hard way when you hit that growth spurt at fifteen and kicked my ass at the family football game." His smile faded, and he jammed his hands into the pockets of his thick flannel jacket. "Holidays are about family, which means they're still tough for Lacey. She wants you there, so do me a favor. At least put in an appearance. You'll just be right next door, and there's going to be quite a crowd, easy to duck out early once you've made an appearance."

AJ saw the defeat coming even as he put up a token fight. "I don't have any gifts or food. It wouldn't be right."

"Do you have beer?"

He snorted. "I'm a bachelor."

"Bring the beer. Now hurry up and get dressed." Wyatt

clapped him on the shoulder. "You can be the one to deliver the good news to Mary Hannah if she hasn't heard already."

"Good news?"

"The woman we arrested at the cabin spilled her guts this morning. Apparently being locked up at Christmas made her sentimental enough to want to go home faster. She provided documentation that the dogs are hers, including some vet records on the adult animals, and she's signed them all over to Animal Control."

"Vet records?"

"A traveling vet. The guy's shady, but the rabies vaccinations appear legit. A lucky break actually, since so many of the animals that land at the shelter aren't current on even their rabies shots. Provided the meth-house dogs pass their temperament test, they're free to go to a rescue. It's like some kind of Christmas miracle."

"I gotta agree. It's sure not the turnout I expected. That's great news." Provided they passed. Provided the *boxer* passed the test. He wasn't more than cautiously optimistic. "I might have rolled out of bed faster if you'd led with that."

"Good point." Wyatt put his mug in the sink. "I was working up to the next part. A suggestion."

Ah, so now they'd gotten to the real reason Wyatt had thought he would balk. "And?"

"If you work with Mary Hannah after work and on days off training a dog—maybe one of those from yesterday's seizure—you could enter it in that big fund-raising event this February."

AJ picked up his mug and turned it round and round.

"She trains therapy dogs for PTSD patients, and as I understand it, that's a long process."

Not to mention he didn't have PTSD. What the hell kind of suggestion was this?

"She also trains emotional-support animals for people who are stressed. There's less time involved. Think about it, because I'm trying to help you. This would be enough to get the captain off your back and maybe even skip visits to the shrink altogether."

"Why am I not hearing this from the captain?"

"He's giving you this chance to keep it unofficial, off the record. That's a gift and you know it."

AJ couldn't argue with that, so he picked up his coffee and downed the rest before speaking. "If I don't do what you ask, I'm gone?"

"That's not what I'm saying. But you can't simply wish this away. Don't say no out of some knee-jerk reaction."

AJ scratched his bristly jaw. Even if his cousin had his best interests at heart, he didn't like being maneuvered this way. "You've taken Machiavellian matchmaking to a whole new level."

"You can't deny this helps your situation at the station, and as for the matchmaking, no one's forcing you to ask the woman out. You don't have to give me an answer right now. Think on it. Talk to Mary Hannah after lunch." Wyatt nodded once, before backing toward the door. "I'm off. I'll see you next door in a half hour. Don't forget the beer." He slid back out the door as silently as he'd entered.

AJ ate the last bite of Pop-Tart, watching his cousin pick his way through the snow to the house next door. A line of cars was parked haphazardly by the McDaniel house and barn. The barn with a studio apartment. Mary Hannah's apartment.

Of course she wouldn't be the only one there. The Christmas celebration would be crowded with family and rescue workers. Wyatt had a point that he didn't have to participate in the matchmaking. There were plenty of other people to exchange Christmas cheer with. He could eat and leave.

Except with that dream of being with Mary Hannah still fresh in his memory, he couldn't deny the truth. He wouldn't be able to resist—the Christmas dinner invitation or the dog-training proposition with her. This attraction to her wasn't letting up. He'd been drawn from the start, but ignoring it for five months hadn't helped one damn bit. He wanted her.

Better to take a more proactive approach and spend time with her. At his instigation. On his terms. Provided he could persuade her to put up with him while they trained a dog.

The thought of sparring with Mary Hannah again shouldn't turn him inside out this much. She was still a prissy pain in the ass who would probably take one look at his bachelor pad and run screaming for a bucket of bleach.

But he'd witnessed a grit to her yesterday that had impressed the hell out of him. Seeing her tender heart later at the shelter? That moved him. She was relaxed around the animals. Less paisley . . . more mess.

The notion of Mary Hannah messy, disheveled from his hands in her hair, had him walking to shower all the faster. He just had to bide his time to find the right moment to get her alone and launch his campaign.

Seven

Apparently *Family Feud* wasn't just a game show . . .

—FEMALE BOXER, FOUR YEARS OLD, SHELTER #S75230

CHRISTMAS AT THE McDaniel house was so different from Mary Hannah's home growing up. Her mother always had a perfectly matched tree like the kinds found in a high-end store's front window, a larger version of her little tree in her apartment.

The McDaniel Christmas tree had been cut from their land. One side was fatter than the other. The whole fir was covered in a hodgepodge of ornaments, some clearly gifts from adopters with photos of their new pet inside and other handmade ornaments signed by Lacey's children.

It was a family tree.

Mary Hannah sat at the base by a pile of discarded wrapping paper, boxes and bows. She gently traced a crystal bulb with Lacey's wedding date stenciled in flowing script.

Mary Hannah slumped back against the wall, enjoying the peaceful nook to observe the chaos that came with any Second Chance Ranch gathering, a mix of relatives and Second Chance volunteers who didn't have anyone else, even two young couples who had each other but were drawn to this extended-family feel. Over the island between the kitchen and the family room, she could see one group was playing board games. Another played cards out in the sunroom.

Inside, the television droned John Wayne movies for the grandfather with Alzheimer's. Mike parked beside him with Trooper, feet on the coffee table, playing his guitar softly.

Total controlled chaos, plus four dogs and three cats mostly oblivious. Trooper inched off the sofa and sidled into the kitchen. He stationed himself by the table to scavenge bites of food that had fallen to the floor—or had been surreptitiously passed down.

AJ backed out of the refrigerator and closed the door, a plate with two slices of pecan pie in hand. He stepped over Trooper on his way back into the family room. He looked so damn good in a green sweater and well-worn jeans.

He knelt beside her. "Wanna share some pie? This stuff's like frickin' ambrosia. There's no way there will be any left by the end of the day."

"Sure, thanks." She took the extra fork from the edge of the plate while he sat beside her. "This is like one of those Christmases you hear about but never see."

Her parents were always so uptight, everything kept calm the way her father wanted. She'd expected to build a different future with her own family.

"The McDaniels have worked hard to get back to normal." He stabbed off a bite of his slice of pie and rested the plate on his knee.

"They deserve this day." Sharing the dish seemed strangely intimate, but not eating would make more of it than if she did.

He shrugged, shoveling another bite into his mouth. "That's why I'm here. To lend support."

"You got guilted into showing up, too, huh?" She scraped her fork along the goopy filling and pecans, leaving the crust. Her sister was allergic to nuts, on top of being epileptic. So that ruled out pecan pie at her house.

"*Strong-armed* would be the more appropriate wording."

"What did you want to do instead?" She savored the taste of pure filling, caramel and nuts. The sugar rush went straight to her head.

"Go fishing. And you?" He ate a piece of her abandoned crust.

"I spent the morning at the shelter taking treats to the dogs."

This sharing food was definitely not accidental. He was tormenting her on purpose. She sucked her fork clean.

He blinked hard once before speaking. "How's Mama?"

"Quiet. Still wary, but she liked the pumpkin peanut butter cookies I made for them." How strange to realize this was the first time they'd spoken with each other, just talked comfortably without there being an official reason.

He set the plate onto the edge of the hearth, flames crackling. "You have a big heart, Mary Hannah. It's no wonder the whole town adores you."

She hugged her knees to her chest. "I am not some kind of saint."

"Do you say that because of Francesca?"

"Shhh!" She touched his knee. "Someone might hear you."

Chuckling, he covered her hand with his, linking their fingers. "I'm certain even if they heard that little bit they wouldn't guess the truth."

She let her fingers curl around his, his palm warm against hers.

"You're right there." She looked around at the group gathered, and God, it would be almost comical to see their shock if they heard about the other side of her. The side that lost control and made the most unwise decisions.

She felt the weight of AJ's eyes in the silence between them. But then they didn't need words right now. The memory was plenty clear of that steamy rainy evening. Of a flirtation that escalated fast and led them into a motel room where they'd peeled wet clothes off each other.

A cleared throat snapped the tension between them. She looked up quickly and found Lacey's teenage son slouching, clothes too big, almost as big as his grin. "Wanna join us for a game of Risk?"

"Sure. Can't have Wyatt thinking his matchmaking is working." AJ stood, holding out a hand. "Mary Hannah?"

The longer she waited the more conspicuous it would be. But her stomach knotted at the thought of taking this step. So simple really, just joining in the chaos and fun.

Leaving the past Christmas traditions behind.

Nathan passed the boxed game to AJ. "Grab a seat. I'll be right back."

Lacey tipped her chair at the kitchen table and asked, "Where are you going?"

The teenager paused on his way to the hall, the cuckoo clock blaring. "Dad always made us wear military hats he picked up around the world when we played Risk."

Everyone at the table went quiet.

Nathan spread his arms wide. "What? It's not like I'm gonna go all suicidal over a mention of Dad." The fact that the kid joked about his attempt to kill himself drew uncertain laughs. Nathan shook his head. "Lighten up and be real. Dad's a part of our past. So deal with it and quit treating me with kid gloves. I'm dealing with it the best way I know how."

Gramps shot to his feet. "I want the Bolivian general's hat. Ups my chances of getting the hot chicks." He winked at Mary Hannah. "Wanna be on my team?"

Looking at the twinkle in the old man's eyes, she knew he was totally clear for one of his rare moments. And there was wisdom there. Life was tough enough on its own without borrowing trouble.

Lighten up and just enjoy the moment. The morning would come soon enough.

Mary Hannah pushed to her feet and hooked an arm through the General's. "I would be honored to have you on my side, sir."

* * *

"THAT WAS REALLY awesome how you handled the General and his Alzheimer's this afternoon." AJ slid two board games on the top shelf of the hall closet, then reached behind him to get the stacks of cards from Mary Hannah. He'd expected to just endure Christmas, but this had been . . . good.

"I'm a counselor." She tucked two of the decks into his hand, her soft fingers brushing his palm. "It's what I do. And truly, it wasn't that tough, just letting him enjoy a family tradition. What did your family do during holidays?"

"Board games like this. A lot of food. Television and naps." He turned to face her, the hall narrow and private. Close. "My dad and Wyatt's father are brothers. Our mothers teach at the same junior high school. Plus other distant cousins . . . holidays were a zoo like this."

"Wyatt has re-created home for you both here," she said perceptively.

She smelled like pecan pie and a hint of smoke from sitting so close to the fire. Her sleek black hair was loose, a stark contrast to her white sweater. A Christmas wreath pin fastened to her shoulder peeked between strands of hair. So quaint and cute and totally Mary Hannah.

"I guess Wyatt has." Except he didn't want to talk about his cousin. He wanted to get to know this more relaxed Mary Hannah. "Do you have family? I don't recall anyone visiting. Come to think of it, we skipped the exchange of histories."

"I have a sister—Sarah Jane. She lives in California and runs a successful Internet business—kind of like Etsy." She sagged back against the wall, smiling. "She's an amazing person. She had epilepsy—still does—but the meds are better these days and regardless she came up with a successful career and life." Their dad had always demanded such order out of fear for his child's health. Turned out Sarah Jane was the strong one.

"Her sister's pretty successful, too." He brushed her hair aside so he could see that little wreath.

"Thanks, but really"—she chewed her bottom lip—"it was tougher for her."

"What about your parents?"

"My father died of a stroke when I was in college." She scrunched her nose. "He had high blood pressure and a fiery temper. Not a good combination. He got angry one day and literally blew a gasket." She winced. "Bad joke."

"Sometimes jokes and sarcasm help."

"My mom died in a car accident the year after my father passed away." She fidgeted with her wreath pin. "I've always wondered if she killed herself. I'll never know. Maybe that's a part of why I decided to be a counselor, to make sense of my life. Okay. Stop. I'm being really morbid here."

"You must have some happy memory, something from Christmas?" He stepped closer.

Her eyes went wide with panic. "This has been nice, but I'm starting to go on sensory overload from all the merriment. I'm going to give some of those pumpkin peanut butter treats to the dogs here, too."

He skimmed a hand along her shoulder, not wanting to push too hard, too fast, but also not ready for this to end. And yeah, he was worried about those shadows that had just chased through her eyes. This was Christmas. "Want some company?"

She hesitated, searching his eyes and toying with that wreath pin. "I don't want to start gossip."

"Then I'll give you a five-minute head start."

A slow smile spread over her face. "Okay, then. Sounds like a plan."

ONCE SHE SNATCHED the container of dog treats from the counter, Mary Hannah grabbed her red wool coat and made her escape out the mudroom door. Checkered curtains fluttered at the gust of frigid air before she pushed the door closed.

Was she freaking crazy? She did not need to be meeting AJ out here. Alone.

Breathing in the crisp breeze, she clutched the container of cookies under her arm and held the rail on her way down the steps. She'd worked hard to rebuild her life, and for the past few years she'd managed holidays better each time. Except for today. And she couldn't ignore the fact that AJ Parker caused that turmoil.

Tupperware container under her arm, she slipped her cold hands into her pockets. She picked her way gingerly over the ice along the covered walkway leading to the barn. Distant squeals carried from the distance of a half-dozen volunteers sledding. She opened the side door that housed the Second Chance Ranch Rescue. Rows of kennel runs housed a dozen dogs, two horses, a donkey and a pig, thanks to the latest round of renovations. Even more animals lived in foster homes.

This place gave her a comfort that had been far too elusive since her life had fallen apart. Sure, she was Sierra's friend, but what if Lacey married Wyatt? If things went south with AJ, that could wreck things for her here.

Even his brief kiss on her forehead had left her tossing and turning all night. That simple brush of his mouth against her skin brought their one-night stand roaring back to life in her memories until she felt the urge to find relief in a deep, foggy medicated sleep. A dangerous temptation. She'd even called her Narcotics Anonymous sponsor this morning and would be attending a meeting next week. She just had to make it through the holidays and then she could lose herself in her work, with patients and here with the animals.

She placed the homemade dog treats on a shelf, opened the last stall and tucked inside to scoop up a scruffy white Cairn-Terrier mix named Barkley. She'd chosen him to partner with a patient she counseled at the VA hospital, the veteran who'd lost a leg and an arm in Afghanistan.

Mary Hannah cuddled the scruffy little scrap, and he licked her chin in appreciation just before his ears perked up. He barked a warning. She turned fast to find AJ in the doorway watching her.

"How long have you been there?" she asked self-consciously.

"Only for a few seconds," he answered with a wry smile. "I thought we could let some of the dogs have an extra run in the play yard."

"Oh, um, thanks. I would appreciate the help. It takes a while since we divide them into groups according to how they play together."

"Good thing I brought us something to drink. It's out on the picnic table."

"I'm not much of a beer drinker," she said skeptically.

"I remember. You ordered a Diet Coke with rum the night we met."

That he remembered the small detail from months ago made her breath catch in her throat. She thrust the Cairn Terrier into his arms. "Take Barkley and I'll open the gates for the other dogs in his playgroup. Meet you outside."

She couldn't decide if she was a coward or just strategically wise, but she ducked into the supply closet to get tennis balls for fetch—and to gather her composure. Three ragged breaths later, she retrieved the dog treats from the shelf, a bag of tennis balls dangling from her wrist. She opened gates along her way outside, her stomach buzzing with nerves. Five bundles of energy raced ahead of her to the snowy play yard. A beagle skidded along the packed ice, tumbling butt over head, then righting himself again.

AJ's laugh carried on the wind, deep, masculine and tempting. Drawn to the sound, she walked closer, couldn't seem to stop her feet if she tried. She pitched a tennis ball past the sprawling oak tree, and the rest of the pack raced past. The bird feeders that stayed full year round swayed, showering seeds.

"Here, catch." She tossed a couple of tennis balls to AJ.

"These treats look good enough for people." He caught each of the tennis balls cleanly in midair.

"They are definitely for the dogs." She saw a thermos and two cups on the picnic table. "I assume that's the drink you brought for us?"

"Hot cider instead of Diet Coke. Be warned, though, it is still spiked with rum." He winked, his blue eyes glinting.

"Cider and rum?" A smile warmed her insides as much as any alcohol. "Nice choice, Detective. Since we both can walk home, that works well."

She swiped her coat sleeve across the picnic table to clear snow off the space beside the thermos and set down the container of treats. In the summertime, baby pools of water were out for the dogs to splash around, but for now it was just ice and snow. Not that the dogs seemed to mind as long as they were free to race frenetic circles around the fenced-in area. The distant warble and cluck of a turkey filled the night as if the bird shouted victory at surviving the season alive.

Her scarf flapped loose from her coat collar. She missed her paisley parka, but between the unwashed dogs, a couple of rips, the sludge and the meth, her clothes had been beyond salvaging. She had to wear her red wool coat for now until she could hit the after-Christmas sales—

What a ridiculous time to worry about clothes or think about the fact she'd chosen to wear contacts today rather than her glasses.

She kicked a ball free from the snow, distracting the dogs.

AJ set down the Cairn Terrier to join in the chase. "Tell me more about this new fella?"

"That's Barkley. He's slated to be in the Mutt Makeover competition. I'm pairing him with a wounded army veteran from Fort Campbell." She opened the thermos and poured the steaming cider into both mugs. "If we have a shelter dog win, that prize money would mean everything to the Second Chance Ranch."

"Barkley should win on the cuteness factor alone." He pitched a ball and the dogs tore off after it.

"If only it could be that simple." She sipped the warm

cider, an after-kick of alcohol tingling through her. The chilly wind tugged at her scarf, and she anchored it with her hand. "You must get very annoyed at all the matchmaking."

He lifted his mug to his mouth. "We could just have sex again—for the sake of peace."

Her hand fell to her side. "Or we could just keep talking. They'll think their plan is working and we won't have to listen to the racket indoors."

His smile was slow in spreading across his face in time with the slow burn building inside her. "Fair enough, then." He toasted with his cider. "Merry Christmas, to you and your Second Chance Ranch family."

She drank along with him to hide how the word *family* stung this time of year. The wind rolled across the fields and tugged at her scarf again, pulling the tail free from her coat.

"Did I say something wrong?" He set aside his mug and picked up the edge of her scarf and tugged lightly.

"No, of course not." Not anything she could share with him. Like the big-city narcotics detective would be sympathetic to her drug addiction that had wreaked havoc on those around her. "I was just thinking that I'm not Lacey's family, not really. I try not to impose on her. Sure, I'm friends with her daughter, but it's not like we're blood related, so I don't want to take advantage."

His eyes held hers for another instant, and he tugged the scarf, drawing her closer. "What would Francesca do? I've seen you be assertive when it comes to what the animals need. You can take what you want for yourself, too."

She jerked her scarf out of his hand and jammed it into the V of her coat. "Thanks for the advice, but I don't recall either Francesca or myself asking for it."

"You're funny." The dimple kicked into his cheek again, such a contrast to his dark, broody self. "I like that."

He seemed more approachable when he smiled. And when he tossed the ball for the pups again and again, while she sipped the cider. She allowed herself to relax a little, to settle into the idea of spending time with him.

Maybe she could figure out why she was so drawn to him. "So you do like animals."

"What made you think I didn't?" He knelt to scratch the beagle on his floppy ears.

"Maybe the fact you don't have a pet of your own in spite of living next door to a rescue. I'm sure Lacey has offered up candidates."

"The moment was never right with undercover work." He shrugged, and God, how his shoulders filled out his navy-blue jacket. "I'm thinking it's time to change that. My schedule here is more regular."

She set aside her mug before the spiked cider stole her restraint. "What made you trade big-city undercover detective work for a sleepy town and small-time stuff?"

"Yesterday was hardly small-time."

"True enough." She shuddered at the memory of the filth, but more than that, the pain in the animals' eyes. "Yet certainly rarer than the work you used to do in Atlanta."

"Call me crazy, but there's an appeal to not waking up each morning wondering if I'll be shot." He refilled his mug and walked away, toward the pack of dogs rolling in the snow.

Guilt nipped as she watched him stride off with those broad shoulders braced. She was so caught up in her own problems she hadn't thought about others, not really. Even if she wasn't on the clock, job-wise, she should have picked up on this vibe from him before now.

She poured out the rest of the cider into the snow rather than risk the alcohol clouding her mind, and searched for the right words. Sometimes there was nothing to say, just let people have peace to work through the weight of emotion.

Her hand fell to rest on the container of dog biscuits. "I'll put these pups back up with a treat and let some of the others out of their kennel runs."

AJ's footsteps crunched on the snow, louder and closer

until she felt the warmth of him standing behind her. His breath brushed her neck. "They're having fun. Let's wait a bit longer."

Oooo-kay. What did he want from her? What did *she* want?

She picked up the box of cookies and turned to face him, dog biscuits between them. "Pumpkin peanut butter treats. I took some to the shelter this morning and they were a hit with the canine crowd."

His hands covered hers over the container. "Great news about the dogs from the meth lab. Will you be going with Lacey to pick them up? Or do you have to work tomorrow, Dr. Freud?"

Her hands warmed even though they both wore gloves. She should just give him the cookies and step away. But she didn't. "I wouldn't miss it. I already called in to work a half day tomorrow afternoon so I can go to the shelter in the morning and be there for the temperament test."

"I've been thinking about those dogs." Snow fluttered down, catching on his lashes and making those blue eyes all the more mesmerizing.

"And?" Brilliant response.

He took the cookies from her and set them back on the table. "The police department wants to sponsor a Second Chance dog for the February competition."

"That's awesome." She relaxed back against an icy-slick trunk. "Who's going to be the dog's foster? Wyatt?"

"That would be me." He braced a gloved palm over her head on the tree.

Now, that stunned her silent.

"I thought we could use one of the dogs from yesterday, if any of them works out, and you would be the trainer."

She struggled to follow his words, tough to do with all the heat pulsing through her veins until she could have sworn the snowflakes steamed on her sleeves. "I train therapy dogs and emotional-support dogs."

"Then you can include some of that emotional-support aspect to help me get over all those bullets whizzing past my head back in Atlanta." He winked.

Her eyes narrowed. "I don't appreciate your making light of my profession."

"Sorry." He raised both hands in surrender. "The department is on me about being a cranky, irritable son of a bitch. This will get them off my back and you can't deny it will be good promo for the rescue to have one of their pups partnered with one of the men in blue."

Maybe he'd been using humor to shield something deeper. Wouldn't be the first time. But she didn't want to analyze him right now. "Sure, but—"

"Good. Then we're in agreement. We're working with one of the Second Chance dogs for the competition."

He angled forward and she readied herself for another kiss on the forehead or on the cheek. She steeled herself to resist. Then his mouth pressed to hers and all her resolve melted away faster than snowflakes hitting a skillet. Sizzling with fire.

Steaming desire through her.

A sigh slipped free, parting her lips, and he deepened the kiss. His mouth angled, his tongue meeting hers just as she stretched up on her toes to get closer. Her arms crept around his neck and she held on, grateful for the tree behind her to keep her from sinking.

His hands cradled her face, a simple touch but it stirred as much as flesh on flesh contact. Her eyes fluttered closed as she focused more intently on absorbing the feel of him against her. Remembering. The chemistry between them was every bit as explosive as before. Even more.

Her fingers twisted in his coat, her hips arching closer, nowhere near close enough with all these layers of clothes between them. Years of abstinence sharpened the edge of desire into a painful ache, almost impossible to resist, especially with her apartment so very close. Her solitary, lonely apartment.

Words began to form in her mind, impulses urging her to just say it. Just ask him to follow her up those stairs to her studio apartment.

A slamming door startled her, her eyes opening wide and her stomach lurching at the prospect of being discovered making out with AJ behind a tree.

Voices drifted on the snowy breeze, familiar voices of volunteers who'd come to the holiday dinner.

"We should help Mary Hannah get the rest of the dogs out before we head home," Debbie said. "Did you bring those rope toys?"

"Sure did," her husband answered, boot steps steady as he lumbered through the snow.

They were seconds away from being discovered.

AJ's hands stroked down her face to rest on her shoulders before he stepped back. Cold air rushed between them, all the more biting against her overheated face.

Her rapid breaths puffed needy clouds into the late afternoon air. "AJ—"

He tapped her lips. "I'll see you tomorrow."

"You will?" She spoke against his fingertip and resisted the impulse to nip and draw it into her mouth.

"At the shelter, to find out if I'm a love match with one of the dogs." He stepped back slowly without taking those mesmerizing blue eyes off her. "Good night, Mary Hannah. Sleep well."

Eight

I didn't realize how much pressure came with the question "Is that your final answer?"

—FEMALE BOXER, FOUR YEARS OLD, SHELTER #S75230

WATCHING THE LAST of her guests drive away, Lacey sagged into a chair on the glassed-in back porch where she kept puppies so she could watch over them. The space was empty now from Christmas adoptions.

She expected the space to be filled tomorrow once Mary Hannah picked up some of the meth-house dogs and pups. She couldn't keep operating as if life were normal for much longer if it turned out she really was pregnant. She still wasn't sure. She was only a few days late, and the home pregnancy test was negative. But she felt pregnant, exhausted, with swollen boobs and feet.

She would have to tell Wyatt soon.

That didn't mean she would have to stop working with animals, but it would curtail her duties, as it had yesterday. Not to mention juggling all of this with an infant would be challenging. Just the thought of keeping up with a toddler again exhausted her. She was almost a grandmother, for heaven's sake.

All of her lectures to her teenage son about safe sex plagued her. She'd definitely lost her credibility in that arena.

But damn it, the condom really had broken. She'd started watching the calendar, and sure enough . . .

She sipped her Waterford crystal glass of lemon water. If ever she could have used something stronger . . . She propped her aching feet on the patio coffee table.

Everyone had gone home or to bed. The volunteers had cleaned up and fed the animals as an additional gift to her. She was lucky in so many ways. Knowing that didn't stop the nerves eating at her until her hand trembled and she had to set the glass down again.

Hands slipped onto her shoulders, massaging. She hadn't even heard Wyatt approach. He moved so quietly for such a large man. Because of his job perhaps. She rested her hand over his.

"Thank you. That feels amazing." She closed her eyes, her head lolling to the side as she savored each kneading roll into knotted muscles.

"Touching you is amazing." He kissed her temple. "I've been waiting all day to get you alone."

"Holidays are crowded. It's family time." She was lucky to have him in her life. She knew that.

Was it so wrong that she wanted to take things slower and ease her way into the relationship? She'd rushed to the altar with Allen because she'd gotten pregnant. But she wasn't a frightened teenager. Even afraid, she'd been so certain Allen was her future. She needed to be as certain this time, regardless.

"What a great Christmas spread you put on, Lacey." Wyatt swept aside her hair, massaging deeper, the calluses on his fingertips arousing against her skin. "Thank you for including my cousin in that family time."

She glanced back at him, his strong handsome features tanned and weathered with a midforties maturity she appreciated. His face wore experience in the creases fanning from his eyes. "The images of a bachelor Christmas made me shudder in sympathy for him."

"What would you have imagined?"

"Beer and fried turkey legs. Maybe some macaroni and cheese from a box. Enjoyed in front of the television."

His laughter rumbled over her head. "That's bad, why?"

She swatted his arm. "You're such a guy."

"Good thing." His hands slid around to the front to graze the tops of her swollen, sensitive breasts.

Usually she enjoyed his touch, but with her emotions in such turmoil, she couldn't relax enough to consider making love. Not tonight. "Well, I appreciate your joining in and putting up with all our casseroles and carols."

"Hey, I didn't say the beer and ball games would have been better." He tucked around to sit on the patio sofa, still holding on to her hand. "Everything's better with you around."

"Flatterer."

"I only speak the truth." He tugged her until she had no choice but to sit by him, curled up against his side. "I'm a cop, honor bound and all."

Her fingers grazed along a scar on his palm where he'd been sliced by a knife when arresting a drunk driver last year.

He linked fingers with her, clasping hands. "I'm safe on the job."

"I know you are, and I'm so very glad of that." She smiled up at him, kissed his bristly jaw, then settled back against his side, breathing in the smoky after-scent of the bonfire they'd built to finish off the evening. "I guess that whole meth-lab raid has me rattled. That woman came after you with a baseball bat. It could have been a knife . . . or a gun."

"This is a small town. Days like yesterday are rare. I'm more likely to get egged than shot."

She flinched. "You don't have to explain yourself to me. You're only doing your job."

"And you would rather that job be something more along the lines of an accountant or a trash man." He stared off into the distance. "Or maybe that veterinarian friend of yours who went to save animals in third-world countries. Anything out of the line of fire."

Where the hell had the vet comment come from? She and Ray Vega had never been an item. Okay, so they'd kissed. But only once and no one knew about that. It had happened too soon after her husband had died, and then Ray left town to do "missionary" veterinary work. He'd said he was coming back in a year, but he hadn't. She'd moved on. She'd dated Wyatt.

Done more than dated.

She searched for the words to reassure him. The last thing she needed was an argument. "Wouldn't everyone prefer to have people they care about stay out of the line of fire?"

"You've been bitten more often than I've been nicked on a case," he pointed out accurately. "Remember that pissed-off guy who tried to get to his ex-wife through you since you were boarding her dog while she stayed in a battered women's shelter? We both know animal abuse is often the window to bigger crimes. Maybe I'm the one who should worry."

The wind howled through the eaves. Beyond the glassed-in patio, the stars dotted the night sky, a view she'd taken comfort in too many times to count. She just wanted this one night to pretend her life was uncomplicated.

She deserved that, right? She would pull a Scarlett O'Hara and deal with the rest tomorrow. "I guess we're both just going to have to start going to yoga together to deal with the stress of each other's jobs."

He hesitated, then surrendered with a sigh and kiss to her temple. "As long as I don't have to wear yoga pants."

"You make me laugh. I like that." She stroked his beard-stubbled face. "Let's just relax, enjoy the night sky and the end of a beautiful Christmas."

"As a matter of fact, I agree." He shifted to reach into his jeans pocket. "I still have to give you your Christmas gift."

"We already exchanged presents earlier." She'd given him new fishing gear, and he'd bought her concert tickets to her favorite country band. "You got me something else? I feel guilty."

And a little nervous. A tingle of foreboding raised the hair on the back of her neck.

"That's not my intent. I'm hoping this will make you very happy."

"We're going on a cruise?" She tried for levity, because oh God, oh God, she hoped this conversation wasn't going where she feared. She wasn't ready for a baby and all that commitment to each other entailed. She absolutely wasn't ready to be married again.

He swept his fingers through her loose curls. "Not a cruise, although that could be a part of the plan if you want it to be." He eased off the sofa onto one knee in front of her, a ring box in his hand with a princess-cut diamond solitaire. "Lacey, will you be my wife?"

WYATT WASN'T SEEING a *yes* in Lacey's eyes.

Clutching the ring box in his hand, he struggled to keep his face impassive, not to let her pick up on the disappointment hammering through him. He'd planned to propose on Christmas Eve night so they could tell everyone today. But the meth house had wrecked his time line, tainting the day. He'd thought Christmas Day would be just as romantic and memorable.

He hadn't considered that he might also be wrecking Christmas for the rest of his life as he remembered being dumped on his ass.

"Lacey, babe." He clasped her shoulder in what he hoped was a reassuring grip. "I have to confess this isn't the response I was hoping for."

"You took me by surprise. That's all." She blinked fast, a forced smile on her beautiful, tired face. "I wasn't expecting you to propose. The ring is gorgeous."

She touched the solitaire hesitantly, like it was a snake. Or worse, since she wasn't scared of snakes.

Snapping the ring box closed, he sank back to sit on the sunroom floor. "That's still not a yes."

"Why would you want to saddle yourself with a woman who's up to her eyeballs in debt buying land to expand an already-zany rescue full of animals?" She gestured to the two tabby cats sleeping on the back of the sofa and over to the empty puppy pens that would soon be full of little ones from the meth-house raid.

"Because I love you, and I thought you felt the same."

"I do love you." She slid off the sofa to kneel in front of him, her hands resting on his legs. "Those are words I've never said to any man other than Allen. And I mean them . . ."

"But you're not ready." He could see it in her eyes.

She closed her hand over his, folding his fingers back over the ring box. "I'm thinking about it, though, truly. I'm just exhausted today, feeling overwhelmed. This should be a happy moment."

"You're right." He stroked back her tangled curls, wishing this day had ended differently. "We'll do this again, the right way, with a dinner and candlelight. We have a whole future together. A family to share. Since you have a grandbaby on the way, we get all the fun of kids without the work. It's a win-win."

She went pale. "You don't want to have a baby of your own?"

Realization sank in. He shook his head, enjoying the glide of her fingers along his face. "Were you worrying I would pressure you? We should have talked about this before now. I'm fine not having a biological kid of my own. Nathan's a great teenager. I'll love him like my own. I'm too old to do the diaper duty and midnight feedings. Besides, there are plenty of little ones to take care of here at the rescue."

"You're a good man, Wyatt." She searched his face with troubled eyes.

"Then what's the problem?" He couldn't stop the disappointment . . . and jealousy. "Are you still grieving for your dead husband?" Hell, he still thought about his ex. He'd gotten over loving her, but her cheating still cut deep.

"No," she said without hesitation. "It's not that. I'll always miss him, but I'm moving forward. Right now I'm still figuring out how to be single. It has nothing to do with you. Can't we just keep on as we are for now? We're having fun and the sex is awesome. Give me a little more time, okay?"

He decided to play it her way, for now. Not that he had any choice. "The sex is awesome, you say?"

"Damn straight." She leaned forward to kiss him, the taste of lemon on her tongue.

He shifted her to recline on the floor, wrapping her in his arms and kissing her thoroughly. If only he could seduce her into understanding how perfect their future could be. Wishing he could stroke away her fears. Because he knew without question, she was afraid of something and he had a suspicion what that might be.

She'd lost a husband already in a tragic way. That had to have left mark beyond some gentle passing. Military or cop, they wore uniforms and stood in the line of fire. So either she still loved her dead husband or she couldn't love him, Wyatt, for fear of losing him to the job.

Either way, he was screwed.

I HAVE ONE name now that belongs only to me, my forever dog name.

The lady with two names picked it. Her name is Mary Hannah. I wondered for a while if those two names explained why she had so much pain inside her. Like when my life was bad and I had three names.

Except her two names were never shouted with a sneer, so maybe it isn't the number of names after all. Maybe it's about the person speaking them.

But back to the day I found out what they would call me.

I was in that concrete place at the shelter, the space they called a kennel run. I was alone and starting to wonder if I had hallucinated those pumpkin cookies from the day before. My solitary confinement had something to do with quarantine because of the meth and how I behaved the day they rescued me. How strange that I could hate my old home and still be so terrified of this new place where at least I was alone.

The noise, though, oh Big Master, the noise was deafening after my other life. So many dogs barking and people talking. But there was food, plenty of food, and no one touched me—more important, no one kicked me—as long as that quarantine sign stayed on my new home.

Quarantine.

I knew that word from game shows. Isolation because of a disease. I was somehow diseased because of my past. So I curled up in a corner on the cot, hoping to escape notice. There were different people who took care of us each meal and cleaning. Some made eye contact with looks that showed a tenderness I hadn't seen until then except in Mary Hannah's eyes. Others averted their gaze, either out of fear of me or to protect themselves from getting attached. I didn't learn until later in life how very many thousands of animals landed in a county shelter.

Then Mary Hannah came back after all.

Her eyes held sympathy and something else that made me want to be more than scared. She stopped at my kennel run again and sat on the floor, tossing in more of those pumpkin cookie treats. She talked to me but still didn't open the gate this time either because of that quarantine sign.

So I listened to Mary Hannah's soft voice, more soothing than the music.

"You need to be a very good girl today for your test, okay? Listen carefully. Don't gobble the food or guard your bowl. And when they put a plastic hand in your dish, don't bite."

She tossed in another cookie as if she knew I'd been too scared to eat the kibble the tech brought that morning. As if she knew this would help level the playing field when they did their food test.

"Be sure to share your doggie toys, okay?" she continued even though I didn't know what doggie toys were. "They're going to handle you, but be patient. It would be nice if you could wag your tail and let people pet you. And above all, please don't try to bite anyone because this temperament test is really important, sweetie."

That was when I realized the day had come for my temperament test. Even with all the game-show help and her tips, I wasn't sure what that meant or what was expected of me.

One of the staff came to get me out of my kennel, a person in a uniform. "Ms. Gallo, it's time. You can watch with your friend through the window."

She touched the wiry man's arm. "Thanks, Owen. I appreciate your letting me visit with her first."

Mary Hannah passed the container of cookies to one of the other kennel techs to share with the rest of the dogs, then followed us down the hall. She whispered words I realized later were prayers.

We passed two other techs walking dogs back to the kennel runs, all of us on leashes and carefully kept apart. But I caught a hint of their stories. A beagle hung his head sniffing the ground, wondering how he'd gotten off track from his people. He'd just slipped out the front door for a quick run to check out a turkey smoker down the road. Would his people look for him?

A Weimaraner struggled against the leash, pent-up energy making her frantic. She'd been left alone for Christmas break with a doggie door. The neighbor came by to feed her once a day, but she got bored and jumped the fence.

I made a mental note not to jump a fence—if I ever got one of my own.

Owen took me into a room with a couple of chairs, a blanket on the floor and a box, while Mary Hannah stayed out in the hall looking through a window with her policeman friend. I couldn't see what was inside the box, but I smelled treats. I would have been tempted to chew my way through the box for those treats, but with those cookies in my stomach, I could control myself.

That Mary Hannah was a smart lady.

Two people tested me—all of us, in fact. I didn't know then we were getting special attention, but apparently the director of Animal Control had taken extra interest in those of us from the meth house. At first, she just watched the test.

A kennel tech—the guy named Owen who had gotten me out of my kennel run—put down a bowl of food for me. Canned food. I'd never seen that before, and wow, it was tempting. Since this was a test, I wasn't sure what I was supposed to do, so I didn't touch it. Not at first. Owen nudged it closer and waited until I took a nibble and then—you won't believe this—just like Mary Hannah said, he brought out a fake hand attached to the end of a stick. That hand poked into the food again and again.

But I was scared of hands in those days. So I sat back. The hand moved away, and I ate again. We did that ritual for a while. A funny game really, but apparently that was okay because they didn't take the food away or stop the test.

Once the food was all gone, Owen petted me and I held still, just like Mary Hannah told me to. Although apparently I didn't do as well with that part of the test. They said I didn't "relax" into the stroke. I didn't welcome the touch, but since I didn't growl, I didn't fail.

The director—Ms. Taylor—stepped away from the door, coming closer to kneel beside me. Then slowly she reached for my paw. I didn't like being held that way, but she was persistent. She kept it up, too, with my other paws, even at one point hugging me and rolling me onto my back, which I absolutely did not like at all. But I still didn't growl and I didn't bite.

I never bit.

She let me go and I shuddered with relief. She made notes on the clipboard and had Owen sign at the bottom before she walked to open the door. "Mary Hannah, she passed."

Mary Hannah smiled so widely I knew I'd more than passed. "That's great, Dahlia. Better than great."

"I'm glad you're taking her, though, because even passing, there's no way she would get adopted here. She would stay curled up in that kennel run, terrified, which doesn't do much to entice people as they walk by. She needs serious socializing."

"I understand she needs socializing, love, training, patience. But first, she needs a name."

"She's yours now. Feel free to choose."

Mary Hannah tipped her head to the side. "Something to do with Christmas since that's when her new life started. Something like . . ." She leaned and wrote on the paper, my test. "There. It's official."

And that's how I finally had one name, sweetly spoken with love in a moment that changed my life forever. I had a long way to go, but finally, I had someone who cared. Someone who thought of me as more than Fat Mama, Bitch, Dumbass, Confiscate #8 or Shelter #S75230.

Finally, I mattered. Me. An individual being, not just a baby-making machine. And finally, I can introduce myself to you.

Hello, my name is Holly.

AJ HAD BEEN to the county shelter on more than one occasion, but never with such an insider's view of what a temperament test entailed.

He'd been allowed to watch through a window, standing beside Mary Hannah. He could swear she'd barely breathed through the process. He'd held her hand, and she hadn't objected. Although the hand-holding wasn't sexual. But it was progress in another way. A new connection.

He wasn't in a hurry to push for more just yet. He'd won a huge victory in getting her to agree to work with him training a dog. He was curious which of the animals would be chosen for their training project, and yeah, he hoped it could be Holly even though he felt bad for all the animals seized from that hellhole.

The poodles and schnauzers had been clipped of the larger mats for comfort, but they still needed baths and professional grooming. They'd passed their temperament tests, too, but he didn't consider himself much of a little-dog guy. Not that he was going to get a choice here. Mary Hannah might choose one of those froufrou pups just to get back at him.

The male boxer was still at a vet clinic, having taken a turn for the worse. He was in critical condition, so he wasn't an option for training anytime soon, if ever. The mama boxer needed her overgrown, curled nails trimmed, then ground down, but by the way the guy Owen had signed the paperwork, and the reassurance from the director herself, the female boxer had passed. Mostly she'd just trembled in fear, but she'd never growled or nipped, even when the director came in and wrestled her to the ground. That dog had plenty of fear but zero aggression now that the drugs were out of her system.

Holly wasn't going to be an easy candidate. But she was the one he wanted.

The *click, click, click*ing of heels echoed as the director of Animal Control—Dahlia Taylor—approached the door again after finishing with the last of the other dogs. She wasn't exactly what he would have expected. Wearing jeans and leather thigh-high boots, she looked more like an edgy New York model than someone who wrestled animals to see if they would be safe in society.

"Well, Mary Hannah," the director said. "If you're absolutely sure, they're all yours for the taking, even terrified Holly."

"All the more reason to get her out of here." Mary Hannah's big heart and generous nature wowed him all over again. He'd almost forgotten there were still pure people like her in the world. "The noise and the lack of human contact in a kennel run is the opposite of what she needs."

"I agree." Dahlia hugged the clipboard against her angora sweater flecked with dog hair. "I just want to make sure you know what you're signing on for."

"Would you question Lacey if she wanted to take Holly?" Mary Hannah braced her shoulders, standing her ground for the cowering dog on the other side of the window.

"Honestly? I know Lacey better than you." Dahlia frowned. "She has more experience in the field. I have to be certain for your safety and for Holly."

Mary Hannah nodded. "Then we'll get Lacey."

"Hey, no need to get defensive." The director pulled the temperament-testing forms from the clipboard. "I want to save these dogs as much as you do, but there are only so many rescue slots to go around. The boxer's lack of socialization goes deep. She's not going to magically turn into Friendly Fido once she walks out of here."

Mary Hannah looked back at the window, and the connection between her and Holly was damn near tangible. "I have to try. AJ has signed on to foster one of the dogs. Since he's right next door and can check in for help with her issues, Holly is the perfect fit for him."

Nice.

No froufrou dog for him after all. He would be working with his favorite—the antisocial one. They should get along well.

Dahlia stepped back. "Fair enough—and thank you." She ducked her head into the room. "Owen, you can release Holly to the Second Chance Ranch Rescue along with the poodles and schnauzers."

AJ blinked in surprise. All the little dogs? They were taking every dog from the cabin—other than the sick male boxer? The Second Chance Ranch van was going to be jam-packed full of crates.

Mary Hannah secured her hold on Holly's leash attached to a harness. "Let's go, girl. Time for your freedom ride."

As she led the dog down the corridor, she smiled at AJ, and joy radiated from her warm brown eyes that was every bit as mesmerizing as the kiss they'd shared last night. Her beauty and passion for this rescue took his breath away.

A low growl rumbled just ahead, yanking AJ's attention off Mary Hannah.

An employee held a yellow Labrador on a leash as he headed back toward the kennel runs. "The owner just surrendered this guy." He shrugged. "Said they don't have time for him anymore and are tired of him digging out from under their fence."

Some of the joy faded from her eyes, and he wanted to tell them to load up the Lab even though he wasn't one of the meth-house dogs. The yellow Lab snarled again, teeth bared.

Mary Hannah secured her hold on the boxer. "AJ, let's backtrack and go out a different door."

He turned with her and reached for the doorknob just as the Lab lunged—

And chomped down on Mary Hannah's thigh.

Nine

PAIN SEARED UP Mary Hannah's leg as the Lab's teeth sank deeper. The attack had happened so fast, her head spun. AJ and Owen launched onto the dog to pry the terrified animal's jaws open. Holly flattened to the floor in fear, ears back.

The Labrador went limp, the male dog's aggression fading as quickly as it erupted. Still, AJ slid between her and the animal, shielding her as Owen made fast tracks in the other direction.

"Clear the hall," Owen shouted, leading the dog toward the kennel runs, his commands growing fainter as he hustled away. "Stay back. Gerlach, open that door and prep a kennel."

Owen and the petrified Labrador disappeared through the double doors into the section of kennel runs for strays and quarantined animals.

Mary Hannah's leg went numb, and for an instant she hoped her jeans had protected her and she would just have one heck of a bruise. She wanted to hold on to that hope but knew she needed to look down.

Ugh. Her head went woozy.

Blood oozed from four puncture wounds through denim. The bite would have been worse on bare skin, but still. *Ouch.* She swayed, and AJ slid an arm around her. Holly whimpered at Mary Hannah's feet, belly flat on the ground.

Dahlia sprinted from her office, flustered, her bootheels clicking double time. A strand of hair actually shook loose from her sleek French braid.

"What happened?" The director's face paled as she looked from Mary Hannah's leg to Holly cowering on the floor. "Did the boxer bite you?"

"No"—thank heavens, although it was still tragic news for the other dog—"it was the yellow Labrador that just went by. He lunged for Holly, maybe she's in heat and he reacted, or was just overwhelmed and scared? I'm not sure. It all happened so fast. The tech has already taken him to a kennel run."

Dahlia drew in a shaky breath, composure sliding back into place as she took control. "Let's step into the clinic to flush out the puncture wounds with antiseptic before you leave for the emergency room."

Emergency room? Mary Hannah balked. Hospitals still brought back too many memories of rehab and losing her baby. But there wouldn't be a way to avoid seeing a physician.

She braced a steadying hand on the wall by a poster for flea preventives. "I guess I'll need to check in with a doctor for antibiotics."

"That looks deep. You may need a stitch or two." Dahlia took her elbow gently. "Come with me. Sadly, this isn't the first time we've dealt with a bite incident, as you know, and I need to follow protocol for filing a report."

Mary Hannah squeezed her eyes closed for a second, the weight of what had happened washing over her. A bite could very well mean the end of a dog's life. She swallowed hard and let herself lean back against AJ's arm as he guided her across the hall. Staff members nodded and waved, eyes filled with worry as she passed the front desk on her way to the clinic.

The discount spay/neuter clinic stocked the basics without frills, an exam and treatment area for the main room, with a small surgical suite to the side. The space hummed with activity. A wall of crates held sick or recovering animals. A vet tech was weighing a Great Dane. The veterinarian was spaying a cat while another tech monitored the anesthesia.

A vet tech Mary Hannah recognized as Vivian came bustling forward with saline solution, antiseptic and a pair of scissors. Her gym shoes squeaked against the tile floor. Mary Hannah eased into an office chair, her leg extended.

Vivian tossed down a thick towel and knelt beside her, all business and focus. "Sorry this happened to you, Mary Hannah, but I'm going to have to cut the leg off your nice trouser jeans to get to the wounds and flush them out." She slid the scissors into the tear in the denim, going slowly to avoid bumping the punctures. "Detective, please hold her in case she passes out."

"I'm okay. Let's just get this over with." Mary Hannah tapped the director on the elbow while Vivian finished cutting away the jeans leg. "Dahlia, the dog was overwhelmed and scared."

"Understandable." Dahlia nodded. "But I still have to document and check the dog's intake record. His owner surrendered him, so hopefully there will be vet records. Maybe we'll luck out and he's up-to-date on his vaccinations."

AJ went still beside her. His eyes shot to the director. "*Hopefully* there are records? *Maybe* he's been vaccinated?"

Mary Hannah already knew the chances were slim to none the dog had a current rabies vaccine. Few animals were ever surrendered fully vetted.

The receptionist leaned into the clinic with a folder in hand. She shook her head ominously as she passed it over to the director.

Oh hell.

Mary Hannah struggled not to wince as the cool cleanser splashed and stung over the puncture marks. "No rabies vaccination on record for the Lab?"

Dahlia thumbed through the paperwork, then sighed. "No veterinary care noted for four years. Definitely not a current rabies vaccination." She snapped the file closed. "You need to get to the emergency room and see a doctor right away."

"I figured as much." She'd always known this was a possibility, working in rescue with neglected animals. She just hadn't expected to feel so shaky.

Or so grateful to have AJ's steadying presence beside her.

LACEY HUGGED THE toilet bowl. Dry heaves pulled at her while her cell phone chimed on the floor beside her with text after text.

God, she didn't remember pregnancy being this draining. Maybe she really was just sick with the flu or some bad turkey.

Or maybe this was different since her last pregnancy had been a long, long time ago.

How was she going to keep up with teaching online classes, running the rescue and parenting her teenage son alone? But the thought of saying yes to Wyatt's proposal just to have help was completely repugnant to her. He deserved for her to be one hundred percent certain that she loved him and would have married him regardless of the baby.

She sagged back against the vanity cabinet, drawing in one unsteady breath at a time until her stomach settled. Not that she was willing to risk standing just yet. Staying as still as possible seemed the wisest move. She reached up for her cell phone to check the texts.

Damn. The number was staggering. Her phone lit up with missed messages from Mary Hannah, Dahlia, three Second Chance volunteers and a slew of numbers she didn't recognize but knew would be requests from people to take in their animals. She prioritized and started with the names she recognized.

Dahlia: MH got bit by new intake, Lab, no rabies vac. On her way 2 hospital. So sorry. Pls let us know if we can help.

Lacey closed her eyes, her head thumping back. This was always an awful possibility working with animals. It had happened before and would happen again. The only question now was how badly Mary Hannah had been injured. Lacey moved on to the next text.

Mary Hannah: Bit by dog on leg. Am OK. Puncture bite only. AJ's taking me to ER.

At least the wound wasn't as bad as it could be. Although the rabies vaccine series for humans wasn't a walk in the park. Another text dinged.

Mary Hannah: We have dogs in van. Didn't want to leave at shelter. Can u meet us at ER? Or should we unload at rescue first?

Good Lord, Mary Hannah was every bit as crazy as she was. Her thumbs flew as she typed:

Lacey: I or volunteer will meet u at ER 2 pick up dogs. Take care of yourself.

She thought through the names of her most seasoned, reliable volunteers to figure out one who lived near the hospital and wouldn't mind being bothered the day after Christmas . . .

Zoe. Her husband worked holidays. They'd celebrated early.

Lacey sent off a text but could afford to wait only a couple of minutes before she would have to leave and get the dogs herself. She would just trade cars with Mary Hannah since she and AJ had taken the Second Chance utility van—an acquisition made six months ago, a big step in expanding her operation.

She'd been so proud to see her rescue logo on the side of the van. Today, she would need to take a barf bag to make it to the hospital. Good grief, she wasn't any better than Mary Hannah, disregarding her health for the sake of getting the animals out of the shelter as quickly as possible. Except Lacey needed to be careful now, in case.

Her cell phone chimed with an answering text from Zoe agreeing to pick up the animals at the ER and bring them directly to the Second Chance Ranch. Relief settled her stomach faster than any antacid. Now she would have time to ready spaces for the incoming animals, making sure each one had music and calming scented infusers. Even bland dog and puppy foods full of protein and probiotics to transition their sensitive systems to the new diet.

She texted Mary Hannah and AJ the update that Zoe would be waiting for them at the ER. Zoe would trade cars so AJ could focus on getting Mary Hannah treated and no worries about shuffling the animals to a different vehicle.

Lacey cradled her cell phone against her chest. How would she manage this if she had a baby, too? How much would her doctor let her do at the rescue if she was pregnant? Would she end up high risk because of her age? Worries piled on top of concerns in her already stretched-to-the-limit life. Fear alone was making her sick to her stomach.

Setting her phone on the vanity, she braced and rose slowly, hoping hard that her empty stomach was done protesting for the day. The floor seemed to rock under her feet for a few seconds before her world stabilized. The tile was cool and soothing under her bare toes.

She took a risk and brushed her teeth, praying the minty

flavor wouldn't set off another episode. She spit and rinsed. So far, so good. She needed to change out of the sweat suit she'd worn to feed the animals and work on brunch.

She opened the walk-in closet, scanning the rack and shelves. She grabbed a long sweater and tried not to think about how it belonged to her dead husband, one of the few items of clothing she hadn't given away. Somehow this cable knit from Ireland had shown up in a batch from the cleaners after she'd purged the closet for Goodwill. She hugged it close, breathing in for an instant and finding Allen's scent was gone, even the memory fading.

Shaking off the whimsical thought, she tugged the sweater over her head, yanked on a pair of yoga pants and grabbed a black, fuzzy pair of fake Uggs. She could pull this off for a little longer, just to give herself time to think.

Her cell phone rang where she'd left it on the bathroom vanity—the tone just for Wyatt—and she snatched it up, her stomach fluttering. Their child moving? Not yet. It was too early for her to be feeling anything.

"Hello," she answered breathlessly. "Did you need something?"

"Hey, babe." His voice rumbled over the phone, low and deep like the bass singer in one of those male quartets. "Just checking to see if you heard about AJ and Mary Hannah."

"About the bite at the shelter?" She shivered thinking about how bad it was and how much worse it could have been.

"Yeah, are you okay? Freaked-out?" Sounds of the police station echoed in the background, phones ringing and shouts for more coffee, then the door closing as Wyatt must have found a quiet room. "I wanted to see if you need help."

"I've got everything covered," she said automatically. She hated being dependent on anyone. The habit from years of independence as a military wife was hard to shake off. Her fingers skimmed over the frame by her bed, a small shadow box with two origami animals that Allen had sent her while overseas. His last gift to her in his last letter.

"Lacey?" Wyatt asked. "Are you still there?"

She cleared her throat. "Yes, sorry. Zoe's picking up the meth-house dogs and bringing them here. She's leaving her car for AJ and Mary Hannah. I'll have a morning shift of volunteers to help me settle the animals and figure out how to swap the vehicles back."

"Good to know." He paused, and she could envision him chugging down coffee. "You do too much."

"The fund-raiser is important to the rescue. Once that's past, things should be easier." If she was pregnant, could she hold off telling the world until then? She would not even be three months pregnant by Valentine's Day.

She had her first doctor's appointment in a couple of weeks; she should at least wait until she knew for sure all was well. Maybe she was making excuses, but damn it, her peace of mind was important. Meanwhile, she would keep breaking the bank with daily at-home tests that kept saying negative in spite of the fact she was too young for this to be some menopausal scare.

"Lacey, I need a favor from you."

Surprised, she sank down to sit on the edge of the bed. He never asked for anything from her—other than to get married. "What can I do?"

"Do whatever you can to facilitate AJ training the boxer for the competition. He really should take some time off, but he's resistant. I'm hoping that prepping for the competition will give him something else to focus on other than working the next case."

His thoughtfulness touched her already emotional heart. "You're a good cousin to watch out for him this way."

"I want to take care of you, too, Lacey." His voice went softer, intimate.

She couldn't decide if she felt smothered or tempted. "I don't want to be a responsibility."

"I know you can handle yourself just fine. I only want to share life's joys—and burdens—with you." He was saying the words any person would hope to hear from a life partner.

She chewed her bottom lip before answering. "You sound too good to be true."

"That's because I am." As he spoke, she could hear the smile expand across his face. He said it with the right touch of humor so as not to come off as arrogant. "I'll let you go. Sounds like you have a busy day ahead."

"I really do need to go get lunch for Nathan and my father-in-law."

Her stomach rolled at the thought of food, but she wanted to treat her father-in-law to a family meal before he went back to the assisted living facility.

"How much longer is your father-in-law staying?"

"We're taking him back this afternoon." Joshua McDaniel had grown exponentially more disoriented by the Alzheimer's since his son died. His good days were so very few and far between now. There hadn't been a coherent moment since he'd joined them at the table to play Risk while wearing the Bolivian general hat. "I wish he could stay longer, but the doctors think this is the best way. He's more at home in the facility now than here, and that makes me so very sad."

"Because you've lost another link to your dead husband?"

"In part." She couldn't deny that hurt. "But mostly just grieving for the General and his loss of independence. He's my family, too."

Wyatt *hmm*ed on the other end. "Is that why you're hesitating to answer my proposal? Because you're worried about losing independence?"

"Of course not." Or was she? God, she didn't know, and her mind was such a jumble. "I rushed into my marriage with Allen. I want to take my time and enjoy the romance."

"Romance doesn't have to end with marriage."

"That isn't what I meant." Her fist twisted in the quilted bedspread.

"You just mean that today your answer is still no. Okay,

then. Know, though, that I'm not giving up on you," he said
before ending the call.

Nausea hit her again and sent her sprinting back to the
bathroom. Without question, her time was running out.

FOR A LONG time I wasn't sure why the dogs on television
seemed to enjoy car rides so much.

My second trip wasn't much better than my first. I was
stuck in a van in a crate, except this time they didn't even drug
me. Having AJ at the wheel with Mary Hannah in the front
seat helped reassure me some. Except everyone was tense.
And no wonder.

That badass Labrador back at the shelter bit Mary Hannah. Twice. I wanted to protect her, but I was too scared.
Too beta dog when I needed to be something I never, never
could be—an alpha dog.

But AJ sure was. He'd alpha-dog stepped in and protected
Mary Hannah the way she deserved. He'd kept her safe, and
that meant a lot more in this world than some people realized. I'd known fear. I sensed Mary Hannah had, too. She
needed a protector.

Thing was, though, AJ needed Mary Hannah, too. That
wounded look in his eyes cut right through me. He could
use some peanut butter pumpkin cookies—metaphorically
speaking. To be plain, he needed someone who cared
about him.

I'm not sure why the two of them pretended not to like
each other, because the attraction was there. The need was
there. And honestly, good people were tough to come by in
this world.

The van hit a bump, jostling me in the crate until my
head hit the top and the other dogs barked like crazy. Yep,
this car-ride stuff was overrated.

But having someone in your life to depend on? That was
off-the-charts important.

The contestants on *The Bachelor* might not understand how important it was to find the right person to love, but the rest of the world did. That's why we watch and hope the rose goes to the right person. I couldn't let Mary Hannah and AJ mess this up. While I might not have been much of a protector, I was smart. I was also a nurturer after whelping all those litters. And this was the opportunity of a lifetime to use those skills on these two, who were deeply in need of some healing.

Whatever it took, I would make sure Mary Hannah and AJ quit fighting what they felt and accept the love there waiting for them.

AJ PARKED THE unwieldy van in an emergency room customer spot, poodles barking at deafening levels since they'd left the shelter. The boxer—Holly—just stared from her crate with those wide whale eyes, shivering in spite of the blasting heater.

He had to find the volunteer who was supposed to take the dogs and get Mary Hannah into the ER. He made fast tracks to her side of the vehicle, bracing a hand on the hood to keep from slipping on the ice. He'd worked undercover in tense situations, dodged bullets and knives. Even taken a knife to the side to divert a perp from stabbing a female hostage. He should have nerves of steel.

But seeing that Labrador go after Mary Hannah had scared the shit out of him. His brain roared with memories of Sheila being held at gunpoint, little Aubrey hiding under the bed in fear with her sippy cup. Emotions slowed reaction time. He couldn't forget that for an instant.

Thank God instincts and training had taken over in time for him to steer Mary Hannah out of harm's way at the shelter before worse could have happened.

Frustration chewed at his gut over the way she kept focusing on the dogs when she needed treatment. She'd demanded the boxer, poodles and schnauzers stay loaded in the van so they wouldn't have to spend even one more day at the shelter. The whole way to the hospital, she'd been on her cell phone making arrangements for them to be transported to the Second Chance Ranch. A volunteer named Zoe would meet them, and they would just swap vehicles so the animals didn't even have to be unloaded.

He didn't doubt for an instant that if Mary Hannah hadn't found anyone to help, she would have insisted he just drop her outside the ER and take the dogs to Lacey himself. She would have hobbled into the hospital all alone.

Opening the passenger door with one hand, he extended the other to steady her. Regardless of how often she insisted she was fine, she still trembled, and her face was ghostly white.

"Take it slow and steady," he said as she stepped on the running board, then out onto the ice. He hooked his arm closer around her shoulders, anchoring the blanket they'd given her at the shelter.

She was wearing surgical scrubs now since she'd gotten blood on her shirt and coat. She looked up at him with a wince-grin. "This blanket outerwear is starting to be my wardrobe staple. Shelter Winter Clothing Line. That's Zoe there in the blue SUV."

Zoe jumped out, a long parka over workout clothes.

"I've got the dogs now. Go, go! Take care of yourself. We'll sweat out the stress with some hot yoga later." She tossed her keys to AJ just as he tossed the other set to her. "I'll get them all to the vet, then Jim is meeting me at the ranch to help bathe and groom them. We're good. Shoo."

Mary Hannah waved. "Thanks, Zoe. You're the best." She glanced at AJ, her jaw trembling. "She's a tiny tank with a huge heart for animal rescue."

AJ realized she was rambling out of nerves. She wasn't as calm as she claimed to be. He secured her against him, unable to miss what a perfect fit she was, her curves soft and too damn vulnerable. His pulse hammered in his ears.

The electric doors swished open, a wall of warmth rolling out combating the cold at their back.

Through some miracle, there wasn't a wait, helped by the fact the shelter had called ahead. They were ushered back, Mary Hannah's vitals taken before she was settled into an exam room. An ER doc swept aside the curtain, chart in her hand, her lab coat stitched with the name Dr. Trujillo. She had sharp eyes and a no-nonsense efficiency that reassured him. He noticed her one piece of jewelry, a West Point ring. She must be a retired military physician.

After introductions and a brief recounting of the incident, the doctor examined the puncture sites.

Stretched out on the exam table, Mary Hannah hitched up on her elbows, watching. "How exactly does this work? Do I get injections in the stomach or what?"

"That's not how we treat for possible rabies exposure anymore," Dr. Trujillo explained, without taking her eyes off the puffy red bite wounds that still oozed droplets of blood.

"Oh, thank God." Mary Hannah sighed heavily with her first obvious admission of fear. "I've witnessed bite incidents before, but the animal was always vaccinated. I never gave this much thought until today."

AJ took in her words, gaining an insight to her volunteer work he hadn't expected. She was more than paisley and pink fluff. She took risks as a volunteer that most wouldn't take for pay.

"It does involve a series of injections." Dr. Trujillo sat on the edge of the exam table, the paper cover crackling. "For today, we inject serum into the wound site."

"You mean *around* the bites, not *into* the bites, right?" Mary Hannah's voice squeaked.

Dr. Trujillo shook her head slowly. "I'm sorry, but yes, into the bites."

AJ leaned forward, elbows on his knees. "That sounds painful."

"I won't lie to either of you. It is, even with numbing. But the sooner we get this done, the sooner you'll be protected."

Mary Hannah drew in even breaths at a near-meditative rate. "Sorry to have so many questions. I guess I should have considered the possibility of a bite before now, given how many animals I handle with unknown histories. What happens after today?"

"Questions are fine," Dr. Trujillo answered as a nurse lined up gauze and injections on a rolling tray. "You'll have a follow-up series of injections into your arm over the next couple of weeks. We'll give you the schedule before you're discharged."

"And even if the dog is rabid, I'll be okay?"

"Yes." The doctor nodded, relaxing into a reassuring smile for the first time. "And if it puts your mind at ease, I've done this procedure before, overseas when soldiers were bitten by wild dogs. The risk there was much higher that the dog was infected, but any risk isn't worth taking since rabies is fatal."

The last word sucker-punched AJ in the gut. Why the hell was he so off-balance over this? He needed to get his head together and figure out why Mary Hannah Gallo had such a way of kicking the props out from under him. Right now he wanted to haul her to him and comfort her. To reassure himself she would be all right.

Dr. Trujillo looked from one to the other of them. "The good news is that rabies is slow moving, and you were bitten on the leg, so we'll kill the virus before it can get to your brain."

Her brain?

Mary Hannah gripped the sides of the exam table. "Let's just do this."

"Okay, then." The doctor stood, jotting notes on the chart before setting it aside. "The nurse will give you a couple of Percocets to help you relax before we begin the injections."

To hell with being objective or detached. AJ reached for Mary Hannah's hand.

"No, Doctor!" Mary Hannah swung her legs off the table, extending her arm as if to physically bar the physician from leaving. "Wait. I don't want any drugs."

Dr. Trujillo turned on her heels, hands in her lab coat. "You don't have to John Wayne this, Ms. Gallo. Nobody will think less of you if you take all the pain meds we can safely dish out."

AJ squeezed her hand. "It's all right. I'll be here with you." As he felt her soft hand go chillier in his, he realized he wanted to be here for her. That for some unknown, inescapable reason, he was drawn to this woman on more than a physical level. "You don't have to tough this out or face it by yourself."

Her brown eyes went wild with pure panic for the first time since the bite occurred. "I can't take the pain meds."

He smoothed a hand along her back, trying to soothe her nerves. "It'll make this easier—"

"No! You don't understand." She jerked away from his touch. "I can't take the pills because I'm a recovering drug addict."

Ten

Out of the shelter and into the unknown. If I'd realized how far the world went past the chain at my old cabin, would I have still left? Put it this way . . . it was kind of like buying a vowel when you had the chance. You just had to do it.

—HOLLY, LEARNING THE MEANING OF *I*

MARY HANNAH SETTLED into the passenger side of Zoe's SUV, with AJ beside her in the driver's seat. He cranked the engine without a word, blasting the heater. In fact, he hadn't spoken to her since she'd told the doctor about her former addiction.

Why hadn't she thought to ask AJ to leave the room? She should have, but her brain had gone on scramble when he took her hand and touched her back. Now she wondered if on some level she'd wanted the information out there between them because of that attraction that hadn't gone away even after five months.

So she'd let him know her secret, the truth of her past that would be guaranteed to make him run in the other direction. And he had. He'd dropped her hand, mumbled something about giving her and the doctor privacy to talk and left.

He'd just left. Taking all that beautiful comfort with him. But then she didn't deserve to take anything from him.

She'd clenched her jaw and breathed through the painful injections into the bite wound. As the door opened and closed to the exam room, she'd seen AJ sitting in a chair staring off into space. He hadn't left the building physically. But emotionally? He had placed miles between them. Miles that probably stretched all the way back to Atlanta. Back to his old life. Back to the reasons why they would never work as a couple. That realization stung worse than the injection.

So she'd signed the release forms and gone along as AJ led her to Zoe's SUV. He didn't speak other than the barest words of "careful" and "watch your step up" before he closed the door. It was such a quiet drive compared to their rushed trip to the ER with the van full of dogs. Still, the signs of an animal rescuer were all around them, from the waterproof drape over the backseat to an extra leash stashed in the cup holder.

Mary Hannah slumped back in her seat, her leg throbbing from the injections jabbed into an already painful wound. The silence between them hurt even more.

Since he clearly wasn't going to speak, she needed to talk first. "I was addicted to prescription drugs."

Eyes forward, he steered the borrowed SUV through the lunchtime traffic. "I didn't ask for the details. It's none of my business."

"You didn't have to ask. I should have told you."

"Why?" He turned onto a side street, a silver guardian angel on the rearview mirror swaying.

Apparently he was going to make her be the one to spell it all out, to take the risk. Fair enough. "Because we spent a night together before I knew you were a cop. Because you kissed me at Christmas. We've started to act like there might be something between us and you're a police officer, a detective who used to work on some kind of antidrug task force and—"

"You kissed me back on Christmas."

And it had been good. Very good. The memory of that crackled between them.

"You're right, AJ, this attraction isn't one-sided. I've tried to stay away from you ever since that first night as Francesca. And I should have kept on trying, given my history."

Finally, he glanced her way, blue eyes glinting with anger—and a hint of something else that looked like pain. "Why didn't you?"

Wasn't that the million-dollar question?

She shook her head and looked away, watching the world outside act normal. A snowplow drove past, slapping sludge to the side. Trash cans lined the street overflowing with wrapping paper and packing boxes. Children played in the yards, having snowball fights, building snowmen and dragging sleds. She'd only ever wanted a normal life, calm and peace.

AJ Parker was anything other than peaceful.

She rubbed her leg, the surgical scrubs a thin barrier over a bandage. "Things just got out of control between us. But what happened today in the ER has been a wake-up call." A reminder of her past, a past she could never afford to forget for an instant. "Like I said before, you're a cop, a narcotics detective, no less. And I'm a recovering drug addict. It's like pairing up a firefighter and an arsonist."

His jaw flexed with tension. "If you meant that as a joke, it's not funny."

"I know. Addiction isn't in the least amusing." She traced the outline of the bandage with one finger, the silence stretching again, and she was damned if she could think of what to say or do now. Her body ached. She wanted to crawl under her covers and hide for the day . . . or a decade.

The SUV jostled along a rut in the road and over chunks of ice. She braced her hand on the dash just as his arm shot across to protect her. Their eyes met and held for an instant, his palm warm against her rib cage, just below her breasts. Her skin tingled, her whole body on overload from adrenaline, good and bad tangled together, leaving her vulnerable.

His throat moved in a long swallow before he jerked his arm back and faced the road again, steering around a corner. "Were you high that night we met at the bar?"

"No," she gasped. "Absolutely not. I've been in recovery for four years and haven't slipped."

"Four years?" His brow furrowed. "How did it happen?"

She glanced his way, almost surprised he'd asked. But he'd at least opened the door for her to explain. She understood on an intellectual level but still wondered how she'd allowed herself to be so . . . consumed. She also knew history could repeat itself if she let her guard down.

Plucking at the surgical scrubs, she settled for the simple answer. "I was in college, and I couldn't handle the pressure, so I medicated. To stay awake, then to go to sleep. The problem steamrolled as I started worrying about applying to grad schools. Next thing I knew, I was hooked."

The memories clogged her throat for a moment before she could continue. "My ex-husband paid for a top-notch rehab center, used by Nashville stars and their families. That's actually how I first met Billy Brock. His teenage daughter was in the program the same time I was."

"The news was full of reports about her heroin addiction." The censure in his voice was unmistakable.

"And I knew my addiction was just as real and as bad as hers. I refuse to make excuses or let that be some kind of cop-out because I used prescription drugs."

"Good for you." He nodded curtly.

Defensiveness snapped and popped inside her like a log that had fallen into a banked fire. "Are you being sarcastic?"

"Absolutely not." He looked at her, the sun glinting through the windshield and reflecting in his blue eyes. "That level of awareness is . . . rare."

While her heart warmed at the hint of understanding and an inkling of acceptance, she couldn't hide from the truth, especially on a day like today when that reality smacked her in the face. This pull she felt to AJ couldn't go anywhere. She had her life in order now and would cope in her usual manner. She would lose herself in her work.

"Thanks, AJ, and I mean that." She shrugged, the blanket

sliding off her shoulders. "But I'm still the proverbial arsonist to your firefighter."

AJ PARKED THE SUV in the gravel lot beside the Second
Chance Ranch's play area. In spite of the twenty-degree
weather, volunteers were out in force. A woman wearing
puffy earmuffs and mittens tossed a tennis ball for three
leggy Labs racing circles in the packed snow. An older gentleman wearing an Elmer Fudd hat walked a former racing
greyhound that had been rescued after breaking a leg. Lacey's son, Nathan, and his girlfriend each carried a fuzzy
husky puppy as they walked toward the farmhouse. The teens
laughed and chased each other, so very young and full of
puppy love. In more ways than one.

Apparently no one in the rescue community was taking
the holidays off.

And damn, he was focusing on the dogs—on anything—
to keep from thinking about Mary Hannah's revelation. She
was a former addict. That admission still rocked him to the
core. He never would have guessed that of her, not in a million years. But addiction wasn't predictable. He shouldn't
be surprised. Disappointed. Hell, even feeling betrayed.

Still, he was.

He opened Mary Hannah's door. "Are you sure you won't
just go up to your apartment?"

"Once I have Holly settled with you, we'll be done."

He didn't believe her for an instant. She would work till
she dropped, and there wasn't a damn thing he could do about
it. He didn't have any say in her life. "Lead the way."

She pushed open the barn door, warm air drifting out.
Heating the place must be tough with all those doggie doors
in the kennel runs letting the animals go through to the outside, but somehow they managed to keep the place toasty.

The inside of the barn hummed with controlled activity,
people wearing volunteer aprons moving in some kind of

Zen-like choreography. Elevator music played with such soothing tones he resisted the urge to yawn. The stalls were all occupied now because of the new dogs picked up today.

A pair of volunteers worked in the corner bathing area, an extra heater on full blast. A poodle was curled up asleep with a dryer pointed on her, and another was having the earlier shave job from the shelter prettied up, half drugged to reduce the stress. Their puppies were nearby, each litter clean and piled on top of one another in a bed under a warming lamp.

Holly lay in the last stall, her head on her paws as she stared at the puppies, her food untouched beside her. AJ took in all the animal gear and paraphernalia around him, realizing for the first time what he'd taken on in caring for this dog.

He swept off his stocking hat and stuffed it in his coat pocket. "This has moved so fast, I don't have anything at my place for Holly. Maybe she should stay here until, I, uh—"

"Don't worry," Mary Hannah said briskly, unlocking the supply closet.

"Can I give you a hand?"

She waved him away. "I've got this. We'll loan you a leash, collar, harness, dog bed and a bag of food to get you started. We also can make tags here for her collar. She has antibiotics to take for her mastitis—"

"Mastitis?" He backed up a step. "Isn't that, uh—" He gestured around his chest.

She laughed, the sound light and floating up toward the high ceiling. Even Holly shifted at the sweet sound. "The shelter vet said since her puppies were pulled so early and abruptly, she developed an infection. After she's been on the antibiotics for a week, if everything clears, she'll be spayed. Be careful that she doesn't get loose. The last thing we need is for her to get pregnant again."

"So, um"—he knelt down in front of the kennel gate,

staring through the wiring at Holly—"she and I are supposed to do what?"

"Over the next month and a half, you'll work with her, make her more adoptable by easing her anxiety, help her connect with people and teach her a few commands—and yes, I'll explain in detail, with flyers that review everything we discuss." Her mouth twitched. "You won't be surprised to hear how well organized my handouts are. You'll have all the information, resources and support you need to prepare Holly for a family of her own."

He smiled back, envisioning all those flyers in some binder or accordion folder, color coded and alphabetized. His smile faded as he thought about how her driving need for organization had pushed her to such extremes in college, even into drug abuse. He'd seen it happen more times than he could count.

Cricking his neck to the side, he looked back at Holly. "I can do that. I'm not sure how it's supposed to make me appear more levelheaded to my boss, but whatever. I'll hit Google, too."

"Never underestimate the power of Googling for articles and advice. But just to be sure, one of our most seasoned volunteers—Jim—will walk Holly to your cabin. He'll review some basics and make sure Holly settles in okay. We don't want any surprises."

He poked his fingers through the gate, wriggling them through to pet her nose. She inched away.

Mary Hannah said, "As a general rule, you shouldn't stick your fingers through the gate like that, for your safety and the animal's."

He drew his hand back. "Are we confident she's not going to bite me? You said the Lab bit because he was terrified."

"That was a different kind of fear and agitation. We wouldn't have placed her with you if we didn't think she was safe. But as with any animal, I would urge common sense. Don't drag her. Don't hit her. If she has an accident in the house, don't shove her nose in it—" She paused, crossing her arms over her chest, chewing her bottom lip. "You know, maybe you're right. Maybe we should wait a day or so after all and ease you into this."

His back went stiff. "You're sending that volunteer along to babysit me. I do know basics of animal care and human kindness. I'm not just going to rely on Google." He scratched the back of his neck. "I lived with a woman once who got a puppy. We went to obedience classes for six weeks."

"You never mentioned that."

"The woman or the puppy?"

"The obedience training," she snapped smartly.

Why hadn't he? Hell, he didn't know why he did half the things he did lately. Mostly, he tried to keep to himself. Was that why he'd missed the signs that she was a recovering addict?

Complex questions, to say the least. He settled for an easy answer. "If I'd mentioned it, Wyatt would have pressured me to foster sooner to help him impress Lacey."

"Fair enough." Mary Hannah knelt beside him, wincing and shifting her weight off the bitten leg. "It's going to be a challenge getting her to come out of her shell."

"How will she win a competition if she won't even let me touch her?"

"Give it time. There are many different levels of success. You can do a lot with before-and-after photos and video footage that shares her story." Mary Hannah focused on the kennel run, her face tipped, the silky black hair sliding to hide her face. "She's a beautiful girl."

Holly wasn't the only one.

His fingers itched to touch Mary Hannah's hair, to test the slide and glide of those strands between his fingers, to tuck it behind her ear again. But everything he'd thought he knew about her had been turned upside down in the hospital, and he needed time to resolve that in his mind.

"What happens now?"

He asked about the dog, wondered about a helluva lot more. Mary Hannah swept back her hair, and her dark brown eyes met his, holding, confusion and awareness swirling like winter flurries in a night sky.

She stood quickly, tucking back into the supply closet, her voice drifting out. "I wouldn't worry about anything other than becoming friends with her. For today, just let her explore at her pace." She stepped out with a bag of food and set it by the gate. "Give her space."

"Space. Got it." He was good at that.

"Keep treats with you at all times." She placed three boxes of dog biscuits on top of the bag. "Keep them beside you. She'll slowly make her way to them."

He watched her build the pile of supplies with neat efficiency, tucking the leash, collar, tags and a couple of booklets into a brown paper sack with the treats. "I'll stop by tomorrow with the flyers and our first session once I can evaluate how things are going in your home." She paused, picking at the tie on her surgical scrubs. "Unless you need me to help now."

"You should take the rest of the afternoon off. You've been through a lot. Maybe you should take tomorrow off as well."

"I'm already late and I have patients to see." She swept a hand over her head and held back her hair. "Let's focus on Holly."

He could tell from the stubborn set of her jaw, she wasn't changing her mind about resting longer. So he scooped up the bag of dog food and the brown paper sack. "I should walk these over to the house. I'll jog over and be back in couple of minutes to meet Jim and take Holly. I assume she'll walk on a leash?"

"We'll find out. If not, Jim has some tricks to get her moving. But every dog is different. Some do better with another alpha to lead the way. Some need to be away from the pack so they have to look to the human."

"God, poor pup."

"I agree." She unlocked the gate, a collar and leash in her hand. "But you can't pity her, not if you expect to make progress. Your instinct will be to baby her, but you have to be careful with that because it reinforces her fears. I'm not saying be hardhearted. But there are ways to build her confidence, to ease her bit by bit outside her comfort zone without pushing too fast or far."

Was she talking in layers? Was it the counselor in her trying to nudge out his locked-up feelings about the past? He'd agreed to this project to appease his boss and his cousin, but he was already feeling itchy.

"This is going to be tougher than I expected." He jostled the bags in his arms until they settled against his chest.

"And absolutely worth it." She slid down to sit, leaning against the kennel wall without touching Holly, just sitting in a nonthreatening manner like she'd instructed him to do. "When you see her shine with confidence and joy . . . it's one of the most rewarding experiences."

"You really believe that's possible for her." Seemed damn near unattainable now, but looking in Mary Hannah's eyes, he saw a glistening hope that reminded him of all the paisley optimism in her outlook. Regardless of what she'd done in the past, her former addiction, he couldn't deny she had a big heart.

"There's something in her eyes that makes me believe Holly can blossom. She may not ever be the dog she could have been if she'd been nurtured and socialized from the start, but she can have so much more than she has now." Mary Hannah looked at the boxer, her eyes filling with compassion. "She will be . . . Holly."

The caring in her eyes drew him in like moths to a lightbulb, making him want to forget what he'd learned about her today. He stepped closer, into the half-open gate.

"AJ . . ." She raised a hand to stop him in his tracks. "I'm the arsonist in this scenario, remember?"

And she sure as hell was making sure he would never forget.

The reminder hit him like sleet against bare skin. And not because he doubted her, but because he doubted himself.

He couldn't deny she lit a fire inside him, one he needed to rethink feeding. Today had shown him too well how vulnerable Mary Hannah was.

Turning on his heels, carrying the food and bag of supplies for Holly, he started to leave the barn, toward his solitary cabin.

Eleven

Thirty-six hours drug-free and counting.
Good-bye, Peppermint Lady. Hello, bachelor
pad. What AJ lacked in decorating taste, he
made up for in a phenomenally large television screen. I fell asleep that night with my old
friend Alex Trebek.   —HOLLY

MARY HANNAH STEPPED through the elevator doors,
stuck in a hospital for the second time in two days.
But this time was different since she was there to help the
patient, not *be* the patient. Normally that was the kind of
thinking that got her through the day when she visited a
hospitalized client.

It wasn't working so well for her today, not after the
sleepless night she'd had.

She wished she could have done as AJ suggested and
taken a couple of days off to rest. Her leg hurt like hell from
the bite, and whatever was in the injections made her stomach churn. But she'd pushed through, showered and readied
for work this morning. She needed to check in on this
particular wounded army veteran—Captain Declan
Roberts.

The holidays were toughest on people already in crisis.

And the Roberts family of three was most definitely stressed to the max since the Captain had been wounded overseas.

Mary Hannah shrugged her paisley bag more securely onto her shoulder, her low-heeled leather boots clicking on the bleached tile. She wore her glasses instead of contacts, a small difference really, but the frames gave her an added layer of protection, a barrier between her and the world. Besides, her eyes were gritty from lack of sleep. Between the dog bite, confessing her battle with addiction and resisting the attraction to AJ, her own stress level was off the charts.

Holidays were tough on more than just her patients.

Christmas decorations still sparkled, garlands draped along the front of the nurses' station. A decorated fake tree towered in a waiting area, without presents now that Santa was done for the year. And on Captain Roberts's door? A construction-paper wreath, made from cutout handprints glued into a circle.

No doubt made by the little boy sitting on the floor outside the door. He leaned over a coloring book, a box of crayons open beside him. Henry Roberts—Declan and Callie's only child, four years old with blond hair and round glasses. The child didn't remember a time when his father wasn't at war or in the hospital. Henry would never remember his father holding him with both arms.

Mary Hannah gripped the handles on her bag until her fingers numbed. She knew she had a vulnerable spot when it came to kids, but there was something about Henry that tugged at her all the more, making her wonder a million times over what her child would have looked like. If her baby would have been a boy or girl. So many questions and what-ifs she would never have answered.

She reined in her thoughts and focused on Henry. He was his own person, not an extension of her lost dreams. She nodded to the nurses behind the station before reaching the too-quiet child.

"Hi, Henry," she said softly.

"Hey, Ms. Gallo." He waved without looking up from his coloring book as he traced alphabet letters with a purple crayon. He painstakingly traced the large *C* on a page of cookies while his snow boots twitched back and forth as if his feet were itching to run and play.

Mary Hannah knelt, struggling not to grimace at the pain to her leg. "Did you get that coloring book in your stocking for Christmas?"

"Yeah, plus some candy, and a video game, too, but Mom says I gotta do school stuff first." He scrunched up his face, hand shaking as he worked so hard to trace. "Gotta work on my motor skills."

"That's a good mommy thing to say."

"Yuh-huh." He colored the spots on a chocolate chip cookie. An aide pushed a food cart past, wheels squeaking and trays rattling.

"Where *is* your mom?"

"In there. With *him*." Henry rarely used the word *Dad*. "They're fighting again."

Low voices echoed through the door, hushed but tense, just barely discernible over the filtering noise of televisions and normal conversations in other rooms. Declan and Callie were having a rough time adjusting to his injuries. The recovery had been long and painful, and life would never be the same for them.

Helping them felt like filling a bucket with a hole in the bottom. She suspected their problems had started before the accident, but neither was willing to admit that yet. She could only keep trying. There was a saying that the therapist could work only as hard as the patient.

Mary Hannah lowered herself the rest of the way. "Do you mind if I sit here with you until they finish their conversation? I wouldn't want to interrupt."

Henry looked up, his green eyes wide behind his round glasses. "Aren't you s'posed to fix them?"

If only it was that simple. "I'm here to help how I can.

I'll visit with them when they're ready. For now, I'll keep you company."

"Sure, whatever." He put away his crayon, closed the coloring book and stashed it in his lion backpack. He tucked his hand in deep and pulled out a Leap Frog learning video. Lights whirled and flickered on the screen.

She leaned closer, her next breath taking in the smell of children's shampoo and waxy crayons. "What kind of game is that?"

"I'm building a farm." Little pigs marched across the screen with numbers on their bellies.

"What's on your farm?"

"Animals and tractors. I like tractors."

She sat silently and waited.

"I'm also planting corn. I like corn on the cob when my friend's dad grills it."

Where was he going with this? She'd found there was always a reason for everything Henry said; she just had to follow his train of thought. "Grilled food tastes amazing," she added, hoping to prompt him. "I like fat hamburgers, too."

"You can have a picnic every day on a farm."

"That sounds fun."

He looked up from the game, his eyes as green as grass, the expression in them far too old for his age. "It's just a game. It's not real."

Professional distance just wasn't possible sometimes. She swallowed down the tears clogging her throat and nose and forced her face to stay mild and reassuring. "Your father is working very hard to get well."

The voices in the hospital room grew louder, the words discernible. Declan's voice growled, "I told you not to bring him today."

Henry's hand tucked in Mary Hannah's, the soft and sweaty stickiness tugging at her heart as it shattered into a million little pieces.

"Told?" Callie sighed with unmistakable weariness. "What

about discussed? God, Declan. When did we stop asking each other's opinions?"

"When I lost an arm and half a leg," Declan said in the next room while Henry clenched tighter, his other hand adding more animals to his farm. "I don't want Henry seeing me this way, like some broken action figure that got tossed to the bottom of his toy box."

"Don't say that." Her words choked on a sob.

"Even you're wincing."

Mary Hannah squeezed Henry's hand once more before she shoved to her feet. She needed to stop this now for Henry's sake. She tapped on the door. "Hello, Declan? Callie? Mary Hannah Gallo here."

The voices inside went silent fast; then, "Come in," Callie called.

Mary Hannah looked at the nurse, who nodded toward Henry, confirming she would keep an eye on him before she stepped out from behind the desk. "Hey, Henry, would you like to pick out some juice and pudding from the kitchen?"

"Sure." He sighed, tucking his game into his backpack. "We can get some for my mom, too. She forgets to eat . . ."

Mary Hannah pushed the door open and stepped inside the hospital room she'd visited so many times over the past months as Declan struggled to survive . . . then regain his independence.

He sat in a wheelchair wearing a sweat suit, the left leg pinned up to the point where his leg had been amputated at the knee. The left T-shirt sleeve was empty. He would get prosthetics soon, which would restore some of his independence but could never replace what he'd lost.

Before the accident he'd been a college athlete, a track star, then afterward a competitive triathlete. The inactivity was clearly taking its toll on him emotionally, but his body could be pushed only so far as he recovered, and he insisted on hiding from the world until he could emerge whole again—or at least on two legs.

Life didn't work that way. The damage he was inflicting
on his family—and himself—with the isolation could prove
just as damaging as the scars he'd gotten in Afghanistan. A
missile hit had toppled his vehicle, trapping his arm and leg.
Even with the scar down his left cheek, he was a handsome,
all-American-looking man, with blond hair a shade darker
than his son's.

"Happy New Year, Doc," he said sarcastically, always
calling her "doc" no matter how often she corrected him.

She understood he had trouble thinking of himself as
anything other than a patient, and everyone around him fit
into that paradigm. "Hello, Declan."

Before she could say more, he wheeled into the bathroom,
and she heard the door lock. The sink faucet turned on, then
a radio he kept in the shower, and she knew from past experience that this was his way of shutting out the world. Of
course it also meant she could speak privately with Callie.

Was Declan offering his wife the comfort of talking out
her pain to someone even if that someone couldn't be him? Or
was he genuinely just checking out? Things to work through
later. For now, she needed to focus on the grieving wife.

Callie toyed with the miniature Christmas tree strung
with popcorn. Her white silk shirt and black slacks were
new, her shoulder-length red hair freshly cut. She'd clearly
tried today. "Aren't you going to tell me to be patient with
Declan? That everything will get better with time?"

"Is that what you need for me to say?"

"Of course not, since it would be a lie." Callie sank onto
the edge of the hospital bed, her head tucked low, red hair
covering her face even as she dragged her wrist across her
eyes.

Mary Hannah sat slowly in the chair beside her. "There's
no denying this is tough, Callie, as tough as life gets."

The young wife and mother glanced at her and whispered, "Most people tell me how grateful I should be that
he's alive, and I am. Really. But everything's still awful."

"Pain is pain. There's no comparing one kind to another." She hesitated. Sharing her own life experiences could be dicey and unprofessional. But she could safely say, "Marriage is difficult even when life runs smoothly."

"That's sure true." Callie sniffled, grabbed a tissue from the box on the bedside table, then threw her head back with a long exhale. "It's like even though he's alive, he's still dead to us anyway because he doesn't want us anymore. I don't know what to do. I thought once his body healed, things would get better, but they're worse. He still doesn't want to see Henry. I can't let him keep hurting our son this way."

Staying neutral was tougher some days than others, but Mary Hannah was here to treat all of them. And while she sympathized with Declan—God knows he'd suffered—the best way for him to heal was to help all three of them. "You need to take care of yourself, too, for your sake and your child's."

"I don't know what's right for Henry." Her eyes held a pain so deep it blurred out the rest of the room. "He wants his father, but his father doesn't want him, so maybe it's best for Henry if I just take him away rather than let him be hurt."

"Do you really believe that will make the situation easier for Henry . . . or for you?"

"Sometimes yes, sometimes no." She wadded up the tissues and hurled them into the trash. "But that's not what you came here to talk about today. You said you had some program you thought would help Declan."

Mary Hannah had come with a concrete idea in mind, but everyone had to be on board. And right now one Roberts male was hiding in the bathroom and the other was somewhere slurping down juice and pudding. "I'm here to talk about whatever is important to you."

"Thank you. Really. I don't know what we would have done without you." Callie smoothed her hands down her black slacks, which still carried the sheen of newness. "Now tell me about the program you have in mind for our family."

"Actually, it's for Declan and Henry, if they'll agree." Mary Hannah reached into her paisley bag and pulled out the flyer and a packet of forms. "I've had a lot of success partnering patients with dogs. They find the training and contact therapeutic. In fact, a few doors down, another patient of mine is here with his service dog."

"Really? To help him with tasks?" Callie sat up straighter, her eyes filling with a hint of wary hope and a lot of skepticism.

"And emotional support. The dog's name is Lina. She was a rescue pup named Thumbelina, orphaned and near death." The Second Chance Ranch had nurtured the litter of pit-bull puppies back to health a year and a half ago. "Now she's eighty pounds of wonderful, trained awesome-sauce."

Callie smiled, her first full-out smile since . . . ever. "I've seen television specials on things like that. It would be a wonderful, amazing miracle if it could happen for Declan."

"I'm glad you think so." She passed over the flyer, wondering how AJ and Holly were managing. What kind of difference would Holly make for him? "There's a six-week program where a shelter dog is cleaned up and trained for the My Furry Valentine Mutt Makeover competition."

"You want us to adopt a *puppy*?" Callie held the flyer between two fingers as if not sure whether to read it or pitch it into the trash with her snotty Kleenex.

"No, an adult dog." The last thing Callie Roberts needed was a puppy to train. Mary Hannah leaned forward, elbows on her knees. "You're under no obligation to keep the dog, only train it for six weeks. There will be people lined up to adopt these dogs. So no worries."

Callie glanced at the bathroom door then back at Mary Hannah. "But Declan can't lift much."

"Henry can, and they'll have to work together." If—please, God—his father would let him into his life again. "I have a dog in mind at the Second Chance Ranch. I'll be helping with the basic training commands. Here's a photo of the dog, a Cairn Terrier named Barkley."

Callie studied the flyer and the picture, her brow furrowed. She looked skeptical but still engaged. "You really think this will magically fix my family?"

"Not magic. And not some guaranteed fix." The family would be repaired through their work, one step at a time, through their own efforts. Mary Hannah settled for stating, "This is just a way to make a start."

"A start?" Callie's eyes watered again, her fist crumpling around the flyer. "We've been at this for so long, I'm ready to end things with him, not *start*."

"I don't believe that."

"How can you be so sure?" Her voice wobbled.

Mary Hannah nodded toward Callie's hand around the flyer. "You got your nails done to visit your husband."

Her hand unfurled, and Callie tucked her French-manicured hands under her thighs. But her eyes glowed with love and a wary hopefulness. "That probably seems like a vain waste of money when we have such an uncertain future with Declan's medical issues."

Mary Hannah smoothed the flyer on the bedside table. "It seems like a woman who hasn't given up on her marriage yet."

Hopefully Declan knew how lucky he was to have Callie in his life. That kind of devotion was rare, something she herself and Ted hadn't shared. Mary Hannah didn't blame him for walking away, after all she'd screwed up so badly. Declan's situation was an accident that occurred during honorable service. But she couldn't help wondering what it would have been like if she'd had unconditional love.

What *she* would have been like.

AFTER A WEEK with Holly, AJ felt like he was hitting his head against the wall even with boatloads of help from Mary

Hannah and Jim, reputed to be the dog whisperer of volunteers. This was an exercise in futility, frustrating the hell out of him rather than settling him the way his boss seemed to want.

Of course part of that could have something to do with Mary Hannah. She came by every evening after supper, always keeping her distance while showing him different training techniques and ways to gain Holly's trust. He wasn't so sure that was possible.

He dropped his bag of carry-out food on the table and sat while Holly watched his every move from her dog bed across the room. "Want some food, girl? Come over this way and we can share. What do you say?"

She didn't move other than one slow blink. She'd been spayed that morning and wore the cone of shame to keep her from licking her stitches. The vet had said it was all right for her to eat a little food tonight if she wanted. She looked too loopy to him to do much of anything.

"Yeah, that's what I thought." He pulled out the cheeseburger and french fries, then flattened the bag into a makeshift place mat for his dinner. Holly's nose twitched, but she still didn't budge.

Who would have thought he would welcome a little food thieving from his dog. *His* dog? For now anyway.

He bit into his juicy burger and chased it down with a fry and a gulp of tea. And yeah, that spot by the window offered him the perfect view of Second Chance Ranch Rescue, lit by motion-sensor lights and two tall lampposts. He watched Mary Hannah's sedan travel down the long driveway toward the barn.

The family that had lived here before—a mother and son—hadn't been fans of the animals and apparently had used this spot to spy on the operation. When their efforts to shut the place down failed, they'd sold their home and moved to Kentucky to live near the mother's sister.

Lacey McDaniel had purchased the property to expand the fences for her rescue. Wyatt had suggested renting her cabin for now, but at some point she planned to transform the cabin into office space and a clinic.

It had been a damn long time since AJ had made plans other than getting through the next undercover assignment. Each time he slipped deeper into the job and further from himself.

Hungry as hell after a long day in which he'd used his lunch break to check on Holly at the vet, he bit into the burger again, grease oozing out and down his hand. He swiped his fingers along a napkin, his eyes tracking Mary Hannah stepping out of her car. The icy branches between their properties glistened, the moonlight throwing a fat beam along the bridge over the frozen stream. Mary Hannah walked that route each night, and he found himself anticipating this part of the day more than he should.

He wasn't some Peeping Tom or stalker, but he couldn't help but notice when she came home from work unless he blacked out the window. Her red coat flashed like a beacon, her steps neat and efficient as she unloaded her work bag and a sack of groceries. She climbed the stairs to her apartment, but he knew she would come over to check on Holly's progress as she'd done every night this week.

His pulse ramped at the thought. Yeah, he wanted her all right, but her past addiction, his past falling for an addict and the fact that she was tied to his cousin . . . it was just too complicated.

Or so logic said.

Attraction never gave a damn about logic—especially when he knew from his night with "Francesca" just how much heat steamed between them. Beyond that, he was surprised to find her kind, and rather funny, too.

Exhaling hard, he tossed down his burger and leaned back in his chair. He picked up a french fry and held it out for Holly. She didn't move—no surprise.

He waggled the fry in her direction. "I wish you could talk to me and let me know what you want."

Still, she didn't do anything except stare back at him.
Granted her eyes weren't as whale-looking anymore. Probably because of the painkillers making her mellow. Mary
Hannah swore they'd made progress, but he wasn't seeing
it. He wouldn't have minded if Holly slept on the bed or
sofa, but she refused to get on the furniture. Period. Which
would probably make her forever family happy.

He didn't want to crate her after seeing how much of her
life she'd spent chained and likely caged. Mary Hannah had
suggested leaving an open crate tucked in a corner where Holly
could retreat if she felt overwhelmed. For the first two days,
she'd slept there. The next couple of days, he'd found her on
the dog bed near the sofa. Last night, she'd snuck into his room
and slept on the rug by his bed. Sort of like the progress he
and Mary Hannah had been making until she revealed her
secret.

But he didn't want to think about that now. He was
focused on Holly, right? And damn, but that progress was
so slow. Maybe by next year Holly would let him pet her.

Except he wasn't keeping her that long. Right? But where
the hell was he supposed to send this sad, broken dog?

Holly stretched up her back end, her mouth opening in
a big doggie yawn. Mary Hannah had told him that yawns
could be a sign of stress. Great. Even fries stressed her out.
His sympathy for the dog mixed with frustration.

The boxer stood and took a wary step off her bed, staggering a little from the meds, but she was moving toward him
of her own free will. AJ held still. Totally. He knew from
experience if he so much as twitched, she would bolt back to
the bed or out the doggie door to cower behind a bush to do
her business before running back inside.

Would she take the food?

God, he wished Mary Hannah was here. She knew so
much more about this dog whisperer stuff.

Holly stood upright and took another stumbling step forward. AJ held his breath. Was she actually coming for the

fry? Mary Hannah had told him to be patient. And how damn crazy that his hand was trembling.

"Hey, Holly," he said softly, "do you want a fry? You can have the rest of my burger, too, if you'll come over here."

She tipped her head to the side and took another step, then another, but not toward him. A log fell in the fireplace, snapping and popping sparks. Holly flinched, halting for a second before creeping forward again. She inched her way to the sofa, stopping beside the coffee table cluttered with magazines, his iPad and the TV remote.

"Do you want to get on the furniture? That's cool by me." Still, he kept the fry in his hand, just in case she changed her mind.

She tapped the coffee table with her paw.

He frowned. "Do you want to shred a magazine? Or for me to bring the food there?"

Carefully, he stood, carrying the container of fries. Holly's muscles bunched as she ducked her head. He stopped at the other end of the coffee table and placed the fries there.

"See, girl? All for you." He backed away, giving her the space she needed, sensing they were on the edge of discovering something, coming to some kind of understanding. Maybe the painkillers had taken away some of her inhibitions.

She thumped the table again, knocking aside the magazines until her paw landed on the remote control. And stayed. Her intent was clear. The dog wanted the remote.

AJ laughed. "Seriously? You want the one thing in the house that is a hundred percent mine?"

He nudged it toward her.

She flinched down again.

He tapped it closer.

"Come on, girl. I thought you wanted this. Chew the damn thing to bits if you want. I'll just get a new one. No big deal."

Her head tipped again inside the cone, and she plunked down onto her butt, watching him, then swiveling her face to the television, then back to him, then the TV again, as if waiting for something to happen.

Waiting for him to turn on the flat screen? Doubtful, but easy enough to test for the hell of it. He dropped into his recliner, turned on the television and started channel-surfing.

Holly relaxed back on the floor, resting her head on her outstretched paws. Her ears up and cranking forward inside the plastic cone like radar dishes pointed toward the screen.

"You like TV?" he asked, still half certain he must be mistaken, but the proof was there in front of him. A relaxed Holly for the first time since she'd arrived. He'd watched TV before, but had he just been too keyed up to notice her reaction? He'd been so focused on training her. "Maybe we do have something in common after all. Mary Hannah's going to be so proud of us for figuring this out."

Holly's nubby little tail wagged.

A surge of victory pumped through him. He was getting hyped to think about sharing the success with a woman he swore he couldn't pursue. A woman he also shouldn't pursue since his career hung on the success of training this dog.

Still, he found himself reaching for the phone to tell Mary Hannah that Holly was a big fan of *Jeopardy!*

Twelve

Winning! —HOLLY

NOW THAT THE holidays and New Year's had passed, Mary Hannah couldn't deny her competitive spirit was ramping into high gear, which sent her need to organize into overdrive. She sat on the barn floor, plastic bins lined up in front of her. She pulled the freshly washed "adopt me" vests from the laundry basket and sorted them by size.

Volunteers filled the space, clumping in groups, some working with the animals and others focused on tasks for the Valentine Mutt Makeover competition. Even the dogs that weren't competing could still attend and be shown. Longtime volunteer Debbie brushed a collie while Lacey printed out new forms. Sierra propped her feet on a footstool and untangled leashes. The echoes of barking and the grooming dryer filled the wide-open space.

Sure, she was overcompensating for the fact she was nervous, and not only about the competition. But also about how it was bringing her and AJ closer. She could still hear the triumph in his voice when he'd called to tell her that Holly was a fan of *Jeopardy!* She's struggled not to laugh, because truly it was so endearing. Seeing that new side to the brooding cop definitely flipped her world. And he kept right on upending her preconceived notions with glimpses of his protective nature and patience.

"Lacey . . ." Mary Hannah pointed to her paisley tote. "If you look under my bag, I brought an accordion folder that has been labeled for adoption applications, fund-raising brochures and animal-care handouts."

Debbie set aside the dog brush and pushed to her feet. "I'll bring it over to you. I need to stretch my legs anyway before they fall asleep."

Lacey glanced up from the computer, swiping a wrist over her forehead. "It's clear who keeps this place organized, and it's not me."

Mary Hannah folded an extra-large vest neatly. "We all have our roles here, and mine just happens to be making sure all food donations are arranged by expiration date so no bag goes bad."

Laughing, Ghita, a volunteer from a local vet clinic, hid her face behind the camera, documenting the day for Facebook. "Wanna come sort my cabinets?"

"For a small fee donated to Second Chance Ranch." A blast of chilly air hit Mary Hannah on the back, and she glanced over her shoulder to find . . . "Dahlia?"

Lacey pushed her chair back from the corner desk. "Dahlia, are you scoping out the competition?"

The über-chic shelter director strode deeper into the barn over to the office area. "As long as one of us wins, I'm happy, because if you take home the prize, you can take in more animals and I know I'm your very favorite shelter director to work with, Lacey McDaniel."

"That you are." Lacey hooked arms with her. "Come see how the two pug sisters you sent here are doing. They both had their eye surgery for the ingrown eyelashes and look fantastic now—"

"Mom"—Sierra passed over a fistful of untangled

leashes—"do you mind if I turn up the heat? It's freezing in here."

Dahlia took the leashes from her and draped them over the hooks. "That's the first time I've heard a pregnant woman complain of being cold. It's usually the other way around. Right, Ghita?"

"Sweetie"—Ghita lowered the camera, her shirt shifting to reveal the tattoo with all her grandchildren's names—"you forget that not all of us are in our twenties. When I hit menopause, I never knew when the next hot flash would hit. It's best to keep things on the cooler side."

Debbie resumed brushing the collie again. "I call hot flashes 'my own personal summers.'"

"Isn't that the truth?" Ghita set aside the camera by the computer. "I was in the grocery-store freezer section, reached in for a Christmas turkey and oh Lord, that blast of cold air felt so good I just stood there, camped out so long the manager stopped by to ask if I needed help."

Mary Hannah snapped a lid on the container for the extra-large vests. "Lacey's a little young for menopause."

And the conversation was clearly making Lacey uncomfortable.

Ghita shook her head. "Plenty of women start in their midforties."

Lacey went paler.

Mary Hannah shot to her feet. "We can debate menopause ages all day long, but I know one thing for sure."

Lacey swallowed hard. "What's that?"

She struggled for something, any distraction, and found that as always her thoughts gravitated to AJ. "The guys are in the garage making some new agility apparatus for the competition."

Ghita grabbed her jacket. "Well then, we need to shuffle our workspace. A woman's never too old to check out the magnificent sight of fine men playing with power tools and oozing testosterone."

* * *

AJ GUIDED THE power saw along the PVC pipe, right over the lines marked and measured. Beyond helping the rescue and the competition, he could work out the frustration over seeing Mary Hannah. Daily.

Tempted. Daily.

Man-cave time was definitely in order today, complete with the scent of sweat, motor oil and power tools in use. All this "getting in touch with his feelings" was damn exhausting. Apparently he wasn't the only one who felt this way.

Mike reviewed the instructions for the bar jump while Nathan assembled some kind of nylon tunnel. Gramps was sitting by the workbench. He was there for the weekend, but the retired general was in one of his nonverbal, Alzheimer's moods today. Still, he seemed to enjoy just watching, with Trooper and Holly asleep at his feet.

AJ set the last of the PVC onto the worktable by Mike. "Thanks for the help building these, although I'm not sure we're ever going to get Holly through that tunnel."

"Happy to help. Even happier to get outside," Mike said. "Don't get me wrong. This rescue is great. Trooper is the best. But that's a lot of people in one house."

Nathan looked up from hooking together the nylon sections. "You're not kidding."

Mike turned over the instructions. "Could you pass the hammer?"

"Sure." AJ unhooked the hammer from the pegboard. "Are you ready for the whole fatherhood gig?"

"Yeah, I think I am." He held the hammer, staring at the tool with his brow furrowed. "My own father wasn't much of a role model to go by, but I like to think I picked up a lot from Colonel McDaniel."

Nathan went still, the tunnel rolling away from him. "Dad was a good guy. You would have liked him, AJ."

"I'm sorry I never got to meet him," he said, and now

that he thought about it, he realized this was Colonel McDaniel's man cave. No wonder Mike held that hammer with a kind of reverence. The tools held an echo of the person.

The garage was organized. Different from the more chaotic approach that reigned in the house and rescue. No doubt something had been moved around in here, but there was still an order and calm about the place that he knew somehow had been set into motion a long time ago.

Mike's thumb worked along the hammer's handle absently. "What about you? Ever think of settling down?"

Yeah, and that hadn't gone well for him. "I just got my first dog. One step at a time."

Mike raised an eyebrow. "So you're keeping Holly?"

"For now," he said noncommittally. Coming to this town was about streamlining life. Not making it more complicated.

Or so he'd planned.

The General stretched his arms overhead, old joints popping. "Time has a way of slipping by, boys. Don't sow those wild oats for too long." His blue eyes glinted with a hint of mischief chasing away the glazed look. "Well, unless they're really good oats, in which case, always remember to wrap your rascal."

Nathan shook his head, muttering, "He can't remember my name, but he always remembers to tell me about condoms."

Gramps barked with laughter. Apparently his hearing was just fine. "Priorities, son. Priorities." He tipped his head toward the feminine voices drifting from the office. "Oh, my wife must be . . . back?"

Nathan's face fell, and Mike's hand went to rest on the teenager's shoulder.

AJ grabbed one of the wooden base posts and a piece of sandpaper. He knelt beside the General, his hand falling to scratch Holly's ears. "Sir, would you mind helping me sand this?"

The older man's face lit up. "Yes, yes . . ."

His voice trailed off, but he took the piece of plywood in his gnarled hands, rubbing the sandpaper along in smooth repetitive motions as the board rested on his legs. The dust swept off the side of the board with each sanding stroke.

And while AJ didn't consider himself to be a mystical guy, he couldn't escape the sense that there was something about this place. The ranch. The animals. The people. Mary Hannah and Holly.

He'd left one family and found another.

And that scared him. A lot. But not enough to make him leave.

THE NEW PLACE where I lived was like nirvana. So much so it was difficult to trust it could be real. I was in a cabin, but it was nothing like the meth-house cabin. AJ's place smelled like fragrant wood burning in the fireplace instead of burning drugs.

It smelled clean.

Mary Hannah said it was messy, but I figured her standards were little too high. AJ put his dishes in the dishwasher. His washed clothes stayed in laundry hampers, and the dirties were in a nice pile in the corner of his room. Sure, he tossed around magazines and he made his bed by tossing the covers over the pillows rather than doing something Mary Hannah called "hospital corners."

Hospital corners sounded overrated to me. I liked how AJ tossed a blanket on the floor beside his bed just for me.

And the food.

Holy son of a mutt, the food here was good. He fed me grain-free kibble so my skin didn't itch anymore. AJ even dropped treats in my bowl and around the house. When Mary Hannah wasn't around he let me have people food, which I really liked. I was almost willing to take it out of his hand.

For now, though, we had a truce. He left it on the floor beside him. I would lie there to eat it as long as he didn't touch me, and we got to watch television together. I wondered sometimes, though, what it would have been like to sit on the sofa or put my head on the footrest of his recliner because feet carried the essence of a human's smell.

How ironic, huh? I finally had a real life, a good life, and I was too scared to make the most of it there at first.

But I kept trying to give back to them by helping them realize they were meant to be together. Like how they thought I was clumsy because I kept getting under their feet, but that was really to help them bump into each other. When they touched, pheromones filled the air.

I also worked my stubby tail off trying to figure out what Mary Hannah and AJ wanted from me all the way to New Year's and into the week after. Because when they were happy, that made me happy. They'd given me everything, so much more than I ever knew existed. I owed them all my loyalty.

So over those two weeks while I worked hard to do what they wanted, I figured out a few things of my own. A car ride was better than drugs because of all the scents that came through the vents. Treats taken from a human's hand tasted better because of the hint of salt from their skin. But the best part of my new world? Running full-out in the snow without a chain to stop me, the wind against my face and sun shining bright.

They told me I would learn more things like commands and how to fetch. They're all amazing, easy joys for me now, but each so difficult to attempt back then.

I didn't understand how locked into myself I'd become until the world began expanding. More than just new scents. More than just my dreams of a honeysuckle world. I'd lived in that cabin with only brief trots in the yard. That had been it. The sum of my existence. Television showed me the world, but that's not the same as experiencing and witnessing firsthand.

Like tipping my nose to sniff the scent of peppermint mixing with the salty guy scent I knew well from sleeping on top of AJ's laundry when he went to work.

They were attracted to each other. Seriously. No question. I happen to be an expert on such things even though I've been spayed. I knew all about mating from my litters.

And I was absolutely certain Mary Hannah and AJ wouldn't be able to resist much longer.

Thirteen

Competition can be a good thing. If only I
knew the rules of the game.   —HOLLY

SHIVERING, MARY HANNAH tugged her black knit hat
over her ears as she walked down the steps to meet the
Roberts family for a training session with Barkley. They'd
called her from the front security gate. She watched as they
drove down the long, icy drive in their new van designed
for a wheelchair.

The past couple of weeks had been a hectic rush of seeing
clients during office hours, plus working in the evening and
on weekends to prepare Holly and Barkley for the My Furry
Valentine Mutt Makeover. They had a month left, and Holly
was having nothing to do with the agility course.

Just seeing her happy and playful, though? Mary Hannah
found that to be a bigger victory than jumping over any PVC
pipe.

Her snow boots crunched into the snow at the base of the
stairs. The Saturday-morning sun crested, reflecting noon
rays off the fresh dusting of snow. She would begin the training session outside and finish inside the barn. While Holly
was already living at AJ's, Barkley had been staying at the

Second Chance Ranch until today. Declan Roberts had been released from the hospital yesterday, and this afternoon, he and Callie would officially take their foster dog home and continue with training in their house until the competition.

She hoped. Declan was still proving difficult.

She'd been so certain this would get through to him. The patient she'd paired with Thumbelina had made amazing progress once the sweet, goofy pit-bull pup entered the equation.

The Robertses' van stopped in the parking area beside the red barn, Callie driving. The side door of the vehicle opened automatically. Declan sat in his wheelchair, the lift sliding out and lowering him. He'd been fitted with a prosthetic arm last week. The leg would come later, once he had better use of the new arm for balance. But he could make only so much progress if his morale stayed at rock bottom.

Henry unhooked the restraints on his car seat and clambered into the front and out the door, swaddled in a hooded snowsuit. He tore off with the energy of a four-year-old forced to spend too much time indoors in winter. He flung himself on the ground and swept his arms and legs back and forth, making a snow angel.

Callie stepped around to her husband as he maneuvered the electric controls to the lift until it settled on the ground. His chair was battery powered, and he steered it forward with his hand, the wheels bumping along the handicapped parking area, shoveled clear, then onto the salted walkway. It wasn't easy or quick, but he managed, his jaw tight, his eyes fiery with stung pride. Her profession made it too easy to read people's thoughts through their eyes.

Watching him struggle was painful but necessary. He had to learn independence. But the tougher part for him seemed to be accepting that he needed to depend on his family as well. Allow them to help, to feel connected, to be a part of their family's journey to health.

Tucking inside the barn door, she waved hello to a couple

of volunteers before leaning over a fenced area to scoop up Barkley. The cuddly Cairn was the perfect little student, smart, trainable and, most important, empathetic. The dog was a natural. Mary Hannah just prayed that once the competition was past, they would decide to adopt him and allow Barkley to continue his training to become a fully certified service dog.

She stepped back out of the warm barn into the crisp winter air. Henry was under a tree now, making his fourth snow angel. His giggles filled the air along with barks from a couple of dogs in the play yard. Between Sierra's pregnancy and this little boy, Mary Hannah's heart was getting a serious stomping. And she felt guilty as hell over that. Especially since Sierra and Mike would be returning home tomorrow and there'd barely been time to visit—or maybe she'd been dodging them on purpose.

Totally unfair of her to do. She had to put that vulnerability with children aside when working with the Roberts family. *Deep breaths.*

Declan powered his chair to the side area they used for training. "Henry, are you going to help or not, son?"

"Yes, sir." The boy pushed to his feet, the puffy snowsuit making balance a precarious thing. "I just gotta get the bag of dog treats outta the van."

Henry waddle-ran to his mom, and she passed him a bag of Cheerios. He dashed back to Mary Hannah. "I have my treats, Ms. Gallo. Barkley likes treats. I give him Cheerios, one for him and one for me, when he does something right." He leaned closer to her. "I gave one to Dad, too, but he said no thank you."

Mary Hannah knelt in front of him, dusting the snow from his arms and hood. "We can't make people do things they don't want to."

"Like how Barkley can't do the water trick 'cuz he's scared of baths?"

"Exactly. We'll just figure out what works best for Barkley."

Henry placed his mittened hands on Mary Hannah's arm and whispered in her ear, "My dad likes to throw the ball."

A longing coated that simple request. Professional distance was tough at moments like this. Damn tough. "Then we will ask him to do that part of your routine."

Henry hesitated, something else clearly weighing on his young mind. He scuffed his Thomas the Tank snow boots along the ground. "Do ya think Mom and Dad will let me keep Barkley?"

"That's not for me to say. You have to talk with them." She glanced at the couple by the gate. Callie stood with her arms wrapped so tightly around herself she must have cut off her own circulation. Declan ignored the cute little scrap of fur racing circles around his chair.

Henry shook his bag of Cheerios. "But you can 'suade them. You make people be smarter without even using treats." He shook the bag again. "You make them get better inside their heads."

"I don't make them, sweetie. I help them understand life so they can be happier."

"Having Barkley at my house forever would make me happier."

"How about we focus on today and teach Barkley how to jump through hoops over there in the exercise yard?" She nodded to the smaller play area that held the new agility equipment AJ and Mike had built. "That's like an obstacle course, um, a playground. We're going to work more on his act with some new equipment our volunteers made. And most important, we need for him to know all the steps and not be distracted by noises."

They'd already taught Barkley to sit, stay and walk on a leash. This would take the training to the next level, thanks to the new gear AJ had taken the lead in building.

Henry shuffle-ran in his bulky suit to the agility course while shaking the bag of cereal. "Barkley, come play, Barkley, come. We're gonna have fun."

As she joined him, her hands in her pockets, Mary Hannah couldn't help but check farther across the field, where she spotted AJ driving toward his cabin. His training session would come later, after she finished with Barkley. She'd spent so much time avoiding AJ because of the one-night stand and his brooding, she'd missed his good qualities. Knowing him made things more complicated, but ignoring him was no longer an option.

Her gaze gravitated right back to his cabin across the field.

AJ opened his door, his voice carrying on the wind as he called, "Holly, let's go outside, girl."

Holly bounded out, a blur of brown fur and energy. He'd made progress with her. She no longer had to be coaxed to walk outside with him. She enjoyed the freedom of running in the yard, sniffing and exploring. He tossed a ball for her and she chased it. But she hadn't yet mastered the art of picking it up and bringing it back. Baby steps.

Still, watching AJ truly give his all to working with Holly touched her heart. Even his insistence that the boxer enjoyed television game shows, although she still thought that was an excuse to chill in his chair and split a burger with Holly while channel-surfing.

The image was so precious and heart tugging, she had to force her focus back on her current trainees.

Callie strode with confident long strides, her bright yellow parka, hat and boots a perfectly matched ski-bunny set that almost hid how much weight she'd lost. No doubt her nails were manicured underneath.

The young mother and wife smiled, her makeup almost covering the dark circles and strain lines. "What do you need me to do?"

"Nothing yet. Barkley and Henry should run some of their pent-up energy off first so they'll be able to focus."

"I don't want to take too much of your time."

"Please don't give it another thought. I love my work."

"If you're sure . . ." Callie acquiesced before joining her son.

The whir of the electric wheelchair warned Mary Hannah that Declan was joining them. The rattle as he jostled along the concrete walkway would have tempted some to offer help. She knew he would rather fall out of the chair than accept assistance, so she waited.

He stopped beside her, wearing a Chicago Cubs parka, shiny new. "I know you think we're going to keep the mutt after the competition. But you're wrong."

She didn't take the bait. "You don't like dogs?"

"It's not that. I'll hang out with the dog for four more weeks, like the doc orders, and that's it."

"You have to do more than hang out. You've got to help train him—you, me and Henry. You and Henry have to reinforce what I show him. I evaluate his progress. And you present your routine at the My Furry Valentine competition."

"You're going to put me, my kid and the dog on display," he snapped bitterly.

"You're going to compete."

"Fine. Whatever." He massaged the metal clamp at the end of his prosthetic arm. "But after that, the dog goes back to you and finds another home."

"You've never had a dog?" She pressed on, deliberately oblivious. "Don't worry, that's why I'm here, to help you. To train the dog and give you any care tips you need. I wrote my master's thesis on training therapy dogs. But to be precise, he is acting as your emotional-support animal— your ESA."

"Emotional support," he sneered. "I know what it means, but it still sounds like a blanket and a cup of tea."

She looked over at him and stared without speaking. Silence was a mighty tool sometimes, far better than a wealth of words.

"Okay, fine, my apologies for being flippant." He looked at his son and wife playing with Barkley, running him up and down a wooden hill. "What's the difference between an emotional-support animal and therapy animal?"

Ah, finally she'd piqued his interest. She rocked back on her heels, keeping her eyes on Callie and Henry, a subtle thing, but she knew if she made eye contact with Declan, he would shut down. It was sad noticing similarities between humans and dogs, but she couldn't escape the truth. Eye contact could be confrontational. She reached into her coat pocket and pulled out a tennis ball.

"Therapy dogs and service dogs are working animals," she explained, tossing the ball up and catching it. "They require extensive training, often more than a year's worth. They have access anywhere. An emotional-support animal is one that provides ease to a patient—documentation of the patient's need is provided by a physician. Emotional-support animals do have rights. They can't be banned by a landlord, but they are not given unlimited access to public buildings."

"Really?" He half glanced her way before catching himself and looked back at his son and wife.

"Really." She pitched and caught the tennis ball again. "And just to clarify, trying to pass off an animal as a service dog, therapy dog, or ESA is a crime and does a grave disservice to the animals that are providing crucial care to people with disabilities."

"Understood." He nodded, massaging the spot where his prosthetic arm met the stub. "So if we take Barkley long term, I'm only getting an ESA."

"That's up to you. Barkley is smart enough to be a full-fledged service dog." *Toss. Catch. Toss. Catch.* "I would hate to see him wasted on someone who doesn't want what he has to offer."

His chin tipped, his jaw flexing. "I've had enough upheaval in my life. I can barely take care of myself." He spit out the words—angry, pained words—but by God, he was talking.

"My wife has to help me off the damn toilet. The last thing she needs is to clean up after a dog, too."

Had she pushed too hard? "We're two weeks in and you're backing out?"

"Now that the dog's going home with us?" He met her eyes for the first time, full of so much pain it swallowed every bit of sunshine. "Yes."

She ached for him and all he'd suffered, but being soft on him wouldn't help him. Her hand clenched around the tennis ball. "The sooner you complete your therapy, the sooner I'll leave you alone."

"That's blackmail."

"It's a fact."

He pounded his fist on his remaining leg. "Facts of my life are pretty much shit."

"Yes, they are."

He glanced up in shock. "You agree?"

"Of course. There's no denying you've suffered. Enormously." She kept her voice neutral. It was a fine line to walk, empathy without any trace of what he might construe as pity, all while pushing him forward. "And the facts are that things will be shittier if you curl up and quit."

He laughed hoarsely. "I thought therapists weren't supposed to curse."

Normally that would be true, but she'd gotten his attention. "Where did you hear that?"

"I assumed."

"Rather than having to assume, here are some facts for you to mull over. You have a wife. You have a son. You may be able to chase off your wife. That's between the two of you." Marriage was tough. She knew that well enough. "But you have a duty to your son. And right now his life is pretty shitty, too."

Mary Hannah dropped the tennis ball in his lap. "You're not helpless. Now pick up that ball and throw it for the dog— and for your son."

He scrambled to catch the ball before it rolled off the stub end of his amputated leg. "Are you sure you're a counselor?"

"I have the diploma to prove it." And God, she hoped her training and instincts would make up for her lack of experience. She was still so new at this, and the stakes were high.

"Your, uh, techniques are not what I expected."

"Are they working?"

Declan didn't smile. He didn't answer. But he put the tennis ball in the clamp of his prosthetic hand and he threw.

AJ GRASPED THE railing on the small bridge over the frozen stream. Holly walked alongside him, trailing her pink leash. Pink, for heaven's sake. He would bet money Mary Hannah had picked up the girliest matching accessories possible for Holly.

Of course he could have bought new ones, something badass. Like a sports team or something braided. Hell, was he really thinking about how to dress up his—the—dog?

He glanced down at the pink, tie-dyed leash slithering a line through the snow. He and Holly had come to an agreement. She would allow him to hook the lead to her collar as long as he never picked up the end.

Crazy, but she walked just fine as long as he never picked up the leash.

She was actually an easy dog to be around. She didn't demand anything and never barked. If she wanted to go out, she sat by the door until he clued in. She never had accidents in the house. In fact, he was pretty sure she was terrified of making mistakes. So much so he wished he could invite her to a "Let's Raise Hell" party, shred some pillows, tip over the trash, steal food off the counter.

Be wild. Be free.

She let loose only during runs around the yard. The rest of the time, like now, she simply watched him with those soulful eyes and walked carefully beside him over the bridge toward the Second Chance Ranch. Her feet left measured steps in the snow, that leash growing soggier by the minute. She knew the path to Mary Hannah's. It was the only place they went for now—other than daily car rides, per Mary Hannah's instructions.

Her laughter hitchhiked on the wind, teasing his ears, the lighthearted sound mingling with a little boy's giggles. Her red coat stood out like a beacon. Or maybe it was just that he couldn't seem to see anything other than her as she worked with that family.

They'd gathered in one of the smaller play yards with the new agility-course gear. Barkley was kicking ass, jumping through a hoop and over the bar like a champ.

AJ stopped at the perimeter fence, one of three layers to ensure even escape artists stayed secure. They had a second fence surrounding the entire property as well, layers of security to be certain the animals stayed safely contained. He'd been given the codes, but few others had them. He appreciated that level of safety for Mary Hannah. In light of the way they'd obtained Holly and some of the other dogs, there was no doubt a rescue could attract pissed-off—and abusive—former owners. Wyatt had even told him there had been break-ins a year and a half ago.

He punched in the code, the gate swinging wide for him and Holly to stride through. His focus still remained one hundred percent on Mary Hannah. He could have waited at his place, but he'd grown restless, oddly looking forward to the training session.

Mary Hannah was such a natural, with the training and the kid. The boy's father sat off to the side in his wheelchair pitching the ball for the scrappy dog to catch as the Cairn Terrier leaped through the hoop, then cleared the PVC bar. Barkley looked stinking cute, like Toto from *The Wizard of Oz*.

AJ stopped at the split-rail fence, chicken wire tacked along to keep animals from wriggling through. He leaned on the top wood bar, one boot resting on the bottom rail. With a new perspective gained from working with Mary Hannah and Holly, he recognized the layers of good in this one moment. The veteran was growing accustomed to his prosthetic arm out in the world rather than in the boring sterility of a rehab center. Playing with the dog gave the wounded soldier and his son a shared activity without any awkwardness.

The barn door opened, the squeak snapping the tight wire of concentration. Barkley dropped the ball. The soldier cursed, and his wife covered her son's ears.

Lacey darted through the open door and into sight with her camera in hand, the shepherd mutt Trooper close on her heels. "Don't mind me. I'm just documenting for the presentation in February."

Henry mugged for the camera with a toothy, little-boy smile. "We made a Facebook page to get fans for Barkley."

Trooper trotted toward Holly, apparently his new best friend for today, but then he liked most dogs.

"Great work, Henry," Lacey said, snapping more photos. "I bet Barkley will have his own cheering section thanks to that page."

AJ pushed away from the fence, hand extended. "I'll take the photos." Having something to do, a purpose for being there, would keep him from looking like some dope who couldn't help but watch Mary Hannah. "You enjoy your last day with Sierra. Let Trooper race out his energy with Holly, before he has to be cooped up in the car tomorrow."

Lacey eyed him with playful suspicion. "You wouldn't be trying to sabotage the competition by getting an inside peek at their routine, would you?"

"I don't think Holly and I are in the running to win the grand prize." He grinned, nodding at the boxer rolling on her back in the snow, her pink tie-dyed leash flopping uselessly like a kite tail. "We'll be lucky if she can bring a tennis ball back by then, much less walk reliably on a leash."

Lacey stroked a hand along Holly's side, gently, until Holly relaxed and let her ears be scratched. "You're doing an amazing job with her. Your instincts are good. It's a great idea to let her trail the leash, get used to the feel of it, learn that it's not there to restrain but an accessory that brings more freedom."

He took the camera from Lacey's other hand. "Visit with your daughter. I've got this."

"Thanks." She sighed with obvious relief. "You can just leave the camera with Mary Hannah."

AJ lifted the camera and snapped a photo of Mary Hannah in motion, jogging beside Henry and Barkley as they coaxed the pup through the hoop. The obstacle was low to the ground now but would be raised slowly over time. He checked the picture. Her beautiful face filled the preview screen, her smile enchanting but at odds with a sadness in her eyes he couldn't quite place. But he wanted to coax it away.

Taking things slow was getting tougher as they worked together training for the fund-raising event. He raised the camera again and snapped a quick group of photos, including the father.

The soldier's wife stepped out of the field of the photos and walked to AJ. "Will I be able to get copies of those?"

"I don't see why not, Mrs. Roberts, but you should ask Mary Hannah or Lacey." The detective in him took in details, and the auburn-haired young mother had a brittle air, like a thin sheet of ice that would shatter if life dealt her one more blow. He'd seen the Roberts family from a distance but hadn't met them in person.

"Please, call me Callie." She leaned back against the fence, tugging at the zipper on her parka nervously, up and down, up again.

Holly inched around to his other side. Not surprising since she was still skittish around new people. Trooper nudged Holly, barking for her to play.

Callie angled to look past him to Holly. "You're paired with her for the competition?"

"For the next few weeks."

"You're working with Mary Hannah, too?"

"Are you asking if she's my counselor?" His gaze gravitated back to the play area and the woman who filled his dreams at night. He sure as hell hoped she didn't look at him as a patient.

"I'm sorry. That was inappropriate of me." Callie pressed her gloved hand against her temple. "I'm still getting used to this new world my family lives in. A world full of doctors and physical therapists and counselors for every one of us. We can't even get a regular pet, for God's sake."

"I'm very sorry for everything that has happened to your family."

"I thought a therapy dog would be more like a pillow."

He glanced at Holly, plastered against his leg Velcro-dog style. His emotional-support dog? And what did that make Mary Hannah? "I tried to tell my boss at the police station that I just need to go fishing, but they gave me an antisocial dog instead."

"Fishing? In the winter?"

He shrugged, trying to shake off a sense of unease, that the conversation was making him face something he'd been avoiding. That Mary Hannah might see him as a patient. "I never would have thought the 'emotional-support dog' thing was for me. But I'm enjoying this. Holly and I need each other. I get to check a box on my eval at work. She needs someone to decompress with, to learn to trust people and pick up training."

"She's one of those dogs from the big meth-house raid, isn't she?"

"She is."

"Don't you worry she's dangerous? That she could hurt another animal—or person? She had to have been exposed to a lot of horrible things in that cabin."

"Mary Hannah says she's timid and undersocialized, but not aggressive. We're making progress. She just takes a while to warm up to new people." He leaned down to pry one of the tennis balls frozen to the ground. He tossed the ball. Holly galloped off to chase it, then raced around in circles without picking it up before she ambled back to his side.

Trooper shot past her, grabbed the ball and dropped it in front of Holly. Then the two of them tore off to run crop circles in the snow.

AJ raised the camera again, snapping more photos, unable to ignore the fact that he was using the task as an excuse to watch Mary Hannah. And with each picture, each additional tug of attraction, he realized how much he needed to take a step back. Especially if Mary Hannah was thinking of herself as his counselor rather than a dog trainer helping with a fund-raising mission.

Until he had the answer to that, he definitely needed distance.

After tucking Trooper into the play yard, AJ started back to his cabin, Holly at his side with her leash trailing in the snow. With every step, he knew his decision to take things slow was fading faster than a snowflake on the hood of a car.

Fourteen

I have the answers now. I wish the people
could hear me the way I hear them.

—HOLLY

THE SESSION WITH the Roberts family had left Mary Hannah feeling drained and energized at the same time. Declan had made major strides, but even with professional boundaries in place, she was still human. His pain affected her.

She had to get herself together before working with AJ and Holly. The last thing she needed was to burst into tears and cry out her pain on his warm, broad chest because that little boy resurrected dreams of having a family.

Damn it, her job and her volunteer work with the rescue filled her days and her life. It was important she not lose sight of that, now more than ever. Was it too much to dream of more?

Eyes fixed on AJ's cabin, she braced herself for another training session with a man who tempted her more and more every day. She did most of her training with Holly outside. The boxer seemed to prefer the outdoors after so long inside, and the socialization with other animals and people was good for her. They just had to be careful not to let her paws get too cold since she still wouldn't tolerate snow booties.

"Hey," Sierra called from her mother's porch, her blond ponytail trailing from her hat. "Wait up. Mind if I walk with you? I just want to get Mom's camera back from AJ so I can help her download the photos."

Mary Hannah stopped, hugging her scarf up to her cold face. "I can bring it when I finish up."

Sierra grabbed the porch rail and picked her way down the steps carefully, wearing men's boots on her swollen feet. "I need to walk off all that lunch I ate." She patted her seven-month-pregnant belly covered in a wool overcoat. "Besides, we haven't had much time to visit and I'm leaving tomorrow."

Mary Hannah winced with guilt. "That's my fault. I've let myself get caught up in work and preparing for the competition. I'm so sorry."

"You have no reason to apologize. I don't expect you to stop working every time I'm in town. It's been nice having you live on the property. Think how tough it would have been to visit if you lived clear across town."

"I've missed you, too, my friend." She gave her a quick hug along her shoulders. "I'm sure you know how much time the rescue can take up. This fund-raiser has kept us all busy."

"How is your dog bite? Does it still hurt?"

Mary Hannah preferred not to think about it at all. "Not bad, really. The bruise from the force of the jaw is actually lasting longer than the puncture wounds. Crazy, huh?"

"You should take some time off," Sierra insisted, trees rustling overhead and showering snow around them. "No one would blame you, with the holidays and the bite."

"I'm fine. Maybe after the competition." The follow-up vaccines made her ill, but she was finished. And the dog had completed his ten-day quarantine and wasn't infected. So she was clear. Safe. And now vaccinated as well. "How can I complain about a little bite when I have patients like Declan Roberts? Besides, I've got dogs to train. Just think what a win could mean for the shelter."

"You wouldn't happen to be rooting for a certain cop and

his gorgeous boxer partner?" Sierra leaned closer, hooking arms. "So? Spill some details about all that time you and AJ are spending together."

"There is no 'us' . . ." There couldn't be, in spite of the attraction that only increased, and talking about him in that way only made it worse. "But I am running late for my training session with AJ and Holly. *Just training.* I really can bring the camera back for you."

"I'm taking a walk away from the watchful eyes of my constantly worried husband." She held up a hand. "Don't argue. I promise to stop asking about AJ."

Good. Mary Hannah changed the subject. "Where's your mom?"

"Asleep on the sofa. I think she's coming down with a bug." Sierra frowned with concern. "She's really been dragging since the big Christmas dinner. I'm worried she's taken on too much with expanding the rescue. That's why I want to help her with the photos. It's something I can do with my feet up."

Mary Hannah understood too well the pitfalls of putting too much pressure on yourself. She took her glasses off and dried the snowflakes off with her scarf. "I can try talking to her about delegating and letting the volunteers do more."

"Thanks, I would appreciate that." Sierra stayed silent for a couple of steps, something clearly on her mind. "What do you think of Wyatt?"

"I'm not sure what you mean?" Mary Hannah punched in the security code to open the gate between the rescue and AJ's cabin.

"Do you think Wyatt's a good match for my mom?"

She pushed the gate closed again. "I thought Lacey wanted to take things slowly."

"Me, too. But I'm picking up vibes that Wyatt wants more. Sooner." Sierra stopped at the frozen stream and grasped the bridge railing.

"What does your mother say about that?" Mary Hannah scanned the wooden bridge, seeing no ice but plenty of salt.

"She changes the subject anytime I mention them dating." Sierra huffed in frustration—or exhaustion—or both?

Mary Hannah thought back to her impressions of Wyatt, not much to go on. For the first time she realized how very superficial the man kept things. He was always smiles and politeness, but never deeper. "Whatever we think or don't think is moot. I trust your mother's judgment."

"You're right, of course." At the other side of the bridge, Sierra stopped and leaned back against a tree. "I just don't want her to stay in a relationship because she's lonely."

"Seriously?" Mary Hannah laughed. "Your mother lives in a well-populated zoo that's constantly overrun with volunteers."

"It's not the same as having a spouse, someone to love in your life . . . Ah, damn. I didn't mean that the way it sounded." She clasped her friend's hand. "I'm sorry."

"No need to apologize," Mary Hannah reassured her, and meant it even though right now the words truly did hit a vulnerable, lonely spot inside her. "I understand what you meant."

"You just don't speak of your ex-husband often."

"I don't want to bore people with reliving my marital breakdown." What a time to realize she was every bit as secretive as Wyatt, keeping things superficial to protect herself from becoming vulnerable to rejection.

"Supporting a friend is never boring. If you ever need to talk, I'm a phone call away."

"Thank you." And how she wished she could take her up on that. Maybe after the baby was born and she didn't have to worry about stressing out her pregnant friend.

Sierra shook her head, blond ponytail swishing. "You always thank me and never take me up on the offer."

Mary Hannah bit her lip, considering spilling all, including the reason that pregnant belly upset her and how very tempted she was to risk letting herself get close to a man again . . . The cabin door opened, the squeak breaking the moment. Then Holly barked as she bounded out, which meant AJ wasn't far behind.

Later that night, after training Holly, after supper, she would make a point of having a real conversation with Sierra, preferably over a bowl of caramel popcorn.

Holly galloped over to the two of them, her powerful paws jettisoning snow behind her.

"Holly," AJ called with calm command, striding down the porch stairs with the camera in his hand. "Sit."

The boxer screeched to a halt and dropped onto her butt promptly, her nubby docked tail wagging.

A sense of joy welled inside Mary Hannah. She was so proud of both Holly and AJ. She blinked back tears. AJ may have groused initially, but he'd gone all in on the training.

Holly leaned forward while still keeping her bottom planted. She sniffed Sierra's belly. Sierra laughed and stroked the boxer's cropped ears.

Holly still kept her eyes averted when close to people, but she wasn't trembling and she leaned into the touch now. Huge progress in such a short time thanks to AJ.

He passed the camera to Sierra. "I assume you're here for this."

"Yes, thanks," she said. "Mom wants to upload the photos tonight. The ones she took of Holly yesterday have been getting so much positive attention for the event. I just know she will find a home at the event. Right, girl?" She gave Holly's ears a final scratch before backing away. "See you later. Thanks for helping with the pictures this afternoon."

Mary Hannah watched Sierra walk the entire way home, before turning to AJ. Just the two of them. Alone. Her willpower dwindling by the day.

WYATT UNLOADED THE last of the dishes so the kitchen would be clean for supper. He'd already sent Nathan out to pick up pizza to have a farewell dinner for Sierra and Mike.

Not that Lacey would be able to eat any. She'd come down with some sort of flu, and he'd done his best to make things easier for her.

Tomorrow, her daughter and son-in-law would leave and he would have her to himself again. Well, relatively speaking. Her son still lived at home, but Nathan was so caught up in his new girlfriend, he was rarely here. And what little time they saw him, the girlfriend was in tow slicking on cherry Chap Stick.

Finally, Wyatt could press Lacey on the proposal.

He closed the dishwasher and dried his hands. He tossed the hand towel in the laundry on his way to the family room. That obnoxious cuckoo clock of Lacey's squawked five in the afternoon. She didn't even stir on the sofa. Her curves called to his hands, each dip and swell enticing even covered with an afghan.

It had been so long since they were together. Her company and preparing for the February event had taken up her time. He only stayed the night at her house when her son was on a camping trip or some overnight school field trip. And when they had sex at his place, she left well before dawn.

Since Sierra's visit, he and Lacey hadn't slept together at all.

He didn't push the point. She was already skittish, and he didn't want to spook her. He dropped into the recliner and picked up the iPad to surf the news. Turning on the television might wake her.

His fist gripped the iPad too tightly, and he forced his hands to loosen. He powered up the tablet and Googled area news sites, looking for coverage on the meth-house bust, seeing what the press knew and checking to ensure there weren't any leaks.

He was concerned about the way the case on the meth-house raid was coming together, with too many loose ends. He was half certain one of the volunteers here at the ranch had bought drugs from that place based on how the individual looked at the meth-house dogs with guilty eyes and had avoided him since the bust. Which shouldn't surprise him since this was a small area.

This was his town, his little corner of the world. His old man and his uncle liked to tout being big-city Atlanta cops. But there was a special talent to keeping the peace in a small town where everyone knew one another and all were connected in some way. Every bust sent ripples throughout the community.

He refused to let any of that touch Lacey or her family. A family he hoped would be his, if he could just persuade her they belonged together. He'd waited too long to give up on his second chance at marriage.

The back door opened and Lacey startled, tossing aside the afghan and blinking fast, her eyes wide with disorientation. She looked at the clock, then over at him in the chair. She didn't smile, either. Not at first. So when the grin spread across her face, it came too late.

Awkward as hell. But he just had to wait one more day to have her all to himself and romance his way back into her life.

The door closed, and Sierra stepped out of her boots before walking into the family room. She braced a hand on the sofa before lowering herself to the couch with an exhausted sigh. "Here's your camera, Mom. I hope the photos generate more support for little Barkley and the Roberts family."

"Thanks, sweetie." She took the camera from her daughter. "I think we can make a difference for that family. They've sacrificed and lost so much."

Wyatt loved Lacey's giving spirit. But he couldn't help wondering if she identified with that military family because of her own loss. Would he ever be able to step out of the shadow of her hero husband? There were reminders of Allen McDaniel everywhere in this house. Not to mention around the town that was so close to an army post.

Patience, he reminded himself.

He pretended to surf for more articles while Lacey and her daughter talked. Maybe he could pick up ideas for new ways to win over Lacey's daughter. Nathan was easier. Just give him money for dates with his new girlfriend and the teen seemed happy.

Sierra propped her feet up on the coffee table and stroked the cat beside her. "I'm sorry I can't come back for the My Furry Valentine event. It sounds like it's going to be amazing."

Lacey leaned her head on her daughter's shoulder. "Your doctor doesn't want you traveling anymore. That's understandable. I'm glad we got to spend Christmas together. Just be sure the baby holds on until after Valentine's Day. Okay?"

"I wouldn't mind a week early, but mid-February? No way. Not a chance do I want to go that early." She rubbed her stomach. "And right now the baby needs pizza. What is taking my brother so long?"

Standing, Lacey combed her fingers through her sleep-tangled hair. "When he's with Kaitlyn, there's no telling how long an errand will take." She sighed. "I'll call and give them a nudge. How about I get you an apple? No? Banana? No to that, too? I have trail mix with M&M's so you can be healthy and decadent."

"Perfect." Sierra smiled. "Thanks, Mom."

Lacey tucked her feet back into fuzzy slippers and scooped up a cat to carry on her way to the kitchen. She always reached for her animals when she was stressed. Wyatt wished she would let him help, but it was tough to get a read off her, and he needed to tread warily.

A little support from the rest of the family couldn't hurt.

He closed the iPad and looked at his soon-to-be stepdaughter. Hopefully. Might as well dive right into his campaign before Lacey came back into the room. "I want to marry your mother."

Her eyes went wide for an instant before she nodded. "I figured as much."

"Do you have a problem with that?"

"Whatever makes my mom happy makes me happy."

He'd been a police officer for long enough to recognize evasiveness when he heard it. "That's not exactly a ringing endorsement."

"It is, actually." She tugged at her blond ponytail absently. "In my family we trust one another's judgment. So if my mom says you're cool, then you're cool." She pushed back to her feet again. "Sorry to be abrupt, but I'm going to get that trail mix."

The cuckoo clock blared as she walked away, each squawk slicing through his aching head. He needed to ramp up his efforts and get her family on board. If not Sierra, then maybe Nathan.

Because biding his time wasn't working, and hell, he'd been waiting for over a year and a half. He'd almost lost her to that veterinarian friend of hers, but the idiot had left town in the interest of being honorable and giving her time to grieve.

Wyatt wasn't letting up for a second. The longer he waited the more he worried she would slip away altogether. So he would keep persisting.

She would be his, one way or another.

I THOUGHT I was so smart because of all those game-show quizzes. I knew all the continents. The US states and their capitals. I considered myself well-rounded, with a solid foundation of knowledge on great artists and classical musicians. Science? No worries. My nose could sniff out elements in a heartbeat. Zero margin of error.

But until I stepped outside of that meth-lab cabin, I didn't realize how little I knew about, well, living. The prospect of walking up a flight of stairs made me pee on Mary Hannah's feet in fear. Getting into a car left me trembling so hard my teeth clicked—which scared people. It took me a long time to understand why dogs enjoyed sticking their head out the window. For the first week, I preferred to curl up on the floor in a very, very tight ball.

There were so many things to learn, it was overwhelming at times. AJ wanted me to walk with a rope attached to my collar. Mary Hannah called it a leash or a harness, but it reminded me of years living on a chain.

He put my food in a bowl rather than tossing it on the floor. I flipped my dish for a long time to spill out the food the old way. Sometimes I still do on a bad day—like during thunderstorms.

And everyone wanted me to learn their words. I understood what they wanted me to do, but getting my body to obey? There was a disconnect that took me a while to overcome.

Sit.

Stay.

Come.

Leave it.

Drop it.

Heel.

But it was worth it all because of the one most important word they wanted me to learn. My name. Finally, I had one name, beautiful, spoken softly rather than shouted. Mary Hannah said the name again and again, while feeding me treats until I really believed that was my forever name.

Living with AJ was good. He needed me. It was nice to be needed, to have a reason for waking up in the morning. Mary Hannah helped me see I could have a purpose and worth. I'll love her forever for that.

As I started to gain confidence and trust, I realized that even though I had a lot to learn, I knew things humans didn't. I knew about the babies growing inside their mothers. Seemed like everyone in this place was either having a baby or thinking about making a baby. Some were happy about babies and others not so much. I loved my puppies, but I also understood that life was complicated and that love came with the great cost of pain, of loss. I knew one of those babies was in trouble, and I hoped the mother could get help.

As I met new individuals, I understood there were

differences in people. Before being rescued, I thought humans were bad.

Now I could sense there were good people *and* bad people. And the good people needed warning because they didn't always understand who the bad guys—or gals—were. I needed to help them recognize not everyone could be trusted.

Because once I stepped outside of my fear enough to observe the world around me, I realized I recognized people from my time at the cabin.

Fifteen

Sometimes even game shows can't distract
from life's pain. Bad stuff happens. Puppies
and babies get sick. Sometimes they die
before they're even born.   —HOLLY

A J HAD SPENT the past couple of hours preparing himself for Mary Hannah's training visit. Given the timing,
it only made sense that they would have supper together.
They'd eaten sandwiches together in the past. But he was
thinking tonight would be right to try more of a real meal
together.

A date.

He had to find out if she saw him as a patient . . . or a
man. Because he sure as hell didn't see her as a counselor
in any capacity. In fact, the last thing he wanted was anyone
jabbing around in his psyche.

And her past drug addiction? Everything pointed to a
steady life, but then he'd been certain Sheila was telling him
the truth about kicking the habit. He shook off the thought.
Mary Hannah was not Sheila, damn it. He had to believe
people could be rehabilitated or this job would truly send
him over the edge.

He placed a folded quilt over the back of a chair near the
fireplace, strategically ready for an "impromptu" picnic. He

always had candles around in case of a power outage, and he lit two of them now, evergreen-scented ones he'd picked up off the holiday clearance rack. He'd also bought shredded barbecue and fresh rolls, some sides, casual, but leaving the door open to be a more intimate dinner if she wanted.

Because without question, he wanted to be with her, and he would deal with the rest later.

A knock sounded at the door. Holly didn't flinch at the noise anymore. She tipped her head to the side. Of course there were only two people who ever came to see him. Mary Hannah, who Holly adored and trusted. And Wyatt, who Holly still didn't know well, so she retreated to her dog bed and eyed him warily. Somehow she always knew which person was knocking before he opened.

Sitting prettily, Holly tipped her head to the side, nubby tail wagging against the braid rug.

"Behave for Mary Hannah, Holly. We want to get on her good side."

His pulse hammering in his ears, he opened the door and even knowing who stood on the other side, she still took his breath away. She wore her red wool coat as usual, but her sleek black hair flowed loosely around her shoulders, her ears kept warm by a simple wool headband. Her cheeks were flushed from the cold, her dark brown eyes sparkling like early stars lighting a night sky.

He cleared his throat. "I'll get my coat and join you."

"Let's work inside this time." She stomped the snow off her boots before stepping over the threshold and sweeping the headband off her ears. "I was outside so long today with the Robertes, I'm still chattering."

Right now more than anything, he wanted to warm her. "I'll take your coat. We can work by the fireplace. I'll toss on an extra log."

"That sounds perfect." She stepped out of her snow boots and passed over her coat, revealing jeans and a fitted icy-blue sweater. She wriggled her toes covered in fluffy yellow socks.

"What do you want to work on with Holly this evening?" He hung her coat in the entryway closet, his fingers digging into the fabric for an instant before he let go.

"Honestly, after her walk today working with the leash, plus socializing with the other animals going there and back, I believe she's maxed out on anything intense. I was thinking we could just sit with her tonight. I have some simple massage techniques you can use to relax her when you're petting her."

Well now didn't that work well with his plan to sit on a quilt in front of the fireplace? "Sure, that sounds like a great idea. I'll spread a blanket on the floor."

She set her paisley bag on the sofa. "I have massage oils as well."

His pulse pounded harder, along with another part of him. "What kinds of oils?"

"Lavender and orange are both soothing, but orange is more for helping with hyperactivity." She pulled out a matching paisley pouch with small bottles clanking inside. She set each one on the coffee table in a row. "Clary sage is good for calming and separation anxiety. Peppermint helps with arthritis or cooling the skin."

"Open all of those and the cabin will smell like a flower shop."

"We're only going to use lavender and sage, just a little while rubbing her ears." She tugged out a small bag of her homemade dog treats.

He shook out the quilt in front of the fireplace, then added another log to the fire. He stoked the embers back to life, coals snapping and popping. "Where did you learn all of this?"

"Some from my counseling background and some from courses in dog training. I'm also a fan of yoga, and there's a yoga that's taught with dogs called doga."

"Seriously? You aren't planning for us to do this yoga, um, doga?"

"No, I promise." She laughed softly as she sat cross-legged

on the quilt. "I'm not expecting you to do any downward-facing dog or cobras."

He pulled a dog treat out of the Ziploc bag. "Holly? Come."

Her nose twitched, and she padded slowly across the room, her long legs making her look a little like a small horse. He knelt, hand extended, waiting until she nibbled the treat from his hand.

He pulled out another. "Holly, sit."

The boxer plunked on her bottom. "Good girl, Holly." He fed her the cookie. "Good girl."

Mary Hannah opened the bottle marked SAGE and reached for his hand. Her cool touch sent a bolt of desire clean through him. She dabbed two drops of oil on his palm, the clean, earthy scent filling the space between them.

She eased back and set the bottle on the table. "Now rub your hands together, then stroke her ears."

He wasn't sold on the notion that putting perfume behind Holly's ears would turn her into a Barkley clone. But hell, he would play along. He also had other hopeful ideas for those oils later on.

For now, he followed her lead and let Holly smell his hand with the oils. She sniffed once, twice, then deeply, her eyelid going to half-mast.

"Well, what do ya know," he whispered, then rubbed her ears, the fur as satiny smooth as the oils.

"Slowly," Mary Hannah suggested. "Barely there. Touch in circles."

Holly's eyes slid closed.

Mary Hannah took the lavender bottle and shook drops on her own hands. "You can watch what I do and try this later."

She set her hands on Holly's shoulders, massaging lightly at first, as if letting Holly get used to her touch, then kneading a bit deeper. "What does AJ stand for?"

He stopped moving for an instant, surprised at the question. "I'm just AJ."

A smile played with her lips. "You're being dense on purpose."

Sure he was. He didn't want to talk about himself or his name or how it linked him to his family. He wanted to know more about her. Intimately. "I'm a Junior, thus the J. So it's not a double name like yours."

"That's the J part." She worked her slender fingers down Holly's spine. "What about the A?"

"You could ask Wyatt or check my wallet." He winked. "It's in my pocket."

She looked over the tops of her glasses with a naughty schoolmarm air. "That seems like an invasion of your privacy. I guess that means I'll have to wait until you're ready to tell me what the A stands for."

He didn't much like his name or being an echo of his father. Definitely time to shift the conversation in another direction. "These oils actually seem to be helping her. I gotta confess when we started working with Holly I was skeptical. But you really do know what you're doing."

"I hope so. Sometimes I have to fly by instincts, and that's scary with so much at stake. We're not just her second chance. We're her last chance."

The intensity in her voice made him realize she identified with this dog in some way. Saving the dog had something to do with her past or making restitution? He wasn't clear exactly, but as a cop he knew motivations were every bit as important as the actions in moving forward.

He skimmed his knuckles across her cheek lightly. "It appears to me you're doing an incredible job at giving her a future."

"Thank you." She leaned into his touch for an instant before turning her attention back to Holly. "How is the case against those responsible for the meth house going? Or are you unable to discuss it?"

He could, to a degree, but honest to Pete, he felt shut out of the investigation. He wasn't sure if it was because of the "burnout" label or something else altogether. "So far every-thing Evelyn Lucas told us has checked out."

She wiped the oils along Holly's chest, frowning. "I hear a hesitation in your voice."

"One of the co-conspirators she named is dead. We found her overdosed in her apartment." Could be coincidental, except he didn't believe in that sort of thing. He smoothed a hand over Holly's head as she stretched on the quilt with a contented sigh. "Another is refusing to talk even though he has all the earmarks of a low-level player who should be begging to make a deal rather than risk taking the rap for the whole operation."

"What are you thinking?"

That he wished he had more information? "That there's someone else involved, someone scary enough to keep them quiet. Someone smart enough to lay low until the dust settles."

"I wish Holly could just tell us everything about what happened in that cabin." She continued to stroke the dog's back even though the boxer had settled into sleep with a soft snore.

"That would certainly make things easier for all of us."

Mary Hannah angled back, leaning against the coffee table. "Looks like she's out for now."

"Apparently aromatherapy works quite well on dogs." Now he had to keep Mary Hannah from packing up her massage oils and heading out the door. "Hey, I have some great barbecue carryout in the fridge. There's enough for two. Why don't you stay for supper? Unless I've misread things and you're here in some kind of counselor capacity."

Her eyes went wide. "Counselor? No. I am most definitely not your counselor. I'm here to help you rehab Holly and train her. Your boss thought this would be therapeutic for you, but that doesn't make me your therapist."

Relief damn near knocked him on his ass. "Good to know. What about my other question? Will you stay for supper?"

Indecision shuffled in her eyes. She was such a logical person, but then there was the yoga/doga side. And the Francesca side. He hoped the sides of her that were in tune with feelings and emotions would win out over that logical part of her. In fact, he was surprised at how very important her answer was.

Her hands slid from Holly to her lap. "Sure, yes, I would enjoy having supper with you."

AN HOUR LATER, Mary Hannah finished off the last bite of barbecue and washed it down with a swallow of beer. She'd enjoyed the surprise on his face when she'd asked for one of the longnecks instead of sweet tea. She'd never considered herself a person who kicked back with a brewski but didn't recall when she'd come to that conclusion.

The time had come to elbow out of her comfort zone and test old assumptions.

She couldn't deny the attraction she felt for AJ grew stronger every day, in a different way from the obvious, out-of-control heat that had flared between them the first time they'd met. As she got to know him more, she liked the man below the moody layers. And seeing him be so tender with Holly melted her heart. She hadn't been able to resist staying for dinner even knowing she was playing with fire.

He'd set out the food on the coffee table, pushing aside her aromatherapy oils. They'd shared the meal casually, the blaze in the hearth warming her cold toes and tempting her senses with a light smoky smell mingling with the oils.

Somewhere about halfway through the meal, Holly had lumbered over to her dog bed, stumbling in a half-awake, lolling manner before falling asleep again. It was a perfect night, actually. Better than any she could remember in so very long.

AJ tipped his beer for a swallow, stretching his arm along the back of the sofa. "What made you decide to work with therapy dogs?"

"My friendship with Sierra. I started volunteering here, and on a whim I decided to turn that time into a research project for school." She rolled the beer bottle between her palms. "I figured out quickly I'd found a calling. I pursued additional courses to become a certified dog trainer. It fit."

"There's more to the story."

Was he pushing for more details about her time as an addict? Was she ready to tell him? She chose to stall. "Maybe *you* should have been a counselor."

"I'm a cop. That just makes me perceptive."

He was right on a couple of levels, but she opted for the safer answer, the one that would leave her least exposed as she trod warily into this new level of intimacy with him. "Remember when I told you my sister has epilepsy? Medication helped, but didn't control the seizures one hundred percent of the time. We tried to make sure she was never alone. My dad even wrote up these exact schedules."

"So that's where you got your organization from."

From her father? God, she hoped not. He'd taken OCD to a controlling level. Even thinking of the comparison made her queasy. "Maybe. But the schedule didn't work because I didn't follow it."

"Hey, you were a kid."

"True. And so was Sarah Jane, who craved privacy, and who could blame her? She was hiding in her closet reading. She had a seizure and hit her head on the shelves full of folded sweaters and jeans." The sounds echoed in her mind even now. The thuds against the wall between their bedrooms. Their mother's screams. Their father's anger.

Later, her own whimpers of guilt over letting her baby sister wander off because she'd gotten tired of always being responsible.

AJ rubbed the back of her neck, soothing her in much the same way he'd calmed Holly. "She clearly survived since she lives in California now."

"She suffered a concussion so severe she had to be

hospitalized. We could have lost her. We'd heard of therapy dogs but couldn't afford the training, not on top of all the medical expenses. So once I started working with the animals, I realized I had a calling here at the Second Chance Ranch."

She'd found a way to help families like hers. To make up for past mistakes.

"You don't charge for the therapy-dog training, do you?"

His question made her uncomfortable. She didn't want him putting her on a pedestal. He needed to see her as she was. Flawed.

"I screen shelter dogs, which reduces the cost considerably if people don't have the money to buy a service dog through traditional channels. I always have a dog in training at the rescue." She shrugged, putting down her bottle by her empty plate. "I do what I can. I'm working with a couple of other volunteers as well, but it takes a long time. We have to raise the money for the medical cost, care and feeding of the animals either through adoption fees—or charity."

"That's why the Valentine's event is so important to you."

"It would certainly bring some welcome visibility, promotion and, hopefully, donations."

"But no pressure on me to work harder with Holly." He lifted an eyebrow, teasing, as if sensing she'd grown uncomfortable with the serious turn.

"None at all." She tipped her head to the side and decided she couldn't just dance around the subject. She wasn't into playing games. She had to know. "Are you flirting with me, with the dinner and conversation?"

"I'm not a flirting kind of man."

True enough. His brooding nature had been obvious from the start. He had shadows, too. That drew her and scared her at the same time.

"You aren't seriously saying you're interested in me romantically?"

He took a lock of her hair and flipped it between his fingers. "And if I am?"

Her mouth dried up. "Ah, um . . ."

"And you're attracted to me," he continued confidently.

She flicked her hair free from between his fingers. "You're cocky."

"I know." His eyes held hers with a blue-flame intensity that seared her to the core.

That heat burned lower, gathering between her legs until she swayed toward him at the same time as his arms banded around her. His mouth settled over hers, warm and firm, tasting of beer and a hint of sweet barbecue.

She skimmed her hands up his chest and over his broad shoulders. He had a lean, muscled strength to him that sent shivers of want through her. He held her with a restrained strength, and she pressed closer, chest to chest, her breasts aching for flesh-to-flesh contact.

The months since she'd been with him had been filled with dreams of that night. Memories that left her aching to be with him again, to find out if that night was as incredible as she remembered.

He kissed along her jaw and down to the sensitive curve of her neck. She stroked his beard-stubbled face, her head falling back to give him better access as he nudged aside her sweater. This kiss, the whole evening in fact, had made her realize attempting to ignore the attraction hadn't worked. She needed to face it. Deal with it.

Embrace it.

A husky moan parted her lips. "Why have we resisted this for so long?"

"I have no idea." His hands went to her waist, her sweater inched up enough that his hands brushed a bare strip of skin. His touch released a fresh hint of the sage on his hands, the oils slick and smooth against her.

Her fingers gripped his flannel shirt. "It seemed the right thing to do at the time."

"And now?" His hot breath fanned against her.

"It seems absolutely absurd." She flattened her hands to his chest and pushed him to his back on the sofa.

He clasped her hips and settled her on top of him. "I've dreamed about that night."

"How ironic. Me, too." She leaned into the kiss, her hair sweeping forward and over him, linking them.

"And here we are." He stared up into her eyes. "God, just look at you."

"I believe you are." And the ardor in his eyes was as unmistakable as the hard press of his erection against her stomach. There hadn't been much looking that first night, just dim lights and frenzied sex.

"I like what I see very much." He tucked his hands into the waistband of her jeans, his fingers caressing. "Yet I'm not seeing nearly enough of you."

"That can be remedied." She toyed with a button on his flannel shirt. "The only question is, do you want me to take my clothes off while you watch or do you want to undress me?"

His eyebrows shot upward. "What?"

A purr of feminine power shimmered through her. "You look surprised. Did you think only Francesca could be bold? She's just me." She rolled her hips against him once, twice, drawing a groan from him.

"And you are beautiful," he said hoarsely, his fingers digging into the curve of her bottom.

"So are you." She kissed his mouth, then his chin. "And once I'm committed to something, I'm all in."

"Oh, really." He cleared his throat. "Tell me more."

"Lucky for us, communication is my life." She pressed her lips to the V of his shirt, enjoyed the taste of salty, masculine skin.

The taste uniquely his.

Her senses went on overload from the scents and textures and pure pleasure pulsing through her. And before she could think, he'd rolled, tucking her underneath him.

The heat and weight of him anchored her. "Madame Communicator, tell me exactly what you want."

"I want to hear what you like." She tugged his shirt from his jeans, her hands gliding up his back, savoring the flex and play of muscles.

"You're full of surprises tonight." He nuzzled her ear. "I want to pull the sweater off you, my mouth greeting every inch of exposed skin along the way."

"Oh." Her breath came in a sigh and request for more.

"Then I want to peel your jeans down and taste the rest of you." He angled back to look into her eyes. "If you think that's something you would enjoy."

Her body flamed at the promise. "I would have thought your detective skills would have told you the answer to that one."

He searched her face. "When it comes to you, I'm not able to think clearly or be analytical. You steal my objectivity."

His raspy admission sent her arching up to kiss him again, her hand cupping the back of his neck. The honesty in him, in the moment, touched her as thoroughly as his hands. And oh God, his touch scrambled her thoughts. The glide of his hands as they tunneled under her sweater, stroking and teasing each breast until her nipples beaded against her bra and the lace was a sweet abrasion.

The lights flickered with a power surge, off and on and off, until the house hummed back to life again. Not that he seemed to notice or care about anything but pleasuring her. His thigh pressed between her legs, and she couldn't have stopped herself from pressing harder if she tried.

And she most definitely didn't try to stop. She wanted that, and more.

As if he sensed her thoughts, his hand slid between their bodies, unfastening her jeans and tucking inside. The oil on his fingertips met the slick moisture of her need. For him. Now.

Her fingernails grazed down his back as she rocked against him, unable to believe how close she was to completion already. He seemed to know just where and how to tease that tight bundle of nerves until she flew apart, her nails sinking deeper into his skin as she anchored herself in the intense pleasure pulsing through her, wave after wave.

Desire still hummed inside her, so much so she could have sworn her ears were ringing.

Ringing?

Her phone. Ringing inside her bag.

"AJ?" she said against his mouth.

"Ignore it."

"Right, of course." She threaded her fingers through his hair.

Holly barked, again and again. She leaped from her bed and ran to Mary Hannah's bag, dragging it by the handles. The ringing stopped.

Then started again.

Sighing, Mary Hannah nudged at his shoulders. "I should at least check. It could be a client emergency. You understand?"

"Sure." He brushed a quick kiss across her mouth before rolling off her and passing her bag over. "Hopefully it's just a telemarketer, and then I'm taking that sweater—"

"Shhhh! I'm answering." She fished her phone out of her purse and saw Lacey's number on the ID. "Hello, Lacey, what's going on?"

"Mary Hannah?" Lacey's voice came across the line shaky, tearful, launching a chill. "I need your help. Sierra slipped on the ice. They're taking her to the hospital. She's having contractions."

Sixteen

Reality series show everything from cooking
to giving birth. Who knew you needed a doctor for that?
                                        —HOLLY

PACING THE HOSPITAL waiting room, Lacey couldn't
remember when she'd felt this helpless since Allen died.
Her daughter had been admitted by the ER doctor and was
in a room hooked up to a million monitors. Her contractions
were real and regular.

Sierra had just stepped out on the front porch with Mike
to sit in the rockers and look at the stars. She'd gotten dizzy
and slipped. Mike had been as pale as Sierra, but he'd been
all action. He'd carried her inside. Contractions had started
just after he'd set her on the sofa.

The pregnancy was only seven months along. Too early.

Her restless feet carried her back and forth between the
waiting room sofas and the vending machine, while Wyatt sat
in a chair off to the side, catnapping. Nathan and his girlfriend
were at home meeting the volunteers to oversee the animals'
evening feeding and snow-blowing clear the parking area. Her
son had matured so much in the past year, come a long way
in healing since his suicidal feelings after his father died. Even
knowing Nathan was doing well these days, she hated to put

so much responsibility on him, but right now she appreciated his help. He would be in college before she blinked.

God, her children were growing up and she felt like she was missing it. Was she so preoccupied with her own problems that she'd fallen short in being their mother? Lately, she'd been so distracted by Wyatt's proposal, the possible pregnancy, even the Valentine's Day competition, that she hadn't focused on her daughter. While Lacey understood she couldn't watch Sierra 24/7, that didn't stop her from feeling responsible.

If the porch had been better salted?

If. If. If. Her life was full of ifs.

Hospital nurses and social workers passed through the waiting area, trying to console her, and she wanted to scream at them that they didn't understand. This was her daughter. Her baby girl. Her and Allen's child. She swiped away her tears. She couldn't even blame it on pregnancy hormones without telling people . . . what?

That she was weeks late but getting negative pregnancy tests? Yet experiencing all the symptoms?

Better to keep her mouth shut until her doctor's appointment.

Footsteps thudded on the other side of the double doors a second before they swooshed open and Mike stepped through, not a smile in sight. Her tall warrior son-in-law looked defeated—and afraid.

Lacey walked fast and took his hands. "What does the doctor say?"

Wyatt startled awake, looking between the two of them silently, waiting.

Mike sagged back against the wall. "The contractions have stopped, and her water didn't break. That's the good news. But she's already three centimeters dilated." A sigh racked through him. "They're giving her injections to help the baby's lungs mature faster. Every day she can hang on gives our child a better chance." Mike swallowed hard. "He's two months premature."

Two months.

Lacey's legs folded under her, and she sat on the edge of the sofa, the fabric rough against her palms. "How's Sierra holding up?"

"She's scared. So am I." Mike plowed his hands through his dark hair for what looked like the hundredth time. "The doctor said it wasn't the fall per se. Her blood pressure is high, dangerously so, and that must have made her dizzy, which caused her to stumble. She's being settled into a room now. She'll have to stay here until . . ." He paused, hauling in a shaky breath. "Until the baby's born."

The magnitude of what happened hit her. Hard. This was real. The baby was going to come early. The only question was how early and how healthy. And how would Sierra's high blood pressure play into this?

Was her daughter at risk as well? "When can I see her?"

"She's been asking for you. One of the nurses promised to come get you as soon as Sierra's settled."

"That's good to know." She pushed to her feet and hugged her son-in-law tightly, bound in their fear for Sierra. He didn't have any family of his own. He'd become like a son to her. She patted him on the back once more before easing away to brush aside her tears that had slipped free.

Mike cleared his throat, his eyes sheened with unshed tears. "I need to step outside, call my commander and let him know I won't be returning tomorrow."

Wyatt stood and thumped him on the shoulder. "Whatever you need, just let me know."

Mike nodded tightly. "Thanks. I mean it."

Lacey's son-in-law turned away, his head tucked as he walked to the elevator, fishing out his cell phone.

Wyatt slid his arm around her and drew her back down to the couch again. "Are you okay?"

Her chin quivered. "So-so. Holding on, but by a thread. I'll feel better when I see her."

A set of doors opened again, and her heart leaped in her

throat until she realized they were the doors that led to the hall, not toward the rooms. Mary Hannah rushed in, a tousled mess, unlike her normally smooth self, with her hair scraped back, wearing jeans and a rumpled sweater.

Lacey held open her arms and hugged her daughter's friend. Her friend, too, for that matter. Their work with the animals had given them a bond of their own.

Wyatt rested a hand on both women's shoulders. "I'll find some coffee from the vending machines." He slipped away without another word, ducking into the nook of hospital fast food.

Mary Hannah eased back. "How's Sierra?"

"Stable for now. Contractions have stopped, but she won't be leaving the hospital until the baby's born."

Mary Hannah covered her mouth with a trembling hand. "I'm so sorry. How frightening. Have you seen her?"

"Not since she checked into the ER. Mike's calling his commander to arrange for more leave."

Lacey squeezed Mary Hannah's shoulders again, grateful to have her there. "Thank you for coming. You didn't have to."

"I wouldn't be anywhere else."

Lacey looked at her. "It's all just so overwhelming. How does life go on when I can only think about being right here until I know that the baby will be okay?"

"We'll figure it out, one day at a time. I checked on Nathan before we left, and he's doing a great job with the animals, Kaitlyn's pitching in. AJ is helping them and overseeing things."

Wyatt reappeared beside them, three cups of steaming java held carefully. All the stress of the past few hours welled up inside her, mixing with hormones and the pungent smell of the coffee. Nausea bubbled up her throat.

"Excuse me." She swallowed hard and bolted for the bathroom.

She pushed open the first stall door just in time, throwing up supper. Had it only been a few hours since she sat down with her family for pizza? Why hadn't she treasured the moment more instead of spending most of the time distracted with worries?

Her stomach as empty as the four-stall bathroom, she leaned against the divider wall, not willing to risk standing just yet. She heard the door open and a pair of brown furry boots strode into sight. Looking up, she saw Mary Hannah yanking out paper towels and dampening them in the sink.

Mary Hannah knelt beside her with damp paper towels in her hand. "Some to clean up and some for the back of your neck. It will help. Trust me."

Lacey dabbed her face, then put the extras on the back of her neck. Sure enough, it did ease the nausea a hint more. "That's a nifty trick."

"I learned it when I was pregnant."

"Thanks. This is probably just the flu. . . ." Lacey stopped short, shaking her head. "But I don't want to talk about me. What about you? I didn't know you'd been pregnant?"

"Years ago, yes." Her brown eyes held a deep sadness. "I had a miscarriage in my second trimester."

"I'm so sorry." Lacey sagged back against the stall wall. "All of this with Sierra must bring back painful memories." She touched Mary Hannah's wrist lightly and found it as icy cold as the tiles.

"I didn't tell you for sympathy. In fact, I prefer not to tell people at all. But I can't help wondering if you're expecting." She tipped her head to the side, holding Lacey's gaze. "If there's even a chance, you really should see a doctor."

"I realize that." Lacey rushed to add, "I have an appointment."

"Soon?"

"Of course."

"Are you unsure about keeping the baby? If you're pregnant."

"If I'm pregnant, I will be keeping my baby." She said it with a conviction echoed in her heart. "I'm just not sure about a lot of other issues. So if you could please not say anything, especially not now. The last thing Sierra needs is any stress or worry."

Mary Hannah frowned, her eyes narrowing. "What about what you need? Looks to me like you could use some support, too."

Lacey had to appreciate her friend's fierceness on her behalf. This had to be so difficult for Mary Hannah.

"You and AJ took care of that by looking after the animals and checking on Nathan—not to mention keeping an eye on him and Kaitlyn so there aren't even more babies on the way in this family right now. Thank you." She had so many people in her life to be thankful for. And yet she still felt so scared.

"Whatever you need, just ask." Mary Hannah dabbed the cool towels along Lacey's neck. She would have made such an attentive mother. "You're not alone."

"The same goes for you, you know." Lacey couldn't help but think how much Mary Hannah kept to herself, counseling and saving others.

Uncertainty shifted through Mary Hannah's eyes, and she started to speak, just as the bathroom door opened, cutting her words short.

A nurse poked her head inside. "Is Mrs. McDaniel in here? Her daughter's able to have visitors now. Family only."

Mary Hannah launched to her feet and extended a hand for Lacey. "We can talk more another time. Please give Sierra a hug from me. I'll see her as soon as they let me."

Luckily the room stopped spinning and her stomach stayed settled as Lacey stood. She needed to stay strong for her daughter and keep her own secret awhile longer. She simply couldn't deal with the added pressure from Wyatt to get married if she was pregnant. Better to wait until she'd seen the doctor.

She followed the nurse down the hall, even managing to smile at Wyatt as he gave Mike the extra coffee he'd bought from the hospital vending machine. Her conscience stung all the harder. Soon, she promised herself. She would tell him soon. She just needed to figure out how to explain the truth she'd been dodging since the day he proposed.

She didn't want to accept his ring.

AJ HEARD THE alarm ring, notifying him that a car waited at the security gate. The digital clock read 11:45 p.m.

He had roughly the same security system as the ranch. He wasn't all that trusting of the world. He'd been brought up on his old man's stories of the latest case, the newest lows of the criminal element.

The camera view showed Mary Hannah outside, her hand compulsively smoothing back her haphazard ponytail. Her instinctive need for order even when she was fraying at all edges tugged at him. He'd known she was on her way home since Wyatt had called him with an update. Sierra was stable. Lacey and Mike were taking turns sitting with her. Mary Hannah had left as well.

AJ had half assumed she would go straight to her place, that their encounter would have scared her off. Or that she would want to be alone after the crisis with her friend. But here she was, and more than likely there was only one reason for her to return rather than just call.

Relief and desire knocked around inside him, more than he would have expected. If they picked up where they'd left off, neither of them could chalk it up to impulsiveness. This would be deliberate. He would have to be prepared to get more involved. No solitary life for him, walled up here in his icy cabin. But the option of turning her away was unthinkable.

He tapped the code to open the gate.

Holly tipped her head to the side, curled up on her dog bed. AJ opened the pantry and pulled out a large dog bone. "Be a good girl and just enjoy your chewy treat."

He jogged to the door, urgency powering his steps. He hated what had happened to Sierra, and he knew Mary

Hannah had to be upset. He was sorry for that but glad she'd come to him for comfort. She didn't accept help often, so her presence here meant a lot.

A damn lot.

The car door slammed outside, and he opened the cabin door with more than a little anticipation. The night air was crisp, the skies clear. Stars were out in full force, winking through tree branches. Mary Hannah made even haphazard wrinkled look chic, her hair scraped into a quick ponytail, her scarf trailing in an uneven drape so unlike her it made him want to kiss away her worries.

She walked up the steps and straight into his arms. She didn't hesitate, and he didn't argue. He just held her close while she drew in ragged breaths. Sierra's condition in the hospital might be stable, but the crisis was still far from over. The night had taken its toll on Mary Hannah.

He backed into his cabin without letting go of her. Once inside, he tapped the door closed again with his foot. He cradled her head in his hand and stroked her shoulders. She fit against his chest, felt so right. She inched away for an instant to shrug off her coat. The wool jacket fell to the floor, a totally non–Mary Hannah move to leave anything lying about. He sat in his recliner, pulling her into his lap, just holding her. Her hair felt like silk against his fingers, her soft curves molding to him. The clock on the stove clicked away minutes. Tens. Then dozens.

Finally, he asked, "Have there been any changes since we spoke last?"

"None that I know of. They promised to call. Hopefully things have settled for the night at least."

"Thank God they weren't halfway home at some middle-of-nowhere rest stop when this happened."

"I hadn't even thought about that. I just can't believe this happened. I should have stayed with her, spent more time with her. That baby, that precious premature baby . . . Sierra's not going to make it the full nine months . . . The doctors are buying days, *maybe* weeks, but not two months. What if . . ." Her words choked off on a sob.

He kissed the top of her head. "You can't think that way. You have to be positive."

"I'm trying." She dragged her wrist under her nose, another gesture so unlike her, relaying the depth of her fears. "But I keep imagining a premie baby and wishing I could have done something to help. If I'd been with her . . ."

"According to what Wyatt told me, the doctors said it wasn't the fall. Remember? She fell because her high blood pressure made her dizzy. You couldn't have prevented that any more than her family who was right there."

"Maybe if I wasn't so preoccupied with things of my own . . ." She looked up at him with such guilt in her eyes, such a weight of unreasonable blame, much like when she'd told him about her sister's seizures. "Then I would have noticed she was light-headed—or should have noticed it even earlier."

"You can't be responsible for the world, Mary Hannah. You didn't make a mistake. You didn't miss a sign. And even if you had, you're only human."

"Believe me, I understand my limitations and flaws all too well."

"Are we going to have the firefighter/arsonist discussion again?"

She shook her head against his chest, the scent of her shampoo teasing his nose. "I'm tired of trying so hard to make wise choices. I'm weary with measuring my every decision."

Angling back to look at him, she cupped his face in her hands. She rested her lips on his and held, just held in an intense way that was every bit as powerful as their earlier tangle on the sofa. Then the kiss changed. She changed. She slid her arms around his neck, her lips parting, her body angling closer.

He tugged lightly on her ponytail until he could look into her eyes. "Mary Hannah, make no mistake, I want you so damn much it's tearing me up inside. But I have to ask. Are you sure this is the right time? I don't want to wake up and find you gone again, pretending nothing happened between us. This time I don't want us to have any regrets."

He knew all about regrets and how they could shred a person for far too long. Mary Hannah helped so many and seemed to have no one protecting her.

"I'm uncertain about a million things in my life, including where you and I are headed tomorrow," she said with unmistakable honesty. "But I am one hundred percent certain that tonight we need to finish what we started earlier."

Doubts vanished. Desire roared up like she'd just poured gasoline on a blaze. The best kind of arson.

"That's all I needed to hear." He took her mouth, fully this time, his hands sliding up the back of her sweater.

Her satiny skin intoxicated him. Everything about her, actually, sent his senses reeling with the need to be inside her. He was done fighting the attraction. Done resisting. She was soft and perfect in his arms, the scent of peppermint lingering on her tongue.

He felt like a man awakened from a deep sleep. All of his senses were alive because of her. She'd tapped into something inside him he hadn't felt in longer than he could remember. With her, he could be real. No walls.

His decision to move to Tennessee, to close the door on his past, had been the right one. Maybe it hadn't been a coincidence the first person he'd seen when he arrived in this town had been Mary Hannah. Maybe they'd been meant to be together all along and they'd both been fighting fate. Hell, he didn't know, but he did believe he could be a different man here. Mary Hannah was all about new beginnings.

Starting tonight.

Seventeen

Paws over my eyes, time for a commercial
break—aka a nap.   —HOLLY

IF MARY HANNAH had any reservations about sleeping
with AJ again, they all vanished. Tonight had shown her
quite clearly how fragile life was. She needed to grasp what
she wanted where she could, when she could. And right now
she wanted AJ.

She needed the release of being with him. Finally. To
finish exploring every inch of his muscled body. Her fingers
flew down the buttons on his flannel shirt, parting the fabric
and exposing the broad expanse of his chest. Her palms
soaked up the feel of warm skin and hard planes.

He held back so much of himself in day-to-day life, but
here, in this moment, he gave his all, every bit of his attention
focused on kissing her, his tongue stroking, his hands caressing. His erection pressed along her hip as she sat on his lap,
and she wriggled to get closer, straddling him, aching for the
feel of him against the core of her.

His growl of approval rumbled from his chest to vibrate
along hers. He wrapped his arms around her waist and stood.

She locked her legs tighter around him as he walked toward the bedroom, carrying her with him.

Each step rubbed a delicious temptation against her. The brush of their bodies. The rasp of his late-night beard. The scent of his soap. And most of all the intensity of his cobalt-blue eyes as he *saw* her. Took her in, flaws and all, yet he wanted her anyway.

That knowledge spurred desire as surely as his touch.

He shouldered open the door to his room, a masculine space of dark mahogany and sparse furnishings warmed by a crackling fire in the hearth. She let her legs slide down until her toes touched the floor. The braid rug gave ever so softly against her socked feet.

Then AJ tugged the hair band free of her ponytail and finger-combed her dark hair around her shoulders. The light glide and tug of the strands through his fingers made her scalp tingle and her nipples tighten. She'd worn her hair shorter for years, only to let it start growing once she finally completed her master's, determined to start a new life for herself.

The ordeal at the hospital and all the memories it stirred had left her raw in so many ways. From Sierra to Lacey, talk of pregnancies and babies hit her where she was most vulnerable. God, she didn't want to think about that.

She just wanted to let the sensations sweep her away. She focused on the feel of AJ's hands as he tugged her sweater over her head. Warm air brushed her bared skin a second before his mouth grazed her collarbone. She shoved his flannel shirt aside into the rapidly growing pile of their clothes, followed by jeans, socks. Until with a slow attention to detail he peeled away her bra. His sigh of appreciation whispered over her and drew her breasts to pebbled peaks.

Her head fell back as she arched into the blissful sensation. Thank goodness his arms banded around her waist or she would have fallen onto the bed.

Instead, he guided her there, gently stretching her out

onto the mattress, kissing his way down her stomach. He captured the low band of her bikini panties in his teeth and let the elastic snap with the lightest tease before he swept off the scrap of satin altogether.

She arched up onto her elbows. "You're still a bit over-dressed for the occasion."

"That I am," he agreed, standing again to push his boxers down and kick them away. His erection strained thick and hard against his stomach as he reached into the bedside drawer and pulled out a box of condoms.

Good thing one of them could still think clearly.

A log rolled in the fireplace, sparks snapping and popping. The hint of smoke in the air was earthy.

She drew in a breath. "I love the smell of a fire in winter."

"The fireplaces are my favorite thing about this cabin. Fireplaces in Atlanta just aren't the same."

Inspiration struck, and she rolled from the bed to stand in front of the stone hearth, the blaze warming the back of her while his steaming gaze heated her front. "Then let's make love in front of the flames."

"Perfect idea." He tugged the thick comforter from his bed and spread it on the floor, tossing the box of condoms onto a corner of the spread.

Only a few hours ago, they'd been together in his living room, hoping for just this outcome. She'd fought hard against that attraction for so long, trying to do the right thing. But she couldn't fight the comfort she found in his touch. Not now.

Her hands in his, he knelt, bringing her to the floor with him. "We're finally going to do this."

"Yes, we most definitely are." She leaned back, her hands on his shoulders, bringing him with her.

The warm bulk of him pressed skin to skin in a sensation like no other. Intimacy. No barriers. He stretched over her, his leg nudged between hers. Her fingers played along his back, his hips, before gliding around to clasp his hard-on.

His jaw clenched, his eyes closing as she stroked, cupping the weight of him. They'd been so close to landing in bed earlier. He'd brought her to release on the sofa, but already her body made that climb again. Desire ramped hard and fast, threatening to spill over too soon.

She writhed with need, her calf hooking around his, anchoring their hips closer, mumbling . . . she didn't know what.

"Mary Hannah . . ." He breathed her name against her neck. "I could look at you all night. It's mesmerizing how the flames cast an amber glow over your skin." He nipped her bare shoulder. "How they send light and shadows along the curves of your breasts." He took one dusky peak in his mouth, his tongue flicking and circling.

She moaned low in her throat, stroking him again, bringing a low growl from his throat.

"No rushing," she whispered. "I want this night to last."

She needed him to keep the outside world from leaching cold through the walls and into her doubts.

The future? The past? So much of it was tangled up in the present, especially tonight. The last thing she wanted was to think of another man, especially not her ex.

AJ pressed another kiss to her lips as if reading her thoughts. "This is just for us. We don't have to think about the future. We're here, now."

Right now was about being with AJ, throwing aside all baggage and accepting the moment and each other. She vaguely registered his arm stretching to grasp the condoms. Between kisses and strokes she heard the rustling of the box, the tearing of the packet, all sounds bringing them that much closer.

He went still over her, the room silent other than the crackle of the fireplace and the light howl of the wind outside. She opened her eyes and found him looking at her, waiting. Once their gazes connected, he slowly, so very slowly filled her, taking his time with that first moment they connected on such an intimate level. The frenzy of their kisses and caresses shifted into something far more familiar. This wasn't impulsive or rushed. This was the two of them. Together.

A ripple shimmered through her.

Then he moved again and again, each stroke taking him deeper, inching her farther up the blanket until she hooked her heels to stay with him and wring every ounce of pleasure from the synchronized movements of their bodies. He whispered in her ear, the hot breath of each word telling her how much he wanted her, how long he'd waited for her, dreamed of having her.

The ways he wanted to take her over and over.

All that brooding intensity made him a powerful, thorough lover, and she was determined to give back as much as she took. She wanted to imprint herself in his memory in ways she had never imagined before. He made her feel bold and desirable with more than his words. She felt how much he wanted her. Sensed it in the tensing and bunching of his muscles as he struggled to hold back his release until she found hers. Sweat popped along his forehead, their bodies slick against each other in spite of the winter freeze outside. The tendons in his neck stood out, and he said her name in a hoarse voice, raw with desire, "Mary Hannah . . ."

No one. *No one* had ever made her feel more wanted than in this moment just by speaking the syllables of her name. Her orgasm built, shattering through her like ice giving way into millions of pieces and letting the wave crash through.

Her arms locked tighter around him as she held on, feeling his own release rock through him with shudder after shudder. The heavy thud of his heart against her chest echoed her racing pulse. He buried his face in her neck as they both trembled in the aftermath. It was different this time, more intense, because this time they both knew they weren't walking away. There was a special, deeper connection this time.

And in the silence of that moment when words floated

through her mind like snowflakes that would melt on her tongue if she tried to speak, she knew. This hadn't just been about sex. There was no going back.

AJ OPENED THE refrigerator and pulled out the leftovers from their supper. Each movement gave him time to gather his thoughts, because sleeping with Mary Hannah again had most definitely knocked him off balance.

The whole evening was so upside down from what he'd planned and expected. He'd thought they could have an affair. They would work the inescapable attraction out of their system and move on, firefighter and arsonist on different paths.

Except he couldn't justify the negative image of her. She'd made a mistake, sure, but she'd done everything right to fix her life and make amends. Her whole existence had become about serving others. He respected that. Which left him in the position of accepting that he wanted to know more about her.

He wanted to be with her for more than the night.

But would she want to be with him when she knew everything about him? Even if he worked through the tangled mess of his past, he was still a cop and there would be other missions to mess with his moody mind.

At the moment, however, the image of Mary Hannah wearing his flannel shirt—only his flannel shirt—wrecked his concentration in an entirely different way. She held a handful of dog treats and worked with Holly on shaking her hand.

"Paw, Holly, paw," Mary Hannah said, extending her fingers.

Holly cocked her head to the side for an instant before flattening to the ground. When all else failed, Holly opted for "down" instead of whatever other command was being given. Mary Hannah laughed softly. "We'll get there, girl. I know you're trying."

She sat at the table, placing a treat on the floor beside her. AJ had learned that while he couldn't reward Holly when she didn't complete the command since that would negate the training, he could find another, easier task to reward her so the session still ended on a positive note. Retrieving the cookie Mary Hannah set on the floor would necessitate Holly coming closer. Getting her trust and even seeking out human contact was an ongoing part of the dog's conditioning that would need to be reinforced long past the Valentine's event.

He pulled out two plates and set them beside the barbecue, rolls and brownies in the middle of the table. He placed two long-neck bottles of beer beside their long-overdue dinner, twisting off the tops. How many more meals would they share before she learned more about him and walked away? Part of him wanted to delay that as long as possible and another part of him pushed to get everything out there now and see how she dealt with the real AJ Parker.

He turned a chair around and straddled it, resting his arms on the back and watching her go straight for the brownie. "Thank you for all the time and work you're putting into training Holly." He thumbed condensation off the long-neck bottle. "And that thanks isn't just for her but for me, too. My boss here was right about the whole emotional-support-dog notion. I left Atlanta because if I didn't, I would end up fired or dead."

She glanced up sharply, then set her brownie on a plate slowly. "Could you elaborate?"

He grabbed the beer bottle for something to do with his hands more than for the buzz of alcohol. "I'd spent so long undercover, I burned out. I was no good to anyone. Not the department, not myself. I took this job with my cousin to slow down and still be able to feed myself."

Although the job had backfired on him in a major way over Christmas and now his escapist coping mechanisms weren't working so hot anymore.

"I know you worked narcotics, but I envisioned more

sting operations like over Christmas." She frowned. "I take it your work went deeper than that?"

He scratched the back of his head, his hair just brushing his collar, which was short for him these days. "You wouldn't have recognized me. I had a magnificent beard. Scruffy as hell. My hair grew just past my shoulders."

"Pictures." She grinned, resting her chin on her hand, eyes wide with mischief. "Please say there are pictures."

"Not that you'll ever see." He broke off a piece of brownie and tapped her lips.

"Spoilsport." She took the bite of chocolate, nipping his fingers, then sucking lightly.

His body went hard at the flick of her tongue over his fingertip. He set his long-neck bottle on the table. He would need all his wits around this woman.

He stroked along her plump bottom lip before continuing. "The highlight of that stage of my life came when I went to a concert between assignments, and these dudes standing next to me were debating about where to score some weed. One of them pointed to me and said, 'Ask him. I bet he sells.' My disguise was rock solid."

"What about your personal life? Wasn't it difficult to have serious relationships?"

Now, wasn't that as sobering as any bucket of cold water? "Having friends or anything more was dangerous to those around me."

Dangerous for Sheila and her child.

Mary Hannah nudged away the chipped plate, searching his face. "Are you going back to that once you've finished your hiatus here?"

He couldn't lie. "That was the original plan. Yes. To return to Atlanta or another large-city force where they can use my skills."

"Was?"

He picked up her hand, loosely linking their fingers. "Are you asking me if I plan to stay in Tennessee long term now?"

"I guess I am." She gripped his hand in response, her chin tipping.

"Uh, I didn't expect you to admit that." He was losing control of the conversation fast. He'd hoped to warn her off, to help her see how unstable his life was, and with her past, she needed, she deserved, a steady man. And damn it, right now he couldn't bring himself to keep pushing her away.

More than anything, he had to have her again, and again after that. He had no idea how he would ever get enough of her.

He tugged her hand until she landed on his lap. "Let's find those oils of yours so I can massage the tension right out of you. What's your favorite scent?"

Purring, she leaned into him. "The scent of *you*."

His arms went around her and he knew. This woman was his kryptonite.

IN THE TWO weeks that followed, it was tough for me to keep straight where I lived. Sometimes AJ took me to Mary Hannah's and we all stayed the night there. Other evenings, Mary Hannah stayed at AJ's. I was just glad they kept me with them and did everything I could to implement my mission to keep them together. Like one day when they started to argue, I sprinted away so they would have to chase me.

For good measure I rolled in a smelly pile of trash I found behind a Dumpster so they would have to give me a bath. I liked nice warm baths with all the scented shampoos, such a treat after living in that cabin. Except I underestimated how badly the garbage stank. Like really stank. Skanky stank.

Mary Hannah turned pale when they found me and said I smelled like "zombie entrails." Which I thought was a little harsh, but whatever. Then AJ chuckled and she laughed, too, and I got so, so, so many baths back in Mary Hannah's big tile shower as they worked on finding something to make the stench go away. They started with Mary Hannah's excellent all-natural shampoos, then on to de-skunk shampoo.

Then they stepped out all wet, having surrendered to using every Googled option. Mary Hannah didn't even complain about AJ tracking water on the floor.

I liked seeing them work together, even when they brought out dish soap and baking soda to scrub me down. They were smiling, and when they resorted to the final Internet suggestion, Mary Hannah burst out laughing. "Feminine hygiene? You mean . . . ?"

He nodded. "Herbal . . ."

Douche.

They poured two bottles of wildflower water over me. I was so overcome by the lovely scent I almost missed what was happening between them. They were drenched, a total mess, and yet AJ was looking at Mary Hannah with this new expression, something special.

"You're so beautiful," he said, sitting in the shower. "Even more so than the first night I met you soaking wet."

"I'm a mess." She pushed back her clumpy wet hair.

"All I can see is your smile." His eyes narrowed, and he leaned to kiss her.

Not one of those out-of-control kisses where I had to stuff my head under the dog bed to get any peaceful sleep. It was a tender kiss. A kiss that said he cared.

That was rare. I knew firsthand.

I hadn't forgotten that other place yet. Even living in a new place, I still saw reminders too often to let down my guard. Seeing familiar faces from the meth cabin made it tougher, too. I wondered where they got their drugs from now and worried they might take me there.

Living that way had been horrible enough before. But now that I had seen the outside world beyond the chain, now that I had experienced a soft bed, good food and a gentle hand, the possibility of returning to my previous life made me tremble all the more.

I tried my best to figure out what they wanted from me so I could stay even after they became a couple. Over time, it became about more than that. I wanted them to be happy all the time. I worked all the harder to figure out what made them smile and use that higher pitch to their voice when they said, "Good girl, Holly. Good girl."

My bond to them shifted from gratitude to something else. Devotion. You humans might even call it love.

I just knew I wanted them to have the very best the future could give them. More than just protecting and tending to each other. They needed to love each other.

And with some smarts gained from many, many episodes of television advice shows, I knew Mary Hannah and AJ were meant to find one house and live there, together. Forever.

It was my mission to make that happen.

Mission. That's a word I learned from a dog named Trooper. He was Sierra and Mike's dog. He explained to me that I had a purpose other than delivering babies after all— and I had been worrying about the puppy issue because I was afraid no one would have any use for me since I'd been spayed. But thanks to Trooper, I knew better. Dogs were created by the Big Master to help and protect humans.

Thanks to Trooper, I fully understood it was my job to help Mary Hannah and AJ realize they were meant to stay together forever. And to make sure that no one from that meth-lab cabin ever hurt them the way I'd been hurt.

Eighteen

The clock is ticking. You're almost out of time
to solve the puzzle.   —HOLLY

TWO WEEKS LATER, Mary Hannah hip-bumped her way
into Sierra's hospital room. She juggled the sack of take-
out food and a shoulder bag of small gifts to keep her friend
from going stir-crazy. A television game show played softly.
Machines chirped and beeped, monitoring the baby's heart
rate, Sierra's blood pressure and so many other details crucial to giving this baby the best chance possible.

"Hello," Mary Hannah called softly. "It's me. I have
thirty-five whole minutes for girl talk before I go see a patient
on the next floor."

Thumbing off the remote control, Sierra lay in the slightly
raised bed wearing a hospital gown, her hair in a side ponytail. "Thank you for keeping me company while Mike runs
home to grab fresh clothes and a shower. He was seriously
starting to look ragged from never leaving my side."

"He's so sweet."

"Mike is, and I love him like crazy. But it's tough to relax
with him staring at my stomach the whole time." Her hands
fell to rest on her swollen belly covered in hospital blankets,

her puffy feet elevated. "I'm going out of my mind in this place, and it's only been a couple of weeks."

"You've made it two more weeks." Mary Hannah set the bagged lunch on the rolling tray, a healthy Panera salad and soup. "That's awesome. I'm here for you anytime you need me to help you pass the time."

"Thank you, and I know it's a miracle that we've made it this far." Sierra blinked back tears. "But still not what I wished for my baby, to be born early, to start his life with weeks spent in a hospital."

"I know it's difficult to keep your spirits up. I wish I could do more."

Sierra tugged the tray toward her. "I have too much time to think. All the aromatherapy in the world isn't going to stop my fears. Let's talk about something else." She pried open the lid to the soup. "Like what's in here to eat?"

"Both the soup and salad are on the approved diet list. They're also guaranteed to be more appetizing than the cafeteria offerings that always seem to include soupy green Jell-O." Mary Hannah sat in the chair by the bedside table and opened her bag with a sandwich inside.

"Oh my God, I owe you a huge payback for this. We're going to have a spa morning together as soon as I'm able. No arguments." Sierra tapped the controls on the bed to raise her head higher, keeping her hand carefully over the monitors strapped to her stomach so as not to disturb them. "Tell me about you and AJ. I need a distraction. I want to hear details, and don't bother denying things have progressed to another level. I've seen the way you two look at each other when you both stop by together."

Mary Hannah sipped her tea, weighing her answer. "We just decided not to fight the attraction anymore. I don't know what happens next. After a messy divorce, I'm in no hurry to risk my heart again. I'm living one day at a time."

Sierra smiled sympathetically. "I guess we both are in our own way."

Guilt pinched. How could she be whining over having a sexy, generous lover when her friend was battling to save her baby's life? "Please, tell me what can I do for you?"

"You're already helping by just being here." Sierra jabbed the plastic fork in the salad topped with fruit. "And the smuggled food is worth its weight in gold."

"That doesn't seem like enough." But it was more than she herself had had at the worst point in her life. No one had come to see her as she lay in a hospital bed mourning the loss of her baby. Her own fault. She'd pushed everyone away.

"Is this development between you and AJ a secret?"

"I can't imagine anything in this town stays a secret for long."

"What will you do when everyone knows?" Sierra forked another bite of green.

"I haven't thought that far in advance." Day by day was so much easier. They were still working their way through the scents in her sack of massage oils, an approach that was turning out really, really well for her. "Right now we're just enjoying the great sex and pretending the rest of the world doesn't exist while we train Holly."

"What happens after the Valentine's event?"

She shrugged with more nonchalance than she felt. "I guess we'll find out."

Sierra studied her through narrowed eyes. "But you always have a plan. This is very unusual."

"Isn't it, though?" More so now that she thought about it. AJ brought out the uninhibited side of her. "I'm even swapping some of my paisley accessories for chevron patterns for the new year."

"You rebel," Sierra teased, laughing.

"That's me, the wild one."

Somehow with AJ, she was. Uninhibited and even messy.

But the moments that rocked her most? Stretching out on a blanket in front of the fire, sharing childhood secrets. Mary Hannah just wanted . . . to be sure she wouldn't get her heart broken again. "Do you ever want to build a tree house and just hide out for a while? With a margarita machine, of course, since there are perks to being an adult."

"Are you kidding? Name the date once I'm free from this place. I'll be there with chips." Sierra grinned, playing along.

"Why wait? I'll come back tonight and bring virgin margaritas and chips. We'll have a girls' night with your mom."

"Just because I can't drink doesn't meant the two of you can't enjoy yourselves. You both deserve to take a break from the Mutt Makeover prep."

Oh, crap. Sierra still didn't know about Lacey's pregnancy scare. Mary Hannah wondered how much longer Lacey intended to keep it a secret. Had she been to the doctor? They needed to talk.

Not telling AJ was more than a little awkward, too, given his family connection to Wyatt. But Lacey was insistent that she couldn't face any more decisions in her life until she knew Sierra and the baby would be okay.

And if they weren't?

That thought was beyond bearing. "The Valentine event is definitely time-consuming, but worth the effort."

Sierra pushed the lettuce around in the dish. "How are the soldier and the kid doing with little Barkley?"

"Reluctantly magnificent," she said with pride. They'd come so far with the dog and with each other. "I have high hopes for them as a family."

"And Holly?"

Mary Hannah rolled her eyes. "She's making great progress, and she's a wonderful companion dog. Very smart."

"Except?"

Her cheeks puffed with her exhale. "She has too many undersocialization issues to overcome before this event." The victories were rewarding, but seeing how deeply Holly had been damaged was also heartrending. "Our goal is to help her feel confident enough to walk into the auditorium, then we'll play a video of her journey. She may not win, but she can soften some hearts to consider adopting other animals like her."

"Sounds like you have a solid plan after all." Sierra set aside her fork and reached out, her hand taped with an IV port. "Thank you for today. For being here. For giving me a few minutes to be something besides absolutely terrified."

Mary Hannah leaned over to hug her friend. "We're best friends. Comes with the territory."

Sierra hugged her back. "I wish you would let me do the same for you."

"I promise to be better in the future about sharing." And she would try. It was just hard to break such a long-held habit of keeping things inside her. "Right now, though, all that's important is keeping you calm and happy. So let's make a list of everything you need me to bring the next time I visit. Anything you want."

"A male stripper?" She wriggled her eyebrows.

"What?" Mary Hannah squeaked. "You're, uh . . ."

"I may be pregnant but I'm still a woman." She patted Mary Hannah's hand on the bed rail. "No worries. I was just joking."

"Well, damn." Mary Hannah picked up her tea. "I was looking forward to interviewing candidates."

Sierra laughed and Mary Hannah joined in, the infectious humor so natural between them and so welcome. She laughed until her eyes watered with emotion. She had much more in her life than she ever could have dreamed of when she lay alone in another hospital bed, detoxing, grieving. "I appreciate you, friend."

"The same here." Sierra held her arms out.

Mary Hannah hugged her again, grateful she'd taken the risk to uproot and move to this little town. She wanted to believe she was brave enough to take an even scarier risk by trusting the growing relationship with AJ.

But to do that, she would eventually have to find the guts

to tell all. A proposition that scared her all the way down to her new pink snow boots.

AJ HELD THE leash while Holly sniffed the snow, her paws leaving a zigzag pattern in the sparkling blanket of white. But hallelujah, she was walking on the leash. Not tugging. Not cowering. Just exploring the world as if the braided leash attached to her collar didn't even exist.

He felt like he'd just won the lottery, he was so damn proud of her.

Mary Hannah strolled beside him, unusually quiet as she walked Mike and Sierra's dog, Trooper. Trees rustled overhead with the movement of a few critters braving the cold.

"How did your lunch with Sierra go today?"

"Great. We had fun."

"Any news about the baby?"

"No change, which is good news." She stopped abruptly and turned to face him. "Look, Sierra thinks we're getting serious and maybe we are. But I need you to know that scares the hell out of me. I was hurt very badly in my marriage, and I'm not sure I'll ever feel okay about wading into matrimonial waters again. I just thought you should know that."

He stopped short at the base of the bridge over the frozen brook. "Um, did you happen to get the license plate number on the truck that just rolled right over me? Because I didn't even see it coming."

She pressed a hand to her forehead and pushed. Hard. "I'm sorry. I'm just emotional after visiting Sierra. Friends also have a way of seeing right through you, and she had a lot of questions about us that I couldn't answer."

He'd been enjoying the hell out of his time with Mary Hannah, but now that she'd brought up the subject, he realized she'd been closemouthed about her marriage. He didn't even know the basics. Not that he wanted heavy-duty details, but she'd taken secretive to a new level on a very significant part of her past. And what did it say about him that it hadn't even crossed his mind until now? "Do you keep in touch with your ex? You mentioned he moved to Ohio."

"We don't talk. I just hear bits and pieces periodically from a few mutual friends, less and less every year." She started over the bridge.

He secured his hold on the lead and stalked after her, hoping Holly wouldn't freak out on the short wooden bridge like she did last time he tried with the leash.

Mary Hannah stopped in the middle, leaning on the icy railing, looking out over the frozen surface glistening in the sunlight. "I'm not trying to be vague. I just don't like to talk about Ted."

Ted. The guy's name was Ted. Was his last name Gallo, or had she reverted to her maiden name? "I'm sorry, then. None of my business." Other than the fact he and Mary Hannah had been getting naked together every night lately. And yes, he was starting to feel jealous. "It's been my experience that a lot of divorced people welcome the chance to vent."

"I don't hate him. He doesn't hate me. I'm not inconsolable over the broken marriage. More just sad." She chewed her bottom lip, her cheeks wind-chapped from the cold. "What? You can go ahead and ask."

"If things were so great, why did you split?"

"I got married for all the wrong reasons." She avoided his eyes, flicking bits of ice off, each fleck landing in a pattering shower on the frozen surface. "I wanted to re-create my childhood but with a new, better ending. And this man walked into my life who seemed to be everything perfect. I chose him for logical reasons, and that was unfair to him. He deserved to be loved."

Still, she wouldn't look at him, and he wondered what she was leaving out. He was good at reading people. Hell, you couldn't work undercover for as long as he had and not be an expert. So the fact that she left big, gaping holes in this story practically stood up and shouted at him.

Not that he planned to call her on it. Maybe half the reason he hadn't let himself think much about her past had been a need to avoid this kind of conversation. When they'd need more answers. For now, Holly shoved her nose through the bridge supports, her body crowding AJ so he had no choice but to move closer to Mary Hannah.

AJ slung an arm around Mary Hannah's shoulders and walked the rest of the way over. "I'm willing to bet you worked yourself into the ground to be a good partner."

She raked her hand along the bridge rail, scooping snow into a ball. "I may be the queen of organization, but that doesn't change facts."

"Mary Hannah—"

She stopped him with a quick kiss before saying, "What about you?" She packed the snowball in her gloved hands. "A trail of broken hearts behind you? An ex or two out there?"

Out of the frying pan and into the fire with this conversation. But she deserved to know more.

"No marriage. There wasn't time to form lasting relationships with the undercover work, and the divorce stats for cops are staggering." He'd watched it happen time and again. "I was engaged once, but she decided she couldn't take the undercover side of my job."

He'd been torn up about it at the time, and now he couldn't even remember the sound of her voice. He knelt and packed a snowball of his own, rolling it around, making it larger.

"You loved her?" Mary Hannah followed his lead, rolling her snowball alongside his.

"I thought I did, but not enough to change jobs. In retrospect, I just thought it was the right time to be married." His parents had introduced them. Her father was a cop. In the end that had made her more leery. "Ironic that now I can't even do the damn job anymore."

He perched the base of a snowman by a tree.

Mary Hannah plunked her medium-sized snowball on top. "Do you still keep in touch with her?"

He shook his head, packing another snowball to start on the head. "Never crossed my mind. That was eight years ago."

Her forehead furrowed, but she kept working, reaching up to break off two icy branches. "What are you not saying?"

That counselor perceptiveness of hers was working overtime today.

"There is another woman in my past. One who meant a lot to me." Even thinking about that time hurt. Bad. "On an undercover op I crossed a line. I let myself get involved with a woman, which is a betrayal on every level."

"What happened?" she asked quietly, sticking the wooden arms on either side.

"She was the sister of a dealer. Everything indicated she wanted out of the gang and had nothing to do with the drug operation." He just rolled and rolled, but it gave him something to do with his hands other than touch her.

"But if you were undercover as a part of that world, why did she get involved with you?"

"She said she thought she could reform me, that she saw something good inside me." He'd seen what he wanted to see, a damsel in distress. "On the one hand it was risky as hell in case she saw through my cover and even more dangerous to think of what could happen to her after the shakedown. That world doesn't forgive people they perceive as traitors."

She dropped to sit in the snow. "Oh God, please don't say something happened to her."

"She's alive, in jail for drug possession and child endangerment." He shrugged, dropping the snowman's warped head on top. "She wasn't as innocent as she appeared, and I wasn't as perceptive as I thought."

"Child endangerment?" She pushed to her feet, holding a handful of icy rocks and pebbles. "Is that your . . . ?"

"No, her little girl wasn't mine. Although I got to know the kid well, an innocent kid." He took half of the rocks from her and worked on the snowman's mouth. "Nobody tells you about that part of undercover work. The children. Intellectually, I knew that drug dealers have sons and daughters, babies. But knowing and seeing, those are two different things."

Mary Hannah pushed two rock eyes into place. "How old was her daughter?"

"Two years old living in a meth house." When she didn't speak, he looked over. "What? No condemning comment about what kind of mother does that?"

Compassion filled her brown eyes. "I've seen plenty of good people trapped in situations that are completely illogical and self-destructive. It happens."

Yeah, it happened. And it also happened that he'd woken up with that little girl during the night when she couldn't sleep in her bed or needed a drink. He'd sung her lullabies, for crying out loud.

"But the kids, God." His voice choked off for a second, the rest of the pebbles slipping between his gloved fingers. "The kids."

She clasped his hand in hers. "There's something more here."

"Aubrey—that's her name—was just sitting there watching cartoons like any other toddler, with her favorite blanket and a sippy cup. Except when we made the bust later, we found her under the bed in agony." The image was burned in his brain, something he would never get over. "Someone had used the sippy cup to measure drain cleaner for the meth."

She gasped in horror. "Is she—?"

"She survived. I called the emergency room in time. I filed my report and moved on." He drew in breath after breath of icy air trying to soothe the fire in his gut. "I went into an apartment for a routine bust—if meth busts are ever routine. I saw a bowl of dog food by the drain cleaner and something flipped inside my brain. It was like I was there again. I couldn't function. A few weeks later, I almost got my partner killed. Something had to change. *I* had to change."

"Then you came here, only to find dogs in a meth house once more." She slid her arms around him, her hair tickling his chin as they stood there beside their lopsided snowman. "AJ, I'm so sorry for what you've been through and the things you've had to see while trying to keep the rest of the world safe."

His hand fell to rest on Holly's head. "That was a bad day, but I'm glad for her sake we were there."

"Still, somehow that isn't giving you peace."

She was too damn perceptive. He pulled in another bracing breath of chilly air.

"I just kept thinking how Aubrey should never have been in that house in the first place. I should have said to hell with the sting and had her removed from that home right away. But I believed Sheila when she said she was getting out and preparing to start a new life for them. I made a mistake that almost cost Aubrey her life." His judgment was faulty when he let feelings get involved.

Mary Hannah stroked his face, the woolly mitten scratchy against his skin. "You're human."

"I'm a police detective." He clasped her wrist. He didn't deserve the comfort. "I'm trained to know better, damn it. I let my judgment get clouded by a beautiful set of eyes and a sad smile."

"I could explain the psychology of deep undercover work, but I imagine that won't help you feel any better about what happened."

"I wish I could say you're wrong, I really do." He rested his forehead on hers, wanting to be different for her. He'd come here to escape the past, only to realize it lived inside him. There was nowhere to go.

More than anything, he wanted to haul Mary Hannah into his arms and say to hell with it all. Plunge into the future and hope he could pretend to be the man she deserved, a man who wasn't always one step away from total burnout.

Holly nudged him again, the press of her solid body a comfort. Then Trooper barked, sprinting across the bridge to chase a rabbit, yanking Mary Hannah with him. Holding the leash, she slid like an ice-skater down the sloped bridge. AJ scrambled to catch her, tough as hell to do with Holly tugging to join her new buddy, Trooper. Mary Hannah's feet hooked at the end of the bridge, and she went flying into a snowbank.

Damn it.

"Are you okay?" AJ picked his way to her where she lay flat on her back with her eyes closed.

His heart lodged in his throat. What if she'd hit her head on a rock? Both dogs sniffed her, whimpering. He knelt quickly, patting her face carefully. "Mary Hannah?"

Her hand shot up fast. And she pitched a snowball in his face.

Icy flakes exploded over his skin. Mary Hannah's laughter tickled his ears. Her arms went around his neck, and she pulled him into the snowbank with her, her lips warm against his. The taste of peppermint brought back erotic memories of massaging her with that scent.

Naked.

He would have thought it impossible to have a raging hard-on while covered in snow, but Mary Hannah was tempting beyond any rationale. He rolled, settling her on top of him so the cold was against his back while they kissed. God, he appreciated how she'd distracted them both from weightier subjects, allowing them to keep things light and dodge the inevitable crash awhile longer.

She was his total opposite, which pretty much made her perfect. His mind started traveling what-if paths the way it always did when he held her, desperate to figure out a way to be the right kind of guy for her.

Holly and Trooper started barking again, and thank God they did, or he might well have made love to Mary Hannah there in the snow where anyone could have walked up on them wrapped in coats, going at it.

Lifting her off him, he sat up, his pants tugging uncomfortably at his erection. He struggled to clear his fogged mind. The two dogs raced toward the fence line, their leashes trailing. Mary Hannah's gasp made him look closer.

The dogs weren't just racing to the gate. They were galloping to greet a small cluster of people, one of whom had a movie camera on his shoulder. A man in a cowboy hat walked ahead with Lacey McDaniel. Two burly guys trailed them looking a lot like bouncers.

AJ pushed to his feet, dusting the snow off his jeans. "Does that guy in front look familiar to you?"

Mary Hannah shaded her eyes with her hand, peering toward the group. Her hand fell back to her side and she smiled. "Maybe you recognize him from the Grammy Awards. Or visits to the Grand Ole Opry."

Holy crap. No wonder the guy looked familiar.

It was country-music-star legend Billy Brock.

Nineteen

Things were getting out of hand fast, talk-show style. I sure hoped these people didn't start throwing chairs.

—HOLLY ON *JERRY SPRINGER*

L ACEY HAD A raging headache.
      She should be rejoicing over the media coverage. She had a country-music icon to her rescue with the local news documenting the entire visit, an incredible benefit of living an hour's drive from Nashville. Billy Brock's presence would be a huge boon for the event and her rescue as a whole.

And even more than that, she should be turning cartwheels over her doctor visit yesterday. She wasn't pregnant. She was just "having her own personal summer."

A perimenopausal pregnancy scare.

Good news. Right? She should have been hugely relieved, but still she couldn't escape a lingering sadness. There would be no more babies. She drank half a bottle of wine and cried until four in the morning before falling into an exhausted sleep.

Once she'd finally managed to put her feet on the floor, she'd tossed on baggy cargo pants with bleach stains and a sweatshirt over her favorite long purple tank top. Her churning stomach totally the fault of wine this time. Her hair was pulled back with a floral neck ruffle normally worn by little dogs.

Yep, she was a hungover fashion plate for sure.

Shivering, she hugged her parka tighter around her and tried to focus on the conversation to get her best talking points on film. The singer was an animal activist supporting his message by visiting each of the participating shelters. The competition was stiff.

Lacey needed to make this interview standout amazing. "The lady walking toward us is a volunteer trainer. Mary Hannah is a mental-health counselor, and she trains service dogs, therapy dogs and emotional-support dogs. She's working with two entries from our shelter, Mr. Brock."

"Aw, just call me Billy, ma'am." His long strides had her double-timing to keep up.

Billy Brock looked like a smoother version of Johnny Cash, a bad boy with a gravelly voice. He'd charmed the world with his country redemption ballads. Hollywood starlets and Nashville divas all claimed to be the subject of his songs, but he never gave names. A gentleman, Billy Brock never told tales.

And then he went right on to break another heart.

The cameraman angled his lens at Mary Hannah and AJ jogging closer with Holly and Trooper loping alongside. They looked so right together, the chemistry and connection building by the day, impossible to miss. No doubt the camera was eating them up.

AJ extended his hand. "Good afternoon, Mr. Brock—"

"Call me Billy, my boy; you make me feel a hundred years old with that mister mess." He shook hands, then swept off his hat. "And hello, Mary Hannah, good to see you again." Then nodded to Lacey. "Pleased to meet you, ma'am."

His gesture made Lacey think of another man who wore a signature cowboy hat, Ray, an unconventional veterinarian who would have been excited about this event. Ray had left town to do mission work for a year, vowing he would return for her once she'd finished grieving. That was eighteen months ago.

She'd accepted the fact he wasn't coming back. It had been a silly crush, a fantasy about a younger man at a chaotic time in her life. She'd moved on with Wyatt. Sort of.

Thank goodness Mary Hannah was holding up the conversation for this interview.

"It's a pleasure and honor to have you here, Billy. Thank you for sharing your time and talent with us."

"I'm an old country singer with a sandpaper voice these days, but if that'll help homeless animals in this area, then I'm all in."

"We're glad to hear it." Mary Hannah brought the dogs forward with a hand gesture. "This is Trooper, befriended in Iraq by Lacey's husband, then brought here after he died in action."

"I believe I remember reading about that story. My condolences, Miz Lacey."

"Thank you. Trooper has given a lot of comfort to our family. He lives with my daughter and her husband now."

Mary Hannah guided the boxer forward, which took a little more finesse. "This is Holly. She was rescued from a meth-house operation and has been paired with AJ for the Mutt Makeover competition."

AJ stroked Holly's side reassuringly, already in tune with the animal. "I work for the local police force. Mary Hannah's training an emotional-support dog for me to help with decompressing from the stresses that come with the job."

Impressive that he explained it so comfortably on camera. He'd come a long way from the initial resentment Wyatt had described when he'd proposed a support dog.

Billy held out his hand for Holly to sniff. "I've heard of dogs like that for soldiers but hadn't considered using them for our law enforcement. Novel idea." Holly dipped her head for him to stroke. "Atta girl, good girl. I wonder if that's the real reason why fire stations started keeping a dog."

Lacey smiled. No wonder this man charmed people far and wide.

"Could be," AJ acknowledged.

Holly dropped to her belly and shoved her nose into the snow. Pedaling her back legs, she burrowed forward, butt in the air. The cluster of people burst out laughing, and Lacey had to admit, Holly was funny, even if she was far from acting well trained.

Billy tapped the cameraman. "Be sure to get that. She's cute as a bug. A mighty big bug."

Lacey scooped up Trooper's leash. "Holly's a work in progress. I doubt she'll be jumping through rings of fire or dancing in a hula skirt at the competition. Only a month ago, she'd lived her entire life as a breeder dog on a chain. We're teaching her to play."

Now *that* was spin.

Billy laughed, one of those deep, throaty laughs that filled wide-open spaces. "She'll be in a category all her own." He looked around the rescue yard, scratching just under his Stetson. "And your other entry?"

"An army veteran and his son are working together with a Cairn Terrier." That wounded family tore at her heart. They'd been through so much so young. "We needed a smaller dog for them due to the soldier's war injuries."

Billy swept his hat off again, turning it round and round in his hands. "That must bring up a lot of memories for you. No one would blame you from wanting to stay away from reminders of the military."

"I do this in honor of Allen." He had been her high school sweetheart. Her first love. Her first lover. She missed him every day.

He held the hat against his heart. "Ma'am, you have my deepest condolences."

"I appreciate that," she said, his sincerity real and

touching. His eyes broadcasted that the sympathy was more than just token words. "If Allen were here, he would invite you to share a beer while he told you all about our zoo."

"I would have liked to meet him."

"He would want you to know he's grateful for all you're doing here today. Thank you for all your support in making the event a success. Even for those of us who don't win, the exposure for our organization and the animals is priceless."

He plunked his hat back on his head. "Well, ma'am, I have the kind of time and money to do projects that interest me." His eyes lingered for an instant with that Cowboy Romeo appeal he was so famous for. "I'm not a slave to the concert tour and publicity hounds any longer. Animal rescue is close to my heart. My daddy was a vet tech in a poor county shelter. I saw a lot following him around at work. You're making a real difference here."

Lacey's cheeks felt hot in spite of the winter weather. She looked to the others, but they were all occupied playing with the dogs. "All of the shelters and rescues participating can't thank you enough."

"You're the driving force behind this. That's clear to see."

She appreciated the thought but had to be fair. "Dahlia at the county shelter has worked with me every step of the way. She has an amazing eye for screening possible service dogs. A win for one shelter or rescue is a win for all."

"I like you, Miz McDaniel." Those deep brown eyes of his melted over her like warm chocolate.

Staring back, she couldn't deny her bruised, menopausal ego soaked up the light flirting that meant nothing in the big scheme of things but made her feel attractive. She allowed herself to savor the sensation because honestly, it hurt no one and was going nowhere.

She barely registered the sound of footsteps crackling through the snow until Wyatt's arm went around her shoulder. "Hello there, Mr. Brock. I'm Wyatt Parker, Lacey's fiancé."

* * *

WYATT COULD STILL see steam coming out of Lacey's ears even two hours after the interview. He probably should be grateful she hadn't cut him off at the knees when he made the impulsive announcement. But he'd been so pissed and jealous watching her light up for the famous musician. Not that he expected her to suddenly dump him for Billy Brock. Except the glimmer in her eyes reminded him too much of the way she used to look at that veterinarian Ray Vega.

A look she'd never once turned his way.

Lacey closed her office door, sealing the two of them inside and alone for the first time since he'd claimed her as his, on film no less, for the whole world to know.

She locked the door and turned to face him, fists on her hips. "I can't believe you did that."

He couldn't help but snap back, "I can't believe you've ignored my marriage proposal for weeks."

"Damn it, Wyatt, my daughter is in the hospital with critically high blood pressure, fighting for her baby's life. I can't think about the future right now. Why can't you understand that?"

"Because you were making excuses before she went in the hospital." He leaned back against her desk, arms over his chest.

She paced, shaking her head. "It's just bad timing. I need to think."

"If you have to think this hard, then I believe your answer is already mighty damn clear." Frustration gnawed at his insides. He'd done everything right, been the romantic gentleman, and it hadn't gotten him jack shit.

She continued to walk restless circles in her small office, her hair shaking loose from that ridiculous hair band. "You're rushing me."

"You told me you fell for your husband right away." And yeah, that stung.

"I was a teenager," she cried, throwing up her hands. "What did I know about love?"

"It lasted for two decades. Sounds like you knew a lot."

Her restless feet slowed. "People fall in love in different ways," she explained as if talking to a junior high sex-ed class. "That doesn't make one better or greater than another. I was enjoying what we had."

"Had?"

"You're just picking a fight." She crossed her arms over her chest, her stubborn stance mirroring his own. "If *you* have changed your mind, then say so."

This was getting him nowhere. In fact, it threatened to derail the progress he'd made. He should have held his peace and kept quiet until all the company left and she started freaking out over her emptying nest.

"Lacey, babe, I'm sorry." He pulled her toward him. Her feet held and he tugged harder until she relented and stood in his arms, her chest to his. She wasn't relaxing against him, but she didn't pull away.

He kissed the top of her head and reminded himself to be patient. Letting his impulsive side show was a mistake. He had too much at stake here with her and at work to be anything but cool-headed. He would win in the end through persistence.

Losing her was not an option.

WITH THE MOON just beginning to climb in the sky, Mary Hannah walked Trooper back to the McDaniel house, her body still humming from making love to AJ. After the interview, they'd returned to his cabin, and the next thing she knew, her back was flat against the door. AJ was wooing her with a corny country accent, singing country songs and teasing her about falling for Billy Brock's line of bull.

She hadn't seen that lighthearted side of AJ often, and it surprised her. But something had happened between them when they ventured into deeper waters, building that goofy little snowman while talking about serious subjects. Was it possible she could trust him with her darkest secrets after all? Could his work actually help him understand rather than lead him to judge her? A tempting notion that stirred hope. And wasn't that a scary thought? It had been so long since she dared dream of a future with a man.

Trooper tugged at the leash as they neared the McDaniels' rambling farmhouse. She let go, and he raced to the front porch. Lacey sat in a rocking chair, wrapped in a blanket with a thermos in her hands.

Mary Hannah climbed the front-porch steps, gripping the rail. "What's wrong?"

"Why do you assume something's the matter? This is an amazing day." She lifted her thermos in a toast. "Our rescue will be in a news feature. Cause for celebration."

"It is. Yet you're still clearly upset." She sat in the rocker next to Lacey, realizing that somewhere along the way Lacey had become her friend as well. The connection they shared wasn't just because of Sierra or the rescue.

"I'm just . . . tired."

Mary Hannah simply sat, rocking back and forth. She didn't speak. People felt the need to fill a silence. That was often a counselor's greatest tool, more valuable than the sagest of advice.

"Wyatt's announcement that we're engaged was not true," she said softly into the night. "I hadn't turned him down, but I definitely hadn't agreed."

"That must have been terribly uncomfortable for you."

"Understatement of the year." Rolling her eyes, she sipped from the thermos, the scent of hot cocoa steaming out. "I'm not pregnant, by the way, so the pressure should be off. But then he announced to the world we're getting married. I need everything to slow down."

Through damn good training, Mary Hannah schooled her features not to show emotion until she got her own under control. "How are you going to handle it?"

"Hell if I know." She sipped her cocoa. "Want some?"

"No thank you."

"It's spiked with Kahlúa and peppermint schnapps."

"Maybe a sip."

Lacey poured the hot cocoa into the thermos cup and passed it to Mary Hannah. "Wyatt's been so patient. He actually proposed back at Christmas." She sipped straight from the thermos. "I kept telling myself I was holding back because I was pregnant when Allen and I married."

"I didn't know." Mary Hannah cradled her cup and inhaled the scent, intoxicating all on its own.

Lacey glanced over, her smile bittersweet. "Allen and I were in love, absolutely, no question on that. Being pregnant with Sierra just pushed up the wedding date."

"But that's not an issue here now." Mary Hannah brought the cup to her mouth and tasted—yum—her new favorite drink. "Do you want to marry Wyatt? Maybe later, not rushing?"

"This is difficult to say . . . to admit." Lacey's head fell back to rest against the rocker before she blurted out, "Wyatt was my gap guy."

"Gap guy?"

"After Allen died," she said slowly, as if prying the words free. "It took me a long time to date again. I had offers before Wyatt, but I wasn't ready."

"Like the veterinarian, Dr. Vega." Ray Vega had made no secret of his attraction to Lacey even though he was ten years younger. The fact that age didn't matter to him only made him all the more attractive to the local women.

"Ray left." Lacey set aside the thermos. "He didn't come back."

Realization lit up like the stars popping through the night sky. "You were waiting for him."

"Ray said he didn't want to be my gap guy. Or something like that." Lacey pulled her legs up under the blanket and rested her chin on her knees. "He didn't want to be the fling

I had in order to move on. It sounded so beautiful when he said it. He said he would be back in a year."

And roughly six months ago she'd started dating Wyatt. "Did Dr. Vega contact you while he was gone on his mission trip? Is he still there now?"

"I don't know because I haven't heard anything from him. Not a single word." Hurt and anger coated each word. "So I moved on. I decided I should have a gap relationship after all. Except apparently I'm not very good at that. Allen was the first man I was with. So I was over forty years old, trying to figure out how to have a fling."

Mary Hannah reached to squeeze Lacey's hand. "You know I'm here to help however I can. I'm your friend as well as Sierra's."

"Thanks. I mean it." She squeezed back before picking up her thermos again. "I can't let this distract me from the competition. I need to make this place a success so I can support my family. I have a son heading to college and a father-in-law with dementia. I don't have time for flings."

Mary Hannah asked the unspoken question that had been hanging in the air, waiting to be addressed. "Are you still waiting for Ray Vega to return?"

"That's a moot point. He hasn't contacted me." She drew a long gulp from the thermos.

Oh, poor Lacey. Mary Hannah's heart hurt for her. "You still didn't answer my question, and that should tell you all you need to know."

Lacey pressed her hands to her eyes, a single tear sneaking free anyway. Mary Hannah started to rise to hug her. The cell phone by the thermos chimed, stopping her. Lacey sniffed twice as she snapped up the phone.

"Hello? Mike?" Lacey listened, her face growing paler by the second.

A dark sense of premonition filled Mary Hannah like clouds covering the stars. She listened to the one-sided conversation, but there wasn't much to go on.

Lacey kept nodding, her throat moving in a slow swallow. "I'll be right over. I'm praying for all three of you."

She disconnected the call, her hand shaking so hard the cell phone dropped into her lap.

"Lacey? Please, what's happened?"

Her eyes shimmering with tears, Lacey said, "Sierra's blood pressure spiked. The doctors said they can't wait any longer without risking her . . . risking her life. They just took her in for an emergency C-section."

Twenty

Sometimes you have to push for alliances.
Even the ones that seem most unlikely.

—HOLLY, ON *SURVIVOR*

AJ HADN'T REALIZED how attached he'd become to this family until tonight. He was a part of a unit. Wyatt had called to tell him about Sierra's premature delivery. Mary Hannah had already driven Lacey over. They were at the hospital. Wyatt couldn't get out of his night shift for another hour, so he'd asked AJ to check on the family.

The family.

He found Mary Hannah sitting alone in the waiting area, her eyes swollen from crying. His stomach plummeted.

"Mary Hannah? How's Sierra? The baby?" He sat beside her and wrapped an arm around her shoulder. God, she was cold and trembling. She was always so in control that he wasn't quite sure what to do for her.

She held a wad of tissues in her hand and scrubbed at her already raw eyes. "The baby's in the neonatal ICU in an incubator. He needs help breathing. Mike's with him. Sierra's in recovery. She hasn't woken yet, but Lacey is sitting with her. They say her blood pressure was so high they lost her once"—her voice cracked before she regained control—"and they had to bring her back."

He held her tighter, tucking her head against his chest. "I'm so sorry." He felt so damn helpless. "I wish I'd been here sooner."

"You couldn't have done anything. As it is, I've been wishing I could help somehow, but I've just been sitting here, scared out of my mind for Sierra and her baby."

"All the more reason I should have been with you. You shouldn't have to go through this alone." He stroked a hand over her hair. "Are you okay?"

She glanced up at him, her expression shifting. "Are you asking me if I'm at risk for relapsing, searching for a hit from the nearest medicine cabinet?"

Hell, he hadn't even considered that, but the fact that she had made him wonder now. "Are you?"

Shrugging his arm aside, she leaned back, her hands pressed to her eyes. "I'm always going to be the recovering addict, and I know to call my sponsor if I'm in crisis."

"That's good."

Her hands fell to her lap, and pain blazed in her eyes. "But I've done things so much worse than take illegal drugs. So much worse." She paused, waiting, then continued, "Aren't you going to ask me what I did?"

His cop instincts tingled, sensing that need to confess. He could tell something was eating her up inside.

"That's your decision whether to trust me or not."

"Maybe you would rather not know."

Did she have a point? He didn't much like the light that would put him in, though. "I've seen the worst the world has to offer. I imagine at times you hear the worst from your patients."

"It's hard to stay clean." Her chin trembled. "So hard."

He stroked her hair back, tucking it behind her ear. "Do you want to talk about it?"

She twisted the hem of her sweater, her eyes darting

around the waiting area before finally landing on him again. "My ex and I always planned to have children."

"Is your biological clock ticking?" He worked to keep his voice level, even though thoughts of little Aubrey were filling his head and clenching his gut. "I can see how that would make it difficult when your friends are starting their families."

A smile flickered across her face as she straightened. "You don't have to look so horrified. I'm not asking you to knock me up."

"That isn't what I thought." Okay, maybe it was. But he would sound like a jackass if he said as much.

She drew in a deep breath, her back bracing. "I got pregnant about six months after we married. It wasn't planned. But I wanted my baby very much. So much that I checked myself into a rehab center right away."

Holy hell. He hadn't expected this and didn't know what to say. He'd seen so many junkie babies during his time on the force, but he couldn't reconcile that image with Mary Hannah. Black and white suddenly became very gray.

"Yes, I got pregnant while using," she said starkly. "And I was almost all the way through the program. I thought I was going to be lucky after all. My baby would be okay." She snorted a dark laugh, slightly hysterical, and swiped the tissues under her nose.

"Mary Hannah, you don't need to do this now—"

"I have to finish. You need to know who I am. What I did." She shook her head. "In my second trimester, I miscarried. It was my fault. Don't even try to convince me otherwise. It's a guilt I'll have to live with for the rest of my life. I'm every bit as horrible a mother as the woman you knew undercover, Sheila. I put my child at risk, and my child did not survive."

Those shades of gray tormented him, but if he said the wrong thing now, there would be no taking it back later. He could sort through his own thoughts another time. For now, he grasped at whatever logic he could find. "You didn't know you were pregnant. And once you did, you tried your best to come clean."

"That doesn't make it hurt less."

"I imagine not. Especially on a night like this." He slid his arm around her again, drawing her close against his side. "But even here on this really tough night, you're staying strong. Acknowledging there's a problem and facing it head-on, going to rehab and staying clean. That's more than ninety-nine percent of addicts I've met are able to accomplish. You went to rehab and completed the program."

Another sigh racked her body, all the louder in the late-night silence of the hospital. "I wonder sometimes if I hadn't gotten pregnant, would I have ever faced the addiction? I only checked myself in because I was pregnant. My baby saved my life, but it's my fault the baby died and my husband left. I can't blame him. There's no way to make what I did okay."

He couldn't argue the point and didn't know how to ease her pain. And he couldn't be sure he would have reacted any differently from her ex. AJ simply held her. His world rocked.

Because somewhere along the way, the firefighter had just fallen in love with the arsonist.

LACEY WALKED DOWN the hospital hall toward the waiting room to update everyone. Sierra was awake and finally stable enough to be moved into a room. She'd insisted on getting in a wheelchair, and Mike had brought her to see their son.

Allen Michael. Four pounds one ounce. He was a good weight. Sierra had almost given her life hanging on those extra weeks to give her baby time to mature. Lacey's hands shook as adrenaline rushed away in the aftermath of the most harrowing night of her life.

She'd already lost a husband. She could not lose their daughter. But right on the heels of that thought was a gut-wrenching fear that Sierra might still lose her child. A pain Lacey couldn't bear for her no matter how much she wanted to.

Security opened the electric doors separating the maternity ward from the waiting area. The hospital was so silent, her gym shoes squeaked all the louder. She almost thought her friends had left, and then she saw them in the far corner. Mary Hannah was curled up asleep, her head on AJ's shoulder. His head was back, his legs stretched out as he napped, too.

Wyatt sat in a chair watching the television on mute with the closed captions scrolling along the bottom. His eyes slid to hers, and he put a finger to his mouth, easing up from the seat to join her.

He palmed the small of her back and steered her away. "There's a bench around the corner where we can talk. And before you ask, Nathan's fine. He was asleep when I left the house. He said he would come in the morning so you can go home and change."

"He's had to grow up so fast." She followed along on autopilot—exhausted, relieved, drained. She sat on the bench, Wyatt dropping into place beside her. "Sierra's awake and they let her see the baby. Mike's with them both now."

"So everyone's okay?"

"They'll be in the hospital for a while, but I'm cautiously hopeful." She couldn't remember when she'd been so scared. Other than sending her husband off to war. Tears welled up and over. He should be here to see their first grandchild. The weight of losing him hit her all over again, and she bit back a sob.

Wyatt tucked a knuckle under her chin. "Lacey, no offense, babe, but you look exhausted. You should go home and rest or you'll be no good to anyone."

"I'm not leaving." She forced herself not to wince at Wyatt's touch, which felt so wrong right now with Allen so very alive in her thoughts, his smile, his even-tempered ways and humor that balanced her. She missed him so damn much.

"You're no good to anyone if you wear yourself out."

"I am not leaving. Not tonight. Sierra's my child. You're not a parent. You don't understand."

His jaw flexed. "I *am* a parent. You just haven't chosen to tell me yet."

Her head snapped back. "What did you say?"

"Are you pregnant?"

She weighed her words carefully, wishing she'd gone to the doctor earlier so she didn't have those weeks of silence to account for. "No. I'm not. I thought I might be for a short while, but when I went to the doctor, he confirmed I'm not pregnant." Then she realized . . . "Is that why you proposed out of the blue at Christmas?"

"Actually, no, not that you'll probably ever believe me." His smile was dark, bitter. "I guessed a couple of days ago when someone made a toast at the dinner table and you lifted that wineglass full of water. I realized how many times you'd passed up wine lately. Even at Christmas and New Year's. I remembered you didn't toast with champagne like everyone else. Everyone except underage teens and pregnant Sierra. You've been drinking water and juice in that favorite wineglass of yours for weeks."

Guilt piled on top of more guilt. If she'd been pregnant, it had been with his child, too. He deserved to have been told, to celebrate the news rather than stumble on the knowledge.

She took his hand, wishing she could change what she'd done. Waiting had seemed so logical at the time. "You have a right to be upset that I didn't share my suspicion with you."

"I'm hurt and disappointed. That's different," he pointed out rightly. "Because I know you're making excuses because you don't want to marry me."

"It's not that. I might—"

"You *might* want to marry me?" He tapped her lips to quiet her. "Pardon me if I'm underwhelmed."

"I want you in my life—" She couldn't make herself finish the sentence and commit to marry him. She loved him but wasn't in love with him. Not the way he deserved to be loved.

There was no denying it. She'd made a mess. A big mess. "I promise to let you know the second I know either way."

"Good," he said curtly, pausing as if he needed to say more, then shoved to his feet. "I need to take a walk."

With regret and an ache in her heart, she watched him lumber away, those broad shoulders stiff. She wanted to be able to lean on that strong chest and take the comfort he would have given if she'd offered even a bit of encouragement.

But tonight had reminded her how very much she'd loved her husband, and she could not settle for less.

I UNDERSTOOD AJ. We were a lot alike even though I'm a dog and he's human.

Fear doesn't discriminate or pick favorites.

I saw it in his eyes and in the way he struggled to hide a wince. The world is a scary place. Letting people see vulnerability was even more frightening, but often impossible to hide. To be honest, my fear was more obvious. There were still times I couldn't stop trembling any more than I could stop breathing. AJ's anxiety was better hidden from humans. But I could smell it.

My great sniffer. Remember? I can sniff more than the leftover pizza a person ate for lunch. My nose enables me to smell emotions and even health issues.

Like how I knew Sierra was going to have her baby early. And how I knew Lacey had the flu even before she went to the doctor. If I could have used human words, I also could have told her she was just having a perimenopausal pregnancy scare. I suspect it took her so long to go to the doctor because she was more afraid of saying good-bye to the mothering part of her life than she was of finding out she wasn't in the family way. I was pretty sure it had something to do with saying yet another good-bye to her dead husband.

But when it came to sensing the emotions, I was more in tune to AJ and Mary Hannah. They were the ones I knew I needed to help. And there was no missing the turmoil inside AJ. He needed comfort, and for some reason he would accept it only from me. No matter how much I nudged, he wouldn't let Mary Hannah be the one he leaned on.

Back then, AJ became like one of my puppies, and that meant I needed to protect him. That urge to protect was the only thing that stood a chance of overcoming my fears.

I just had to figure out a way to let AJ know he was in serious danger. Because I recognized a person very close to him.

A person who'd made regular visits to my old home in the meth house.

WALKING INTO AJ'S cabin, Mary Hannah was still in a fog of exhaustion and emotions. Lacey had woken them at the hospital to let them know Sierra and the baby were stable. They should go home to get some real rest now. She would call when she needed backup.

The night was so damn surreal. She and AJ had walked to his old Scout as if the conversation back at the hospital never happened. Was he just processing what she'd said? Or waiting for the crisis to pass before dumping her?

The drive back to the cabin had been quick and uneventful on the deserted roads, the rest of the world still asleep for the most part at four in the morning. The silence between them stretched. She considered asking him to just drop her off at her apartment, then decided to follow his lead for now. She was too drained to make decisions she could trust.

A quiet little voice inside her reminded her she was only delaying the inevitable.

She stifled a yawn that brought tears to her eyes—or maybe the yawn was a good excuse. AJ opened the front door and called for Holly to come out. He angled sideways, Mary Hannah's body barely brushing his as she walked inside the warm cabin.

Absently, she picked up magazines off the sofa and stacked them on the coffee table. Her gaze skated to the hearth with logs stacked. How she wished they could go back to that night they'd lain in front of the fire and made love. She snagged a crocheted afghan trailing off the recliner and folded it. She draped it precisely along the back of the sofa.

Holly padded back inside, shaking snow off her coat.

AJ locked the front door and set the security code. "Quit looking at my house like you want to dust."

"I'm not a germophobe." She forced a smile and smoothed the afghan. "I just like order."

"A person could eat off your floors," he said wryly, teasing predictably.

"A person would *have* to eat off your floors because they can't find the table under all those files."

"I'll concede, it's cluttered with work. I'm still wrapping up loose ends on the meth-house bust."

God, they were just going through the motions, but it was all so forced. AJ was too nice to give her her walking papers right after she'd torn her heart inside out to share her past with him after her friend nearly died. But Mary Hannah couldn't escape the feeling that all their actions were stilted, that it was only a matter of time until the other shoe dropped. After her admission, something had changed between them back at the hospital. She felt self-conscious and vulnerable.

She just wanted to crawl into bed and curl up against his warm body to sleep. "You need more baskets to put things in."

"Baskets? Mess isn't mess if it's hidden?"

Now, wasn't that a loaded statement? She should just quit being silly and go to bed. She slept here more often than she stayed at her place. He'd driven straight here. Going to her apartment now would require more effort and bring up questions she didn't want to answer.

She tugged off her boots and lined them up by the front door.

"Have you always been this, uh, organized?"

"Since I was a little girl, yes." She walked into his bedroom.

"That's a lot of pressure to put on yourself." He pulled a T-shirt out of his drawers and passed it to her.

She unzipped her jeans and kicked them free before folding them by habit. "So my psychiatrist has told me more than once." She flinched. "Shit. I didn't mean to say that."

"Then I didn't hear it." He peeled off his clothes, down to his boxers.

When had they gotten into this routine? It made her stomach jumpy.

Steeling herself, she slipped out of her sweater and bra and pulled on his T-shirt, the cool cotton sliding over her skin and carrying a hint of his scent mixed with laundry detergent. "I really don't want to talk about my messed-up life anymore tonight."

He flipped back the covers, inviting her to slide in beside him. He pulled her close to his side before turning off the bedside lamp. The moon shone through a part in the curtains.

Holly padded into the bedroom, straight to her new dog bed under the window. She turned around three times before settling with a huff and resting her face on her paws.

His heart beat beneath her ear, a steady soothing sound that should have lulled Mary Hannah to sleep, except now she felt wide-awake. "I do put a lot of pressure on myself. You may have noticed I'm a bit of a perfectionist."

"Nah. Really?" He toyed with a lock of her hair.

"Be nice." She tickled his side lightly.

He captured her wrist and kissed her pulse. "I'm growing fond of paisley."

This small-talk game was tearing her apart inside. She couldn't just not talk about what she'd told him earlier tonight. She had to explain. Not justify. So he would understand the choices she'd made even if there was no excusing them. "I had to keep my scholarships."

"College expenses can be crippling."

Except it wasn't about the money. "My dad had the means, but he had expectations, and if I didn't meet them, the stress at home would make things very . . . difficult for my mother."

"Difficult?" He went still against her.

"Are you asking if he was abusive? Not in the traditional sense. He was just very controlling, as if he could make my sister well by managing every aspect of our lives." She wasn't making excuses. She just wanted AJ to understand, except maybe she was seeking some kind of forgiveness after all. "I'm positively mellow in comparison."

"That's no way to grow up."

"Even in college, I still couldn't stop feeling the need to keep the peace. So I studied my ass off to make perfect grades. And it wasn't enough. College was different from high school. I was just one of a group of honors students who'd been valedictorian. I got scared, really scared. I went to the campus clinic and they gave me something for my nerves. That helped for a while, until the classes got harder. I got another B—"

"You mean D?"

She shook her head. "When I say I needed to be perfect, I mean perfect. There was enough stress with Sarah Jane's seizures. I moved on to meds to help me stay awake, then ones to help me sleep. By the time my father passed away of a heart attack my junior year, it was too late for me. I was already addicted to prescription drugs and living a lie with Ted."

"I'm sorry."

"Me, too. When I realized I was pregnant, I used Dad's life insurance to check myself into a really good rehab program outside of Nashville. There's an irony in that."

"It worked."

"It did. For me anyway. The place catered to a lot of the Nashville scene. The rich and famous sent their kids there to detox. That's how I met Billy Brock, since his daughter was there."

"Now you help counsel others." His hand stroked up and down her back.

Finally, she asked the question that was keeping her awake, that had been tugging at her since her revelation at the hospital. "Will you ever be able to look at me the same way? Won't you always be suspicious of every move I make? Wondering if I'm another Sheila?"

He was quiet for a long time. Or perhaps it only seemed that way since she was holding her breath.

"Maybe you're too scared of what we're feeling. This connection between us is messy, Mary Hannah. It doesn't fit into one of your orderly binders."

As she looked into his eyes, the moonlight streaming across his handsome face, she realized he could very well be right. She was every bit as afraid as Holly had been that first day in the meth house. Chained to her past. Afraid of the outside world.

She had rehabbed the drug addiction, but maybe she wasn't done fixing the rest of her. Maybe she'd never brought her heart back to life enough to let anyone in. And AJ—this man who helped her to see that truth, a man who just might give her another chance at love—deserved a whole lot better than that.

Twenty-one

Let the games begin.   —HOLLY

MARY HANNAH HAD visited Sierra every day for the past two weeks. But today was different. A momentous day for her friend. Sierra and baby Allen were being discharged this afternoon. Mary Hannah had offered to keep her company until the afternoon release. They waited together in the hospital room as Sierra looked forward to a new life with her son and Mary Hannah braced herself for the end of her time with AJ once the Mutt Makeover was finished.

Things couldn't be any more hectic with the competition only a day away. The morning after the event, Sierra and Allen would fly home and Mike would drive back. This had been such a tumultuous time, being so happy for her friend yet feeling like a failure herself. She'd failed her baby, her ex-husband and now she was failing AJ because she couldn't trust herself not to screw up all over again.

She cradled the tiny infant her arms, six pounds now and no one would guess what a rough start he'd had. He was perfect. Ten angel toes and ten tiny fingers grasping at the air. He wore a cap now, but hints of feathery blond hair showed. Such perfection.

Her heart squeezed, and she blinked back tears, refusing to taint a moment of Sierra's hard-earned joy. "I'm so happy for you." Mary Hannah rocked the baby. "I'm going to miss watching this little guy grow up. I wish we still lived in the same town."

"I hope you'll come visit us." Wearing a loose sweater dress and fleece boots, Sierra walked slowly around the room, pulling her folded gowns and slippers off the closet shelf. "Take a vacation. Come to North Carolina. We'll go to the Outer Banks and make a holiday of it with AJ along. And you're always welcome on your own any other time, too."

"I'm going to take you up on that offer."

"Thank you for sitting with me this morning. I feel bad for Mom that she's had to worry about me on top of getting ready for the event." Sierra placed the nightclothes in the full suitcase resting at the foot of the bed beside an infant car seat. "Then my crew piling in on her for a couple of days to rest before leaving. She pushes herself too hard."

"You're one to talk about taking on too much." Mary Hannah nodded at her friend's laptop computer case. "You're working on the magazine even in the hospital."

"Just some light editing and a quick couple of military mommy blogs." She closed the suitcase and zipped it shut. "You should submit some articles. Let's do a feature on the therapy dogs for military PTSD."

"Just tell me the word count and when you want it turned in."

"Oh, um, I can't pay you yet."

"I can live with that." Mary Hannah tucked a tiny hand back into the blanket swaddling. "It's good exposure for a great cause."

"Someday I hope the e-zine will generate an income."

"You'll make it work. You have your mother's drive and creativity."

"Mike insists he wants me to follow my dream, but I know he worries about money." She eased down into a chair beside Mary Hannah, gripping the armrest and sitting slowly, wincing as she settled. "I write freelance articles and that helps."

"You're an inspiration that marriage can work." She kissed little Allen's forehead, his skin unbelievably soft and sweet with the scent of baby wash.

"What about you and AJ? How are things going? Do you have big plans for Valentine's Day?"

The words stung. "Between dress rehearsal tonight and the Mutt Makeover tomorrow, we'll both be too exhausted."

"I hope I'm not prying, but I noticed you've both been to visit but never together. Have you broken up and been keeping it from me out of a misguided sense that I should be wrapped in cotton right now?"

"We've both been busy balancing work and preparing for tomorrow." She looked at the sleeping infant in her arms. The past two weeks she and AJ hadn't exactly broken up, but she'd been distancing herself, preparing herself. Only in bed did she let herself be with him unreservedly. "We have good chemistry and too much baggage. If I was counseling us, I wouldn't give us a chance in hell."

WYATT HAD BEEN walking a careful line, not pushing Lacey on the marriage issue. Finding out she wasn't pregnant after all had been a big fat blow.

Perimenopause, she'd told him.

He didn't really want a kid. But he did want Lacey. He refused to let her push him out of her life. She'd told everyone he was only joking when he'd said they were engaged, that he'd been trying to get better ratings.

She'd been pissed, but she'd said they would talk after the competition. Good by him. That gave him more time. He closed the full dishwasher and pushed the start button.

Turning, he leaned back against the counter and watched Lacey's son at the kitchen table with his laptop. An ally on the home front wouldn't be a bad idea.

"Whatcha doing, Nathan? Video games?"

"Signing up for SAT and ACT prep courses."

"That's cool, kid." He'd always planned to go to college someday, get the degree needed to advance in the department like AJ had done. He'd just never gotten around to it.

Nathan shrugged dismissively. "I'm just filling them out to get Mom off my back."

"You don't want to go to college?" he asked carefully. His own dad had hounded him to go.

"I want to . . . someday."

"But?"

Nathan pushed back from the table, a tangle of awkward skinny arms and legs, having grown six inches in a year. "I'm worried about my mom being here alone."

"Because of your grandfather being so out of it with Alzheimer's?"

"Partly." He tapped the edge of his laptop absently. "She shouldn't be all by herself."

Wyatt hesitated, not wanting to overstep and risk Lacey's wrath again. "I'll be around to help her. Your mom won't want you to put your life on hold for her." He himself had run all the way to Tennessee to escape his family's disappointment and scrutiny. Leaving could be—liberating. "What do *you* want to do with your life?"

"I'm not my dad," Nathan said defiantly.

"You're not supposed to be."

His green eyes turned earnest, a kidlike vulnerability edging past the teenage attitude. "So you don't think my dad would be disappointed if I don't join the army?"

Wyatt didn't like to think about the fallen patriarch, war hero. His old man would have wanted a son like Allen McDaniel. He couldn't help but feel the man's ghost looming around here every time that damn cuckoo clock chirped. "I didn't

know your father all that well since he deployed so often."
Why couldn't Lacey see he wanted to be here for her, every
day? He would do anything to provide her with a full family
and pampered life. "But from what I've heard about him, I
believe he would want you to follow your own dream."

"Um," Nathan said hesitantly, cracking his fingers nervously, "I was thinking about the Coast Guard Academy,
but it's really tough to get into."

"You're a smart kid. If it's what you want, I say go for
it." He was proof positive that if a man wanted something
badly enough, he could make it work. He needed to remember that and keep the faith in pursuing Lacey. Low profile
always won. "So, kid, how about finding something warmer
to wear? AJ should be here any minute to go snowmobiling.
We need to get a move on if we're going to enjoy the fresh
snow before your sister and the baby get home—"

The back door opened, letting in a blast of cold air.

"Hello?" AJ called. "You two ready?"

Holly bounded past him, big wet paws slapping the floor
as she ran into the kitchen. She stopped short in front of Wyatt,
the hackles rising on her back. She growled softly, not loud
enough for anyone else to hear, but Wyatt couldn't miss it.

Shit. He'd always hated that dog. The day of the meth-
house bust, he'd been so focused on making sure he talked
to Evelyn Lucas first and coached her on the best way for
them both to get out of this mess with their lives intact. He
would help her only if she kept her mouth shut. She'd played
along to the letter.

He'd just never considered he might have to see any of
those dogs long term. At least Holly couldn't talk.

AJ HELD HOLLY'S leash, tucked just inside the stadium for
dress rehearsal. Tomorrow the My Furry Valentine Mutt
Makeover event would finally happen and close this chapter
of his life.

The echo of barking dogs of all breeds and sizes reverberated up into the stadium. The ground level was still being decorated. Staff hauled in flatbed trucks piled high with bales of hay and a few decorative wagon wheels. Hammers and power tools clanged and whirred as a massive doghouse was built around the entrance for contestants. Agility courses were being assembled on one side, complete with the piece AJ, Mike and Nathan had made. On the other, workers wearing Billy Brock T-shirts constructed the stage and sound system for the musicians.

Mary Hannah and other seasoned volunteers with the rescue were assisting with the dress rehearsal. Lacey would be there tomorrow, but this evening she was with her family settling the baby.

Tonight, he and Holly would do a walk-through and sound checks as much for the dogs as for the people. Tomorrow, his work-mandated project with Mary Hannah would be officially complete. His boss would be satisfied.

And Holly would go up for adoption.

His throat closed at the thought. Despite the fact that this had been the plan from the start. Right? Prepare her for a forever family. Except these past weeks made him consider another plan. He wanted to talk it through with Mary Hannah, to consider moving in together and keeping Holly.

Except Mary Hannah had been erecting walls between them since the baby was born. Since the night she'd bared her soul then promptly retreated inside herself. They slept together. They worked with Holly. But they didn't talk, not about anything important.

Still, he knew. She was pulling away. He was losing her.

She stood silently between him and her other entrants, the military family.

The wife, Callie, held her son's hand while her husband sat in his wheelchair with the Cairn-Terrier pup in his lap.

Holly barked, again and again.

Mary Hannah looked down, forehead furrowed. "Quiet, Holly."

Holly rarely barked, but she did understand that command. Normally. Apparently not as readily today.

Callie fidgeted from foot to foot, her eyes darting around the arena. "You said Barkley was a stray that landed at the shelter. What happens if his owners show up here and recognize him? What if they decide they want him back? Maybe this public forum isn't such a good idea after all."

The kid—Henry—looked up fast, his bottom lip trembling. "Barkley's mine, isn't he, Miss Mary Hannah? My mom and dad said I can keep him."

Mary Hannah knelt in front of the four-year-old. "Whoever adopts Barkley has nothing to worry about. Shelters have rules. People have a certain amount of days to check for their missing pet, and then for the good of the animal, we find a new home. As long as your parents agree, you can be that home."

She was such a natural with the child. The image of her with a baby of her own—their baby—filled AJ's mind with absolute perfection. For the first time in longer than he could remember, he was able to look at a child and not feel pain thinking of Aubrey. He envisioned her happy, growing up safe and loved.

Mary Hannah would never put her child or any other child at risk. He knew that with total certainty. Just as he knew the rigid demands she put on herself would make it all but impossible to trust herself again.

"And Holly?" Henry asked. "Are you and Mr. AJ gonna keep Holly?"

She avoided AJ's eyes. "That's for him to decide."

Callie's hands shook as she rested them on her son's shoulders. "Let's not bother them right now, Henry. I'm sure Mary Hannah has other things to do for the show."

She tugged her son, clearly anxious to leave. Henry

looked back over his shoulder, waving. Declan steered his electric wheelchair alongside his family. Something tugged at AJ, an instinct he couldn't deny, honed from years on the job.

Mary Hannah frowned. "I think I should go speak with them."

AJ grasped her arm, stopping her. "Hold on for a second."

She tugged back. "Can we talk later? This isn't a good time."

"It's important," he insisted, growing more certain by the second. "That woman, Callie Roberts, she's on something."

Mary Hannah's eyes went wide. "What do you mean?"

"I mean she's twitching and fidgety, uneasy to the point of paranoia, and we haven't seen that kind of thing from her before. I'd bet my job that she's on some kind of controlled substance."

"Maybe it's just dress rehearsal nerves?" Mary Hannah stared at the woman's retreating back. Callie looked over her shoulder twice, absently chewing on her thumbnail.

AJ's hunch only strengthened. "My gut says she's exhibiting all the signs of a meth addict."

MARY HANNAH FELT like an idiot.

AJ's suspicion about Callie made perfect sense. So much so, it should have been obvious to a trained counselor. How could she have missed it? She of all people? Guilt hammered her. This was so much worse than having gotten a bad grade on some test in school. She'd failed a human being.

A family.

She just prayed it wasn't too late to help them. "AJ, thank you for seeing what I should have picked up on months ago."

"Don't beat yourself up over that. I think she must be using more than usual because she wasn't showing signs like that the last time I saw her. We've all been surprised by someone at some point. Addicts are good at hiding their problem."

"I know." God, did she ever know. Maybe she'd seen what she wanted to see in Callie, what Mary Hannah had wanted to be herself, a good mother, a loyal wife.

This wasn't the place for a confrontation with Callie, but Mary Hannah had to do something, at least make sure the woman wasn't so stoned she might be a danger to her family driving home. "AJ, could you talk to Declan and Henry while I speak with Callie? I just want to make sure the family's safe for now and set up a time to speak with her privately as soon as possible."

"Sure, but you have to remember I'm a police officer."

"And you have to know I can't break client confidentiality."

"Fair enough."

They walked past a group of Girl Scouts sitting on a quilt with three toy poodles, then wove around an elderly couple grooming a Labrador. Finally, they reached the Roberts family as Callie opened a tote bag of snacks. Their tenuous peace would be blown to bits by this secret.

AJ tightened his hold on Holly's leash, but she still strained at the harness. "Declan, I saw a station set up with water and treats for the dogs. What do you say we get Henry and the dogs out of this chaos?" He glanced at Mary Hannah. "Do you mind staying here and texting when it's our turn to walk through?"

"Sounds great." Mary Hannah turned to the young mother. "I see a couple of diet sodas in there. Care to share? I see a blissfully quiet spot to sit over by the bales of hay."

"Oh," Callie said, jittery, "of course. Lead the way."

Holly tugged and pulled at the harness as AJ led her away. Clearly the distractions of so many people and dogs were upsetting her even though they'd tried to desensitize her to large settings.

Mary Hannah shook off the distraction and focused on

Callie. Sitting on a bale of hay, Mary Hannah unscrewed the cap on her diet soda. "I can hardly believe it's almost time for the competition. Are you planning to keep Barkley?"

"Of course we are," Callie said, not sounding the least bit happy about the prospect. "I know it's the right thing for Declan and Henry. How silly to be jealous of a dog. But Barkley gets more affection from Declan than I do. Although that's not saying a lot, actually."

"He's connecting with the dog. That means he's healing. It's going to take time, but this is an important first step."

"As you've already pointed out more than once, my husband and I are not good at communicating." She picked at the plastic bottle, her nails ragged today. No manicure in sight. "We've spent more time apart than together. Now we have all the time in the world and I don't know what to say to him."

"Extreme stress has a way of making us say and do things we might otherwise never consider." She guided the conversation as best she could in this public setting, trying to assess Callie's state of mind. "I want the best outcome possible for you and your family."

Noticing Callie's pupils, her speedy pulse throbbing along her temple, rapid speech, a million other signs that should have been obvious, all confirmed for her what AJ had already guessed. Callie was using, and not just weed, but hard-core drugs, because damn, there were tiny pinprick marks between her fingers. Needle tracks in unexpected places indicated Callie was too good at hiding the signs for the habit to be new.

Callie sipped the soda, her hand shaking so badly she sloshed a dribble on herself. She swiped her wrist across her chin. "Oh, damn it, I'm a mess. I should go to the restroom and clean up." She grabbed her purse like a lifeline, her foot knocking over the insulated food sack on the ground. "I'll be back in a few minutes."

Mary Hannah knew with total certainty the frazzled woman was going to the restroom to shoot up. "Callie, please sit down. If you don't, I'm going to follow you to the restroom. I know what's in your bag."

And in that instant, Mary Hannah could feel the full force of that temptation only a hand's reach away. Memories flooded her of the moments she enjoyed using the drugs and the easiness they could bring to a scattered, scared mind. She wasn't thinking about meth, but she thought about *her* drugs, the ones that she'd clutched with the same choke hold Callie used on her purse.

She got the draw. Totally.

But she also felt the mental and emotional barriers she'd put into place to help her stay strong. She trusted herself now in a way she'd feared she never could. Even after all life had thrown at her this past month, she hadn't slipped. She was coping. She could handle life.

What's more, maybe her messed-up, horrible past was a way to bring her to this place where she could help other people.

"Callie, you need help. You don't have to do this alone." She expected Callie to argue; God knows Mary Hannah had been in denial about herself until forced to face her demons.

After only a few seconds, the young mother's face crumbled. Tears streamed down one after the other. "I'm just trying to cope."

"I understand." Empathy filled Mary Hannah, along with relief that this first crucial step had been taken—acknowledging the issue. "And I'm here for you every bit as much as I am for Declan and Henry." She kept her voice low as a couple passed with their overexcited schnauzer.

"Why would you want to help me after what I've done? This is beyond unforgivable." Callie held her purse all the tighter, talking faster, her voice pitched higher with panic. "And your boyfriend is a police officer. Is he about to arrest me? If I go to jail, what happens to my son? Or what if I don't go to prison, and child services decides to take my son anyway?"

"Continuing on your current path isn't going to work. You have to know that. Especially not now."

"I don't think your suggestion last week of doga—yoga with a dog—is going to fix this for me." Her laugh was shaky but reassuring.

"I can recommend a first-rate rehab clinic." One she knew well from her own experience. "You'll need to take this step quickly. AJ is the one who guessed. He's going to want to talk to you."

Callie's eyes went wide with panic. "Can't we just go to his cousin instead?"

Mary Hannah covered her hand. "AJ is a good, fair man. We're going to get you help. The path won't be easy, but there is an opportunity here to regain control of your life."

"You don't understand."

"Then tell me."

Her throat moved in a nervous swallow. "His cousin will be more, uh, sympathetic."

Oh God, Callie couldn't possibly be saying what Mary Hannah thought. "I'm not sure I'm following you. You'll need to be more specific."

Callie chewed her chapped bottom lip before blurting out, "Your boyfriend's cousin knows all about the drug traffic in this area. He provides protection for my supplier."

Shock rippled through her. Wyatt? Mixed up in the drug world? A dirty cop? Mary Hannah looked quickly and found Declan in the distance with Henry as the boy took a dog biscuit from a person in a big St. Bernard costume. But where was AJ?

How was she going to tell him about this? The betrayal Sheila had dealt him sent him into a burnout tailspin from which he was only just beginning to recover. What would it do to him when he learned his own family member had been deceiving him on such a fundamental level?

Without question, she knew AJ would do the right thing. But at what cost to himself?

The hair on the back of her neck stood up with that sensation of being watched. Please, no.

Already knowing the answer in her gut, she shifted on the bale of hay, and damn it all, the private corner wasn't so solitary after all. By a stack of bales, AJ stood holding a couple of water bottles.

And there was no doubt he'd overheard every word.

Twenty-two

There are winners and losers at every game.
Make your next choice wisely.   —HOLLY

AJ WANTED TO deny what he'd overheard back at the stadium. But those few words still rattled inside his brain as tangibly as the clanking of the tools behind his seat in the Harvester Scout.

Once Mary Hannah had seen him, he'd backed away from her before Callie Roberts could notice his presence. For the whole dress rehearsal, he'd kept his silence and gone through the motions like an automaton. Thank God Mary Hannah had been visiting a client before dress rehearsal, so they'd come in separate cars.

The second his part of the rehearsal was over, he'd taken Holly and left. Clearly, his dog was grateful as hell to get out of there.

His dog?

He would think about that later. For now, he focused on driving to confront Wyatt, to get to the truth. His cousin would just be finishing up his shift. AJ needed to reach him before Wyatt went to Lacey's. No way in hell could this confrontation happen in front of Sierra and the new baby.

If his cousin caught wind that AJ was onto him, it could put others in danger.

Not alerting their boss first was skating close to the edge, forcing him to make the kinds of decisions he'd had to make while undercover. Sometimes, you had to trust your gut. Right now he still had only a tip, the word of a drug addict who could be playing them. Could be.

But wasn't.

The truth rang through in her words and in an odd way made sense. The day of the meth-house bust replayed in his mind, how when the tip came in Wyatt had leaped at the chance to volunteer for the Christmas Eve takedown. He'd handpicked his team, even the animal rescuers, doing everything he could to ensure that he got to Evelyn Lucas first. He'd even arranged to be alone in the police cruiser with her all the way to the station in order to get their stories straight.

Childhood memories roared through his mind, each one more painful than the last. Back then, Wyatt, the oldest cousin in the family, had been the easygoing leader of the second generation in a tightly wound cop clan. He'd used that good ol' boy charm to disarm his detractors, then plowed ahead doing things his own way. AJ had appreciated the quiet bullheadedness when Wyatt had talked him into coming to this small-town force. But what the hell? Had Wyatt picked him because he thought AJ would turn the other cheek on this kind of shit?

Anger simmered as he steered the Scout into the back lot where Wyatt parked his truck, and sure enough, there it was, under the halogen glow of a streetlight. Theirs was such a small police department he wouldn't have to worry about much traffic coming through to interrupt them. Waiting, he picked up Holly's leash as she sat in the passenger side.

Less than five minutes later, Wyatt walked out into the cold night, his steps loose and easy. For one final second AJ allowed himself to consider the possibility his cousin walked like an innocent man because he was one. Not because he didn't give a crap for the law he'd sworn to uphold.

And then the second passed.

AJ opened his door and stepped out onto the salted concrete of the cleared parking lot. Holly bounded past before he could close her in. He wasn't used to her embracing a new locale so quickly. But since she stayed by his side, he held the leash and approached his cousin.

Wyatt looked up. "Hey, AJ. What are you doing here? Catch a night-shift call?" He spread his hands. "Oh, wait, you wouldn't have brought your dog."

Had Holly just growled? Unmoving at his side, she panted puffs of cloudy air into the night.

AJ looped the leash around his hand an extra time. "How long have you been providing protection to local drug traffickers?"

Wyatt stopped dead in his tracks. His right eye twitched, but not his hands. AJ watched both.

"What the hell, AJ? You're not even going to ask me if I'm innocent?" Wyatt scratched under his hat, a wry smile twisting his lips. "You're already jumping to the why?"

"I already know you're guilty, and I have a reliable witness." Anger burned hot as hell inside him, not just for what his cousin had done but for thinking that AJ would look the other way. He'd brought him into this mess to help hide his own criminal activity. No doubt Wyatt assumed AJ wouldn't second-guess him when it came to police business.

They were family.

"AJ . . . Cousin . . . Come on, it's just a little cash. You need to see the bigger picture here," Wyatt said softly, his hand resting slowly on his 9mm. "Wasn't there a time when you were undercover and you did a line of coke to earn trust so you could get the big fish? Every now and again we have to dabble with the bad guys to catch them."

"You're saying you took kickbacks in order to find more

criminals?" Holly plastered herself to AJ's leg while he shuffled those pieces in his brain.

They still didn't add up.

"Exactly. You understand." Wyatt smiled.

AJ shook his head. "But I didn't do anything for my personal benefit. Whatever way you look at it, you're on the take."

"You just don't get small-town politics and how to keep the criminal element reined in. And I'm guessing if your witness was as reliable as you claim, you wouldn't be coming to me for confirmation." He stepped closer, clapping AJ on the shoulder. "Now let's just forget this conversation happened."

Holly most definitely growled.

Wyatt stepped back.

AJ continued, leveling a no-bullshit stare. "You're going to turn yourself in."

"Why would I do that?" His eyes narrowed.

"Because if you don't, I will. And then it won't go as well for you."

Wyatt studied him as if gauging his conviction. "Isn't this the point where I pull a gun and kill you so you can't ruin my life?"

"Should I have worn my bulletproof vest?" He didn't think his cousin would shoot him, especially not in the back lot of the police station. Still, he felt his mortality in that second, and his lone thought was of Mary Hannah, wanting to hold her one more time.

Wyatt's hand fell away from his gun. "I'm not going to kill you." He backed toward his truck. "I'll go to the captain and tell him about the rumors. I'll beat the rap or cut a deal. There are enough people on the force who feel the same way I do. You know that."

"I hope to God you're wrong." AJ eased his phone out of his coat pocket.

Wyatt went stiff, his hand going back to his weapon. "What the hell are—"

"My cell. Nothing more." He tapped two buttons on the keypad. "I just sent our taped conversation to the captain. So if you're thinking of running, you still have about two minutes to rethink that plan, go inside and turn yourself in. You're not going to be able to lie your way out of this."

Wyatt's eyes took on a frantic gleam AJ had seen dozens of times during arrests, the moment the perp unraveled, realizing there was no going back.

Wyatt held out a hand. "Come on, cousin. Remember all the times I had your back when we were kids? I even had your back now. I dragged your ass here to keep you from losing your shit in Atlanta when Sheila went to prison. I got you that damn dog so the captain wouldn't fire your butt when you started to spiral again. And you can't cut me enough slack to turn this thing around now? We're blood, you and I."

"I know. That's what makes this so hard."

Wyatt's shoulders went back, the frantic edge going to desperation as his fate became increasingly unavoidable. "I can make this right. I know I can."

AJ forced out the hardest words he'd ever said. "Wyatt, you're going to have to turn yourself in. That's the *only* way you can make this right."

Wyatt paled for a second. Stilled.

Then he laughed, throwing his head back and shaking, before he looked at AJ again with a cynical sneer. "You're just like your old man after all, a toe-the-line hard-ass. But a damn good cop."

Somehow that didn't make AJ feel one bit better.

For decades, he had looked up to his cousin. Watching Wyatt walk back into the police station hurt like hell. His idol from childhood had gone so damn far astray it was incomprehensible. Sure, people were flawed. Human. Hell, there had been truth in what Wyatt said. There were things AJ had done during undercover operations he wasn't proud of. Lies he'd told. Mistakes he'd made in situations where all choices were bad ones.

But he had never, never chosen selfish gain or taken his eye from the goal. Protecting others. Protect and serve. Somewhere along the way, Wyatt had lost sight of that and let the job become about his power, sway, influence.

How strange to find that in his messy life of peanut butter Pop-Tart meals, he was more like orderly Mary Hannah than he'd realized. There were rules for the world he moved in, and it didn't matter how long he'd spent undercover, the rules were still damn clear to him. It was important that the guardians of that order stay honest. There was a reason for police procedures and a code of honor he believed in.

And here in this moment of feeling so close to Mary Hannah, needing her and understanding her, they'd never been further apart.

THIS HAD TO be the world's worst Valentine's Day ever.

Lacey stood in the wings of the Mutt Makeover competition as Billy Brock entertained the crowd with a song from one of his platinum-selling albums. The music did nothing to lift her spirits. Even the sight of happy dogs with their families backstage didn't provide the usual joy. She'd held such high hopes for this day, and now her world had been shattered by news of Wyatt's arrest for drug trafficking. Small consolation that he'd turned himself in and his lawyer was hopeful he would get a good deal. How could she have so misjudged him? Small consolation that at least she wasn't pregnant with his child after all. She was just entering menopause early.

A widow.

And alone.

Damn Wyatt for being the worst kind of bastard and for wrecking her life. She should be celebrating at this event as well as rejoicing in her new grandson and her daughter's health. Bitterness made her want to scream at him, at the whole damn world.

Billy finished the number and gripped the mic stand. "My next number is a song I wrote for my daughter. I'd like to dedicate it to all my friends out there with the Second Chance Ranch Rescue who've given hope and healing to countless numbers of God's creatures in need. The tune just happens to be called 'Second Chances.'"

Tears stinging her eyes, Lacey pressed a hand to her mouth and another to her stomach. The words flowed over her, lyrics about broken dreams and the pain of betrayal. Dressed all in black with a face that had seen life and lived it hard, Billy sang the country ballad about imperfect people. People saved by second chances.

A hand fell to rest on her shoulder and she jerked, looking back to find Mary Hannah. The sympathy on her face was more than she could stand. Only pride kept her from bolting.

"Lacey, how are you holding up?" Mary Hannah whispered.

Of course Mary Hannah knew even though word hadn't been leaked yet. AJ must have told her.

"My boyfriend is going to jail. But hey, at least I'm not pregnant. Only getting old," Lacey said softly but flippantly, because dark humor was really all she had right now. "I'm just wondering how I was fooled."

"We all were. He deceived his own cousin, a very smart cop." She fidgeted with the strap of her paisley bag. "Um, have you spoken to AJ?"

Lacey shook her head. "Only briefly. He stayed at the station following every step of Wyatt's processing. He said they were keeping things quiet while they bring in other players, part of Wyatt's deal."

Mary Hannah took Lacey's hand. "Is there something I can do for you?"

"Your support means a lot. I'm sorry to be irritable. You've worked so hard to make today come together."

"And it has. I know it's probably small consolation to you right now. But we all love you, and you have a huge, unconventional support system. This crazy zoo of a family." She nodded toward the entirety of the stadium beyond the wings, full to the top row with supporters for the cause. "Your Second Chance family loves you, and we're all here for you, no matter what."

"Thank you." And she meant that.

"Thank *you*," Mary Hannah said with undeniable gratitude. "You're the one who built this haven for all of us. It's only fair we get to give back to you after all you've done for us and so many others."

Mary Hannah slid an arm around her shoulders and held on through the song. Lacey felt that support all the way to her soul. She still hurt like hell. But she would be okay. She'd survived worse and come out stronger. She had an amazing family at her side. A family she'd built and no one could take that away.

NUMB WITH SURPRISE and a million other emotions there hadn't been time to process in the past twenty-four hours, Mary Hannah stood in the winner's circle with Lacey, Barkley and the Roberts family. Confetti poured from the rafters, sticking to the scruffy terrier's fur until he sparkled like a little diamond in the rough. She was so relieved and happy for the pup and the Roberts family.

Callie was still fidgety in the earliest hours of her promised detox, but she held on tightly to Declan's hand and Henry's with a grip that reflected her determination and grit. Mary Hannah recognized that desperate need to do better, and she planned to make sure Callie got as much help as she needed to ease her transition now that she'd admitted she had a problem. Callie had been a rock for her family through so much more than any woman should have to bear.

The crowd roared with cheers and applause, feet stomping their support for the family. And Barkley hadn't won simply because of sympathy for Declan Roberts's disability. The Cairn Terrier had performed his routine flawlessly, jumping through hoops and bounding over barriers. Each feat was rewarded with a treat from little Henry, who stood in front of the crowd like a brave soldier, showing no nerves or fear.

Declan and Henry had even added a final trick to the routine Mary Hannah hadn't known about. At the end of the act, rather than simply hopping onto the wheelchair, the scruffy little dog had bolted away.

Straight to Callie Roberts.

Barkley barked and barked. When she looked confused and tried to shoo him back to the arena, Barkley tugged on her pants leg. She looked out at her husband and son. Henry nodded. Declan reached into the side pocket of his chair and pulled out a rose. For her. The crowd had gone wild.

The Roberts family still had a long road ahead of them, but they'd clearly bonded again with a deep love that would carry them through. Little Barkley would be right there beside them, completing his training to become a full-fledged service dog.

Mary Hannah scanned the line of other contestants until her eyes finally found AJ standing alongside the massive red doghouse. Holly had won an honorable mention for most moving story, but as expected, she'd been overwhelmed by the crowd and refused to perform even the most basic tricks. AJ hadn't forced her. He'd stood by her side and leaned toward a stagehand, indicating they should cut straight to the video. Holly had visibly relaxed.

Mary Hannah couldn't have been prouder. She hadn't even expected him to show up today and now realized she should have known better. AJ was there for her just as he was there for Holly. He was a man of deep honor. A man who'd been wounded by the past—and the present—and still kept moving forward, doing his best to help those he loved.

Yes, she suspected he loved her in spite of her efforts to keep him at arm's length emotionally for weeks now. She'd been running scared from the truth. Maybe Francesca had known long before she did that AJ was the right man for her. She was learning she didn't need to maintain rigid control to make good decisions. She could relax sometimes and trust her gut to still make a good choice.

She loved him, too.

She felt a tug on her hand and realized Henry was pulling her.

"We're s'posed to go now," he explained like a little pro.

She winked, walking with him down the steps and back through the huge doghouse door, followed by the rest of the contestants. The sound system blared a recording of Billy Brock's "Second Chances," the words about healing sinking into her with each step.

Once they were backstage, Henry squealed with excitement and knelt to hug his dog. "We did it! Me and my dad and Barkley, we all won, Mom."

"Yes, we did, sweetie." Callie looked over his head at Mary Hannah, her eyes sheened with tears as she mouthed, *Thank you.*

Callie had already agreed to check into rehab tomorrow. They didn't know it yet, but Billy Brock was paying for her stay in the same exclusive clinic where Mary Hannah had met Billy's daughter. Life had dealt the Roberts family unimaginable blows, but they were on the road to recovery. They had friends and allies to be sure they came through all the hardships.

Mary Hannah wished her ex-husband could have been as forgiving as Declan. As understanding as Billy Brock. Seeing these broken people come together to hold a hand out to one another filled her with hope for their futures—and hers. For so long, she'd told herself she hadn't deserved her ex-husband's forgiveness or support through her time in rehab. But maybe she had. Despite wishing he'd forgiven her, she knew he wasn't the right man for her.

What's more, maybe it was time to forgive herself. AJ had been quietly encouraging her to do just that for weeks now. But she'd been too stubborn to see it.

It was time to accept her second chance at life with a man she loved more than she'd ever imagined possible.

AJ PULLED UP to his cabin, the headlights shining on Mary Hannah sitting on his front steps, despite the cold and the snow. Their time had finally come to talk. He just hoped she didn't plan to say good-bye.

But even if she did, he intended to fight for her the way her ex hadn't. AJ wasn't going to let this amazing woman slip through his fingers.

He loved her. It was just that simple and that complicated. Perfectly Mary Hannah. He just had to find the right words. He stepped out of his vehicle, Holly following him with her honorable mention medal still attached to her collar.

His boots crunched in the snow as he closed the space between them. "Congratulations on your big win for the Roberts family and the rescue."

The Second Chance Ranch had raked in big winnings and well-deserved recognition. There would be enough money and support for the free-roaming cat shelter and expanded office space. The other animals they'd taken to the event all had adoption applications pending, with more people interested in adding a Second Chance pet to their family.

And Mary Hannah had played a huge role in making that happen. He was so damn proud of her.

"It was a team effort," she said simply. "Let's stay outside and give Holly some time to run."

"I'd like that and so would she." He unclipped the leash

and freed the dog to race around the fenced area, her galloping paws sending chunks of snow flying behind her. Finally, he had Mary Hannah to himself, and he didn't have a clue what to say.

She walked alongside him, her hands stuffed in her coat pockets. "I've done the most unexpected, illogical thing, so prepare yourself."

He quirked an eyebrow. "Okay, I'm ready."

She stepped in front of him, stopping so they stood face-to-face in the moonlight. "I've fallen absolutely in love with you."

He blinked in shock. She had surprised him. Utterly. But happily. His hands cupped her shoulders. "Mary Hannah, I—"

She kissed him quiet then eased back a whisper. "I have more that I need to say. I'm not sure exactly how or why, and I always know the 'why' of everything. I don't even have your birthday in my planner. But I am absolutely certain I want to write it there with five stars alongside the date."

"Five stars?" he asked, looping his arms around her waist, hardly daring to believe his luck. He'd been so certain she wouldn't be able to see beyond the pain of her past, the mess of his life in general. He'd underestimated her.

Something he would never do again.

"Five stars," she explained, "means that's the most important birthday."

He pulled her closer, a laugh sweeping aside the shards of pain that had lingered inside him from his day at the station. "You rate birthdays by the level of importance in your life?"

"Acquaintance, one star. Friend, two. Close friend, three. Family, four. And you"—she nipped his bottom lip—"are in a class all of your own."

He slid one hand up to cradle the back of her head, her long hair tangling around his gloved fingers. "I am so very glad to hear that because I love you, too. So much more than I ever imagined possible. Which is strange as hell, because

I thought I was in love in the past. Now I know all my life was just building up to this moment where I was worthy of you."

Her brown eyes glistened with starlight and maybe a hint of tears. "Don't put me on a pedestal. It hurts so damn much when I fall off." She cupped his face in her mittened hands. "And I will. I have my flaws like anyone else."

"And I love you all the more for them, as I hope you'll keep right on loving me in spite of mine."

"Absolutely, for the rest of my life."

She arched up to press her mouth to his, kissing him, and God how he enjoyed kissing her back without fearing each time would be the last. She was his, and he was hers. Forever.

He pulled her closer, the feel of her rocking the ground under his feet. The heat between them protected them from the winter chill.

Holly barked, jolting him back to the present a second before she plowed right into them, knocking them onto a snowbank. Then the boxer rolled onto her back in a way AJ had come to realize was her own happy dance.

He rubbed Holly's belly. "Good girl, Holly, good girl."

"We owe her extra treats for life for bringing us together." Mary Hannah rubbed the boxer's ears. "Do you think she knew what she was doing?"

AJ looked into Holly's brown eyes, then up to Mary Hannah's. "I'm absolutely certain."

Epilogue

Saying yes to the dress is easy once you've found the right guy.   —HOLLY

A YEAR AND A half has passed since the My Furry Valentine Mutt Makeover, and a lot has happened to me and the Second Chance Ranch crowd. But one of the most life-changing events of all?

I sleep on a real bed now.

Absolute bliss.

AJ and Mary Hannah's bed is nothing like the stinky mattresses on the floor in my old home in the meth house. They have something called a pillow top. It's so high up off the floor I have to jump.

Well, eventually, I jumped, thanks to the tutoring I received from Mary Hannah's cat, Siggy. But the first few times when they patted the foot of the bed for me to join them, I just turned and went back to my big paisley dog cushion under the window and chewed on a remote control.

AJ likes to think he tricks me by buying new remotes without batteries so I won't gnaw on the one that works with the television again. The truth of the matter is that I let him win. I've learned from watching AJ and Mary Hannah that a good relationship involves compromise.

For example, AJ is messy. That hasn't changed. He still leaves his fragrant shoes all over the floor. Hiking boots. Work shoes. Sneakers. But Mary Hannah says that's okay as long as they stay on his side of the room. Her side is as neat as a pin and happens to be the part folks see if they walk past the open door on their way down the hall of this fabulous new house.

The summer after the Mutt Makeover, Mary Hannah and AJ got married, bought land near the Second Chance Ranch and built a home of their own to start a family. A big brick two-story with lots of rooms for children. One of those rooms already smells like fresh paint. Pink paint, with puppies and kittens and paw prints stenciled along the border.

The baby is only six weeks old, though, so she sleeps in a bassinet in our room for now.

Mary Hannah is rocking her little girl to sleep, nursing her and singing songs while I watch over them from the foot of the bed. I keep them safe. They're my family.

And our extended family is huge with all the Second Chance Ranch people and critters. I never knew there were so many good people in the world until AJ and Mary Hannah rescued me from that meth house. They say I rescued them, too. I like to think so.

AJ walks into the room and kisses Mary Hannah before kneeling beside the rocker to kiss his daughter on the top of her head. "How are my three girls?"

Isn't that awesome how he always includes me in everything?

Mary Hannah strokes the back of his neck. "We missed you today while you were at work."

"Missed you, too." He kisses his wife again.

They do that a lot.

The baby just sleeps on. And by the way, her name is

Abby. Named for her dad. Yes, believe it or not, the A in AJ stands for Abner. Even Mary Hannah didn't know until they applied for a marriage license. Abner Zachary Parker Jr.

She laughed hard when she learned that, then kissed him again. Like I told you, they do that. A lot.

Mary Hannah eases her sleeping daughter from her breast and adjusts her nightgown. "How *was* work today?"

"Good, even better than good since I have you to come home to." He'd weathered the storm of controversy at the station when his cousin went to prison. AJ is more focused than ever on the job. There is even talk of him being sheriff one day.

AJ holds out his arms for Abby, and Mary Hannah passes over the swaddled infant. He cradles his daughter with a devotion I understand well. Babies are a gift to be treasured. He walks with her to the bed and sits beside me on the pillow-top mattress made all the softer with a fat comforter. He lets me sniff the top of her head covered in fine dark hair. Abigail Mary Parker smells like baby shampoo and innocence.

My new favorite scent.

I even stole one of Abby's tiny blankets out of the laundry and hid it under the bed for comfort during thunderstorms.

Mary Hannah stands, arching her arms over her head in a languorous stretch. The scents change in the room. And I realize AJ is staring at his wife with *that* look.

"God, you're beautiful," he says softly, reverently even.

He's a smart man, that AJ.

Mary Hannah's arms swing down again. "All day long I've been fantasizing about us pulling out the massage oils and pampering each other. If you're interested."

"I am most definitely interested," he says without hesitation. "I'll settle Abby in her bassinet while you find the oils."

That's my cue to jump down and hang out on my old dog

bed for a little while. They'll let me back on the bed eventually.

I turn in a circle three times, then shove my nose underneath the cushion to grab the remote in my mouth before lying down. I rest my head on my paws, close my eyes and savor the sweet smell of peppermint.

SIERRA MCDANIEL HAD ordered a drug test for a whacked-out Pomeranian, then milked a nanny goat to bottle-feed a litter of motherless pit bull pups. And it wasn't even noon yet.

The Tennessee summer sun baked her hair faster than the professional highlights she couldn't afford anyway. She checked the latches of each kennel run attached to her mom's converted barn/animal rescue, complete with doggie doors and an air conditioner. Someone had tampered with the locks and let all the dogs out last week, torquing off their cranky neighbors even more.

But then who wanted an animal rescue next door? Even if next door was an acre away on either side.

She double-checked the detoxing Pomeranian sprawled on a puppy bed, looking loopy. The fur ball had bitten a teenager, and the cops had soon deduced the dog discovered a hidden bag of pot, started chowing down on the weed and objected when the outraged teen tried to recover his stash. Animal Control had called her mom's rescue for the pup that Sierra now called Doobie even though his real name was Lucky.

God, what she wouldn't give to be a *regular* English Lit grad student at Vanderbilt, living in a crappy apartment with flea-market furniture. Rather than going to the local college and living in her childhood bedroom of pink ruffles and faded boy-band posters. What she wouldn't give to have her dad come home today with his unit.

But he wasn't, and no amount of wishing could change that.

She could, however, honor his memory by doing what he would want. So she spent every spare moment between summer classes and her grad assistantship duties pitching in at her mother's Second Chance Ranch Animal Rescue. Not that her mom would ask for help with the rescue or her own job teaching online classes year-round. Even though Sierra saw the pain and struggle in her mother's eyes, to the rest of the world Lacey was the ultimate independent military wife, giving all for her man. Holding down the home front. Raising Sierra and Nathan to be the perfect military brats.

Oh, hey, and caring for Grandpa McDaniel while Alzheimer's sucked him deeper into the quicksand of dementia.

As if that wasn't enough, Mom decided to save homeless and abused animals in all her free time, starting up a nonprofit rescue organization that didn't pay a dime. The nanny goat—freshly milked—bleated in agreement from across the yard, bell clanking around her neck before she went back to chomping grass.

Seriously, weren't goats supposed to be gifts for third-world villages?

Huffing her sweaty bangs off her brow, Sierra yanked open the door to the mudroom on their rambling white farmhouse and quickly slammed it closed behind her, muffling the din of barking to a dull roar. Checkered curtains on the door fluttered. Through the window, Tennessee fields stretched out as far as she could see, dotted with other homesteads. Her family only owned a couple of acres total, fenced in, but even still, half the neighbors complained.

Some more vocally than others, threatening to file an injunction to shut the whole operation down at a county council meeting scheduled for next month. Another problem for another day.

She scuffed the poop off her gym shoes once, twice, then gave up and ditched her sneakers in the sink. They landed on top of the black galoshes Lacey used for kennel work, sending their old calico kitty soaring away. Sierra eyed her own purple monkey rain boots with a stab of regret that she hadn't tugged them on this morning.

She padded into the kitchen to wash her hands and grab another cup of coffee before they had to leave for Fort Campbell. Not that an IV dose of straight caffeine would help her face what waited for them at the Army post when that planeload of returning troops landed. When *Mike Kowalski* landed with a living, breathing reminder of the father that hadn't returned.

Her chest went tight and she mentally recited William Butler Yeats to soothe herself. *I will arise and go now, and go to Innisfree, And a small cabin build there, of clay and wattles made—*

Footsteps thundered down the stairs, followed by the reverberation of General Gramps's Army cadence marching across her ears seconds ahead of him entering the kitchen, overpowering her literary ramble.

"They say that in the Army the coffee's mighty fine . . ." Her silver-haired grandfather wore a smile and his old uniform, high-stepping his way to the gurgling java maker.

He didn't so much as shoot a look her way, but she knew the drill. Yeats was done for now. Gramps had his own "poems." At least it was a clean one today.

She repeated his chant like a good soldier. "They say that in the Army the coffee's mighty fine."

They'd played this game for decades. Her life had been military issue from the cradle.

"Looks like muddy water and tastes like turpentine." He snagged a chipped mug from a mismatched set of crockery as he continued chanting his current Jody of choice.

"Looks like muddy water and tastes like turpentine."

"They say that in the Army the chow is mighty fine."

"They say that in the Army the chow is mighty fine," she echoed, childhood memories curling through her like the scent of Kona blend wafting from the pot as he poured.

He lifted his mug in toast. "A chicken jumped off the table and started marking time."

"A chicken jumped off the table and started marking time."

"Hoo-ah!" her grandpa grunted.

"Hoo-ah." Happy times with Gramps were few and far between lately. Even if this moment ached as it reminded her of her dad, she could hang tough and enjoy a ritual of semi normalcy in the crazy house. "We need to leave in about fifteen minutes. I have to shower fast and change."

Preferably into something that didn't smell of dog poop and goat's milk. She washed her hands, double-pumping the antibacterial soap.

Gramps opened a Tupperware container and scowled, the light mood fading fast. "Croissants? What is this? A fancy-ass French bakery or a real kitchen? I need a soldier's breakfast."

So much for normalcy. He'd eaten breakfast three hours ago. Eggs, bacon *and* pancakes, with their family Labrador snoozing on his feet. Except reminding Gramps of that wouldn't accomplish anything. Her grandfather, Joshua McDaniel, a two-star general and veteran of three wars, remembered less and less every day.

"How about a muffin on the run, Gramps?" She patted the pan of apple nut muffins still warm from the oven. "We have to get to Fort Campbell."

He glanced down at his open uniform jacket her mom had aired out for him. Probably at about four in the morning since her supermom insisted she never needed anything so mundane as sleep. But Sierra could see her mother fraying around the edges, the little weaknesses slipping through, such as lost files and forgotten errands.

And God, that thought sounded petty to nitpick, but this was a crummy day, going to pick up a dog her father had found overseas—as if there weren't already enough animals here at her mother's rescue. As if there weren't already enough reminders of her dead dad. She blinked back tears. Was it so wrong to want some part of her life that wasn't military issued and full of good-byes?

Sierra pushed aside dreams of Innisfree and patted her grandfather's shoulder, right over the two shiny stars. "General, you *are* looking mighty fine today."

"A good soldier never forgets how to polish his shoes or shine his brass." He grimaced at the rare second's understanding at how much of himself he'd lost.

"Mighty fine shiny shoes and brass they are, General."

"I taught your dad, too." He looked up at her quickly with eyes as blue as her own. "Maybe he can show you when he gets back today. It's not too late for you to get a commission, you know. They let women in the Army now."

"Sure, Gramps." She didn't even wince anymore at references to her dad coming home. Alzheimer's had its perks for some. Like not knowing your son got blown up by a roadside bomb.

Gramps straightened the uniform tie, shirt buttons perfect even though he couldn't zip his own jeans anymore. General Joshua McDaniel had drawers full of track suits and T-shirts he wore with his American Legion ball cap. All easy to tug on. Yet, his fingers worked the buttons of his uniform jacket now with a muscle memory of long-ago tasks, a mystery of Alzheimer's that she'd learned not to question.

At least her mom would be happy about the uniform, and Lacey could use some happiness in her life. If getting this dog made her smile, then so be it. Sierra would suck it up and pretend seeing the mutt didn't make her want to stand in a Tennessee cornfield and scream Emily Dickinson dirge poems at the top of her lungs.

Knowing who brought the dog made it tougher. If things had been different . . . well . . . Hell. She still wouldn't have been here waiting for Mike Kowalski.

But she would have thought about him returning home today, would have lifted up a prayer of relief that he'd made it back safely, then moved on with her life. Instead, she could only think about her father. His funeral. The twenty-one gun salute still echoed in her ears louder than the pack of barking dogs outside.

Sierra willed away tears with a couple of lines from a bawdy Shakespearean sonnet and grabbed a muffin for herself. The family just needed her to hang on here a little while longer until she could move out in a guilt-free way only her multitasking mother could have devised.

Lacey had used some of the insurance money to renovate the barn loft into a studio apartment. Noisy. But with total solitude for Sierra. She could live there while she finished graduate school next year. She would have some independence, and Mom would still have an emergency backup for when General Gramps wandered off to get eggs, milk and Diet Cokes for his wife who'd been dead for ten years.

Or called out for a son who'd been blown up in Iraq.

Ever the soldier, General Joshua McDaniel marched one foot, then two, then started up again with his coffee on the way out of the kitchen. "They say that in the Army the training's mighty fine . . . Last night there were ten of us, now there's only nine . . ."

Her stomach knotted with the realization.

Gramps knew on some level that his son was gone.

She had about three seconds to grieve over that before

she also realized—damn—Grandpa was tugging the car keys off the hook by the door. What had her mom been thinking leaving them there? They couldn't do that anymore.

"Uhm, General, the motor pool is sending over a car," she improvised.

He looked back, blue eyes confused, keys dangling.

She plucked the chain from his hand and passed him the muffin while hiding the keys in her jeans pocket. "Don't forget to eat."

"I'm not hungry," he grumbled, "and I don't forget jack shit."

"Of course not."

"Where are my keys?"

"Haven't seen them." Easier to lie sometimes. Safer, too. Gramps may have muscle memory for uniforms, but not so much when it came to driving a car.

"Allen must have taken the Chevy to go out on a date with that girl Lacey. Now Millie"—he stared straight into Sierra's eyes and called her by his dead wife's name—"make sure that freeloading son of ours doesn't leave the car with an empty tank."

"Sure . . ." She patted him on his stars, something tangible left of the indomitable man she remembered.

Pivoting away, she raced up the back stairs, leaving her grandfather in the kitchen where he was stuck somewhere in the twentieth century. She wouldn't have minded escaping back a decade or two herself. Or maybe more.

But Innisfree was clearly out of reach today.

STAFF SERGEANT MIKE Kowalski never had anyone waiting for him when he returned from overseas deployments. And yeah, both times, he'd wondered what it would feel like to be the focus of one of those star-spangled reunions with family all around.

But not this way.

He just wanted to hand over the dog to the McDaniel family. Keep his cool around Sierra. Then dive into bed for a decent night's sleep on clean sheets.

Well, after he dived into a six-pack of cold beers.

He hitched his hand around Trooper's leash. Thank God, the short-haired tan and brown mutt looked enough like a Belgian Malinois that most folks assumed Trooper was a military working dog. Shit would hit the fan eventually over how he'd circumvented official channels, but he would deal with that later. He'd spent his life getting out of trouble. Even joining the Army had been a part of a plea bargain with a high school mentor.

Bluffing and bravado came easy to him. After all, he'd learned from the best growing up with a con artist grandmother who'd scammed Social Security checks in the name of three dead relatives.

A hand clapped him on the back just as his battle buddy Calvin "Pinstripe" Franklin hefted his rucksack over his shoulder. "Sergeant Major's gonna chew your ass over bringing this dog back."

"Won't be the first or last time that happens." Mike adjusted his hold on the leash and his duffel, his guitar case slung over his back. He'd come by the nickname "Tazz" honestly. Wherever he went, a whirlwind of trouble followed.

"For what it's worth, Tazz, I think what you're doing for the Colonel's memory is cool." Their boots clanged against the cargo hold's metal floor one step at a time as they filed toward the open load ramp. A marching band played patriotic tunes with a brassy gusto. A John Philip Sousa marching song segued into "The Star-Spangled Banner."

"A lecture and a write-up aren't all that intimidating after what we've seen." Most folks had flashbacks of sounds, gunfire, explosions. For him? It was the smells that sent him reeling. The acrid stench of explosives. Jet fuel. Singed hair.

Blood.

Focus on the scent of clean sheets, damn it. "Quit sweating, Pinstripe. You'll draw attention to us."

"You must not have been chewed out by the Sergeant Major lately, or you wouldn't be so chill," Calvin said, trudging ahead along the metal grating. *Clang. Clang.* "Just keep your head low. It'll go a lot easier for you if you don't make a big deal out of things now. Low-key. Walk down the ramp. Hand over the dog to his new family. Come party with us. There's a keg with your name written on it. A babe, too, if you play it right, a military groupie ready to give a soldier a warm, lap dance welcome home."

He winced. Hand over the dog then party as if this was no big deal? Except it was more than that. Facing the family of his fallen commander. Facing the Colonel's daughter. Sierra.

Low-key.

Keep it low-key.

His hand slid down to scratch Trooper's head, bristly fur clean and flea-free thanks to the under-the-table care from the veterinarian at their forward operating base—FOB. Mike flipped Trooper's ear back in place, then patted. He wasn't sure who it calmed more, him or the dog.

Mutt at his side, he stepped from the belly of the plane and into the blinding afternoon sunlight. U.S. of A. soil. Fort Campbell. The Army post sprawled along the border of Tennessee and Kentucky. The scent of fresh-mown hay rode the breeze, blanketing the smell of jet fuel just enough that Mike could shove thoughts of war to the back of his brain.

He'd made it home alive. Adrenaline evaporated from him like water steaming off the hot tarmac. His arms dropped to his side. His duffel slid from his fingers as he breathed in the scent of wheat and barley so thick it was damn near an intoxicating brewery of aromatherapy.

Soldiers jostled by, bumping his shoulders, but his boots stayed rooted, his body weighted by an exhaustion a year in the making. Then the world tilted. His arms jerked.

Trooper yanked free.

Crap.

His guitar strap slipped. Mike regained his footing, but too late. Trooper shot forward toward the roped off area of bystanders. Toward families. The band. Official post personnel.

Media.

Trooper's full-grown size, powered by puppy energy and a lack of sense, turned the mutt into a speeding, barking missile. Mike jockeyed from foot to foot, gauging which way to go. Was the dog headed for the big grill puffing burger-scented smoke into the wind? Trooper's nose definitely lifted to catch a whiff of something as he plowed forward.

The overgrown pup knocked over a tuba stand. Uniformed band members skittered to the side just as the massive brass instrument toppled and "The Star-Spangled Banner" warbled to a premature end.

Calvin jogged alongside him mumbling, "Sergeant Major's gonna be pissed."

Screw it. Low-key was clearly out of the question now. Mike hitched up his bag, which conveniently knocked his guitar in place again, and charged forward. He shouldered sideways past the orderly line of soldiers.

"Trooper, come," Mike ordered.

And the dog ignored the command.

Of course.

Trooper could sniff out an intruder in the dead of night. The mutt could dodge land mines to fetch a ball. But at heart, he was still a puppy accustomed to free roam of his world.

Mike picked up speed, boots pounding as he raced toward the loping mutt. He didn't think Trooper would hurt anyone. The dog hadn't shown feral tendencies since those first few weeks at the camp. But one false move from this dog—already on shaky ground with his entry to the U.S.—and it would be all over. His promise to the Colonel would be broken in the worst way possible.

Where the hell was Trooper going? Mike scanned the crowd of faces. Women with babies on their hips and in strollers. Men, too. Families as well as some hoochied-up girlfriends. A sea of waving flags and signs.

Welcome Home.

Love My Soldier.

People and signs parted like the Red Sea as fifty-five pounds of dog dodged and wove. Mike could only follow until the masses veed open to reveal . . .

The very family he'd been sent to meet. The McDaniel clan. Except his eyes homed in on the one that had drawn him from the first time he'd seen her at a platoon baseball game cheering in the stands.

Sierra. The daughter of his mentor. Off-limits. Untouchable. And total Kryptonite to a man who'd spent twelve long months dreaming of her citrusy scent to escape the pungent stench of war.

Mike had all of three seconds to soak up the sight of her blond hair shining so brightly in the sun he could almost smell lemons. Three seconds before . . .

Trooper leapt into the air and knocked Sierra flat on her back.

Also available from
USA Today bestselling author

CATHERINE MANN

SHELTER ME

A Second Chance Ranch Romance

When Sergeant Mike Kowalski returns home from Iraq, he brings his fallen commander's dog, Trooper, to the McDaniel family's Second Chance Ranch Animal Rescue center—where he catches sight of Sierra McDaniel. Between her ranch duties and grad school, the last thing Sierra needs is another dog…or the distraction of Mike's charming smile. But Trooper has a mission of his own, and when Mike returns to lend a hand, he and Sierra discover how perfect they are for each other…

"A story about the redemptive power of love told with heart. With *Shelter Me* Catherine Mann delivers another unforgettable romance."

—Cindy Gerard, *New York Times* bestselling author

catherinemann.com
twitter.com/CatherineMann1
penguin.com

ALSO AVAILABLE FROM
USA TODAY BESTSELLING AUTHOR

CATHERINE MANN

GUARDIAN

★ ───────────────────

A DARK OPS NOVEL

After a dark ops malfunction, Major David Berg finds himself the defendant in a military trial. It's a race against time to root out the truth, and Major Sophie Campbell isn't making that any easier. The hot JAG wants to bring down David's unit and fast. All Sophie has to do is ignore David's unflappable charm and unnerving good looks. But these adversaries have more in common than secret, mutual desire. There's a traitor somewhere in the dark ops and now, to find him, David and Sophie must work together—relentlessly, tirelessly, and so intimately it could be damn near fatal.

"Catherine Mann weaves deep emotion with
intense suspense for an all-night read."
—Sherrilyn Kenyon, #1 *New York Times* bestselling author

CATHERINEMANN.COM
TWITTER.COM/CATHERINEMANN1
PENGUIN.COM

M1561T0914

Taking a risk may be all that saves you . . .

PROTECTOR

★ ———————————————

A DARK OPS NOVEL

FROM
CATHERINE MANN

Assigned to the investigation of a mob boss whose luxury cruise ship is reportedly a hub for terrorist activity, Captain Chuck Tanaka is going undercover. His target: Jolynn Taylor, the mob boss's daughter.

Ever since she saw her beloved uncle murdered, Jolynn has stayed far away from her father's crooked empire. But after her father falls ill, she finds herself on the run, one step ahead of unknown enemies. Only Tanaka stands between her and certain death . . . but can she trust him?

PRAISE FOR CATHERINE MANN

"An exciting storyteller, Catherine Mann weaves deep emotion with intense suspense for an all-night read."
—Sherrilyn Kenyon, #1 *New York Times* bestselling author

"Exhilarating romantic suspense."
—*The Best Reviews*

penguin.com
facebook.com/CatherineMannAuthor
facebook.com/LoveAlwaysBooks
catherinemann.com

M1089T0412

Reckless passion is right on target . . .

FROM
CATHERINE MANN

RENEGADE

A DARK OPS NOVEL

Tech Sergeant Mason "Smooth" Randolph lives to push
boundaries. But he never anticipated how far outside the
box he would land when an in-flight accident sends him
parachuting into Nevada's notorious Area 51—and into the
handcuffs of sexy security cop Jill Walczak.

PRAISE FOR CATHERINE MANN

"Riveting action, relentless suspense, heroes to die for—
Catherine Mann delivers!"
—Suzanne Brockmann, *New York Times* bestselling author

"One of the hottest rising stars around!"
—Lori Foster, *New York Times* bestselling author

penguin.com
facebook.com/CatherineMannAuthor
facebook.com/LoveAlwaysBooks
catherinemann.com